LUKAS WITH A K

KAMERON TYLER

For Lukas.

CONTENTS

ACKNOWLEDGEMENTS

This book would not have been possible without the love, understanding, encouragement, and support I have been fortunate enough to receive from my teachers, my mentors, my friends, and most of all, my family.

Nor would it have been possible without the bold leaders within this world's many queer communities, who charged faithfully toward adversity so that I might enjoy a more meaningful, just, and happy life.

MAY 20, 1999

As I ran onto the dark blue football field behind my school, all I could hear was the huff of my own breath. Nothing else in the world seemed to exist. I looked back to make sure no one had followed me, and then I peered up at the moon until I could feel my heartbeat slow. Only then did my surroundings begin to feel real again.

At Santana High, prom officially ended the school year, meaning I could have begun my summer break earlier in the day. But nope, I just couldn't miss the year's last hurrah. What an idiot.

My body shivered in the moonlight behind the building, and I wanted to kick my own ass for being so stupid. The moon seemed to agree. The pale, glowing face in the sky seemed completely judgmental the longer I stared. A faint cloud billowed quickly from my mouth and disappeared in front of the stars. It was May. Why the hell was it so cold? It even smelled like cold. My ears were numb and my toes were freezing in my loafers.

I gazed toward the school again, imagining how much I'd confused my date. It was probably safe to say that in the gym, her friends were reminding everyone they warned her not to come to the dance with me. I lifted up my wrist to check my watch, hoping it was close enough to the end of the night for me to apologize quickly, and then leave. I figured if I went home to sulk, at least I wouldn't die of hypothermia.

It was 11:33. Close enough.

But the second I turned around, the gym doors flung open, and my best friend Michael jogged toward me. It felt like a weird dream to see him coming onto the football field in a suit instead of his uniform.

"What the hell's going on with you? Lorena finally tries kissing you, and two seconds later you're halfway to Texas!"

"I'm tired," I said. "I'm going home."

"Going home? She's finally into you and now you're going home? Alone? You've wanted a chance with her for weeks! You said so yourself!"

He wasn't wrong. I had said so myself. In fact, I'd verbally wished, a lot of times, that Lorena Alcantar would give me the time of day, mostly because I never in my wildest imagination thought she would.

As I looked into Michael's big dumb eyes, it donned on me that he honestly had no clue what was really going on. For the past few years, I'd hoped for some small chance he knew me better than I thought, but I was quickly beginning to realize that was wishful thinking at its finest. "I don't want to talk about this," I muttered, trying to walk past him, but he pushed his hand on my chest and stopped me from leaving.

"You don't want to talk about *what?*"

I looked up at him and thought about how strange it was that my best friend was this big, macho football player. If I didn't know him, his size alone would scare the shit out of me, and so would the way his eyebrows came down over his eyes sometimes. It made him look meaner than he really was. His stare traveled through my glasses, and all at once, I felt guilty, and scared, and frustrated. It was finally about to happen. The moment I'd convinced myself I could dodge until graduation was here, a year too early.

2

Michael took my silence as an answer to his question and shoved his hands into his pockets. "Luke, you've been acting weird all night, and somehow you still have a chance to get laid. Why are you going home? It doesn't make any sense. Something's wrong with that. I thought I was your best friend, man. Just tell me what it is!"

My brain was working in overdrive to respond, but nothing came out of my mouth. As much as the idea of this happening had plagued my mind since freshman year, I'd always come up with a way to swerve before hitting this question head on. A part of me thought I might be able to change the subject as fast as I could, but the rest of me was exhausted from doing that dance too many times. Michael was the one person I trusted most in the world. He'd been a brother to me since we were kids. He'd always stood up for me. He literally took a beating for me once. Even when he knew I was wrong, he was always on my side. Logic told me this would be no different.

"Michael, I don't want to get laid by Lorena, okay? That's the last thing I want." I felt my eyebrows raise, and hoped I'd said just enough for him to understand. My stomach felt like it was about to drop into my legs.

It appeared to work. He cracked a smile. "Dude, I get it. I *totally* get it."

"You do?" I asked, puzzled by his nonchalance.

"Yeah, man. It happens to all of us." He put his hand on my shoulder in solidarity, and I knew immediately that he did not, in fact, *totally get it*. "You're nervous because tonight might be your first time having sex. But that's normal, dude. When I lost my virginity, I was so nervous I probably seemed like some kind of babbling idiot."

Right now you seem like a babbling idiot, I thought.

I imagined shaking Michael by his massive shoulders and yelling that the only thing I was nervous about was telling him the secret I'd kept locked up for years, on every spring camping trip, during every winter day we played video games, through every summer night conversation laid out on his old trampoline.

A freezing breeze numbed my cheek and the music from inside thumped softly in the distance. "I don't want to get laid by Lorena because I don't want to get laid by *girls*," I said carefully. Then I inhaled a deep breath, and it all seemed to stop – the wind, the music, time. Although I'd said the most clear and honest thing that I had in ages, somehow, Michael seemed even more baffled than before.

"I don't like girls," I added. "I'm… I'm not like you."

For a minute, he seemed as frozen as everything around us. Then, without a word, his face melted from confused to distraught, as he pieced together the meaning of my vague confession. I could feel him realizing the rumors he'd defended me from were true. He felt like a fool, and it almost took the air right out of me.

When he turned away, I realized I hadn't seen Michael this dumbstruck since the night his dad caught us smoking pot in his backyard and he knew he was about to get it. "Say something," I told him.

He looked around like someone might be watching and then said, "Don't say stuff like that. You don't mean it."

"Yes I do," I shot back, edging on angry that this thing I'd contemplated for years might even be questioned. "Believe me, I mean it. And I can't lie about it anymore, Michael. I'm done with that. I'm fucking tired and sad all the time and I don't want to lie about it anymore."

"Well then stay the hell away from me," he answered, as nervously as I'd just spoken, and started toward the school. He stopped midway and looked back, his face hopeful I would tell him it was some kind of prank. "What's everyone gonna say?"

I honestly didn't have an answer to that. I'd spent so much time worrying about what Michael would say, I hadn't thought about anyone else. I stared blankly at the colorful lights through the school windows, and a flood of horror came over me. A wave of fear, and panic, and dread. In the pit of my stomach, something told me I had just cut my best friend loose from my life, and unleashed a truth that wouldn't serve me well in Santana.

Michael continued toward the school, and as he walked inside and the gym doors closed behind him, the dark wind returned, and gave cold reality a whole new meaning.

ONE

I didn't see Michael again until the first day of senior year. Every plan for our last summer break together was canceled when he decided to spend the summer in Albuquerque with his mom.

Before he left, I begged him to talk to me, but he hung up every time, finally declaring once and for all that we didn't know each other anymore. If anything, coming back to school had proven him right. We passed by each other in the hallway after second period and he looked right through me. The only time he'd ever ignored me was in the fourth grade, when I beat him at tetherball in front of the girl he liked. He didn't talk to me for a week, but even then, I didn't lose any sleep. I knew we were still friends and he'd get over it. This was different.

It seemed like the longest day of my life. And when the last period of the day finally came around, I slowly bit my nail down to the skin while I stared at the clock in Study Hall, wishing I could make the time go faster if I concentrated hard enough. But as it clicked and clicked and clicked, I realized the clicks still seemed an hour apart. I wondered if the whole year would be as slow.

Suddenly from behind, a paper ball hit the back of my

head, interrupting my cynical haze. I turned around to find Michael's stupid football friend Xavier laughing like a hyena in the last row. Sitting next to him, Michael stared at me. He wore his letter jacket, and looked every bit like any other jock at school. I turned back around, until another paper ball was hurled my way. This time, it fell over my shoulder, rolling onto the desk in front of me.

I unraveled it to find a tired, familiar message: *FAG!!!*

Xavier had already pulled similar stunts in both classes we had together earlier in the day, and during lunch. Saying nothing and letting him bore himself into stopping apparently hadn't worked. And just like each time before, the hushed laughs from around the room only made Xavier proud. Instinct took over, and without any kind of plan, I pushed myself up and walked to the back of the room. I felt myself moving on autopilot. My hands smashed the paper back into a ball and darted it toward Xavier's forehead. His eyes widened and the room fell silent. Everyone, myself included, thought he was about to get up and pummel my body into pulp right there. My teacher snappily asked what I was doing, but I didn't answer. In fact, I didn't look away from Xavier for a second.

"Faggot this, faggot that. *Faggot, faggot, faggot!* Is that the only word you know, Xavier?" I looked around the classroom. The whole class was still watching in suspense. "I don't know about everyone else, but I think if you insist on sending me love letters, you should switch it up. Quit writing the same thing over and over and over. It's the first day of school and I'm already bored with this shit."

As soon as I finished talking, I felt a rush of warmth in my face and a drop in my stomach and a shake in my sweaty hands, realizing that by finally reacting, I'd given Xavier exactly what he wanted. How was it that standing up for myself was the one thing that made me feel the most defeated?

I apologized to Mr. Garcia for the disruption, but he simply answered by returning his attention to the book he was reading, muttering for me to take a seat. I was furious with embarrassment.

Xavier chuckled behind me. "*Somebody's on her period.*"

The whole classroom started laughing, and as Mr. Garcia ordered everyone to settle down so he could read, I felt myself becoming even more flustered. I took a deep breath and pulled my hood over my head, looking back at Michael one last time. He was already peering back at me when I glanced his way, and there was nothing behind his eyes. It was like looking at a stranger. I couldn't believe it.

I turned around and stared at the chalkboard in the quiet, and all I could think about was how different things were. We used to shake things off so easily, with a playful shove into a locker, or some wise crack about how the other was a loser. (He was a dumb loser and I was an ugly loser.)

There was something inside me instinctively waiting for life with my best friend to resume, and I had to keep reminding myself that he'd been killed by that guy who didn't know me anymore. Or maybe he was just a hostage to that guy? There was no way to tell. After every fight we'd ever had, I would be the first person to make a move toward reconciliation. It always seemed Michael was physically incapable of being the bigger person. That, or I was just the first to tire of fighting every time.

The desire to confront Michael after class bubbled up inside me. I imagined grabbing his backpack, pulling him into some corner, and making him talk to me. That's the kind of thing I could do before everything changed. Now, though, probably not.

"Should I kick their asses?" asked my cousin Sam, painting her nails next to me on her bedroom floor after school. Her bleached hair was pulled back into a ponytail, and she stared with precision at her work, determined to create the illusion of a professional manicure.

"Yes please," I answered sarcastically. "Michael and Xavier both. And while you're swinging your purse in circles taking them out, maybe you can get the rest of their jock friends too."

She laughed at the thought. "You know, you're better off anyway," she said, blowing the paint dry. "I never understood why you wanted to be friends with Michael in the first place. He's an idiot and you're not, he's obsessed with football and you're not, and he's girl crazy... which... enough said."

I rolled my eyes. "It's not that I wanted to be best friends with Michael. It's just been like that for so long, I forgot what it's like *not* to be his best friend."

And that was true. Michael and I became friends when we were in the first grade, mostly because we sat next to each other in class. Sheer proximity can be enough to attach two six-year-olds. Not to mention, there isn't nearly as much variety in the interests of children. For the first years of our friendship, Michael and I had the exact same hobbies. We both loved playing outside, watching TV, and eating junk food. It had only been for the past few years that his attention and mine seemed to turn onto diverging roads. Once high school came around, I wanted to spend my time reading myself into any place besides the New Mexico nowhere that was Santana, and Michael couldn't decide which he liked to play more: football, or seemingly every girl in our class.

Despite about a thousand warnings from me, Sam was one of those girls in the tenth grade, and ever since, she didn't care for Michael. "Well, I could think of a thousand better things for you to be than Michael's friend," she said, dropping her nail polish into her purse. "I really do think it's a blessing in disguise."

"Maybe," I conceded.

"And they better have gotten picking on you out of their system today," she added. "If they do anything else, just let me know. We'll send my dad in to scare the shit out of them."

I couldn't tell if Sam was kidding or not. Uncle Carlos

was the head honcho of the Santana Police Department, and there was no doubt in my mind that if she were to actually tell him about the kids at school, he wouldn't hesitate to make an appearance on behalf of his favorite nephew, regardless of the reason for their idiocy. I shuttered at the thought of how exponentially worse that would make everything. "Please don't," I laughed.

Sure enough, the next few weeks saw plenty more nasty notes, numerous shoves from a variety of varsity meatheads, and not one, but *two* unfortunate incidents involving mashed potatoes in the cafeteria. It never happened when Sam was around, which I counted as a win, and I didn't tell her about any of it, just in case she really thought about getting Uncle Carlos involved.

None of it came from Michael, but every time something did happen, he was there and he watched, just like the first day of school in Study Hall. A part of me thought it might be better if it were him throwing food on me, or pushing the books out of my hands. Then maybe he wouldn't have seemed like a ghost. Mostly, I hated myself for even caring, and that was a feeling I had since before I told him the truth about me in the first place. I always hated how much it mattered to me what he thought. I hated how deep his reactions could drive me into the ground.

In fact, that unsettling feeling finally erupted in me three weeks after Michael had gone to Albuquerque for the summer.

What started as an accidental scrape against my dresser one June morning became a daily ritual, a hiding hole in the day, where nothing seemed to occupy my mind other than the sweet burning pain of a thin line running down the bottom of my forearm. Dramatic? Maybe. And it really wasn't even because of Michael. It was because I'd made myself so afraid of what would happen when he came home at the end of the summer. All I could hear in my head was the echoing of his voice asking what everyone would say about me. I spiraled so badly, I convinced myself my life would be turned into a living hell once senior year started, or even that someone might kill me.

It hadn't even been a year since a boy named Matthew Shepard was beaten with a two-by-four and tied to a fence, left to die for being gay. His picture and his story were plastered all over the news, and more and more, my brain replaced his memorialized face with my own. I stopped sleeping, and my thoughts only became more irrational, until making those shallow slits up and down my skin was a calming distraction, an instant cool for my inferno paranoia.

By the Fourth of July, my mom had taken notice of the long sleeves I wore despite the dry heat of the summer. One day, she grabbed an arm and pulled up my sleeve to reveal the scabby lines scattered underneath. It took her less than an hour to make an appointment for me with a psychiatrist at her hospital, and for six weeks, I was assured and reassured by a nice woman named Dr. Carver (the irony, right?) that I wouldn't be murdered with a two-by-four.

I was also introduced to the enchanting power of sleeping pills.

Since I hadn't slept a full night in weeks, Dr. Carver prescribed sedatives I could take when it was time for bed. I couldn't remember the last time I'd waited for night to come before I took a pill, though. After only a few days of the sedatives, sleep was what I looked forward to the most. There was no time I felt better than when I felt nothing at all. I slept away the rest of the summer, and when school began, I started to come home at the end of every day only to head straight to my room, twist the blinds shut, pop a pill, and throw myself onto the coolness of my comforter. Within minutes, the weight of my eyelids seemed to melt down the weight of the stress everywhere else in my body. For a while, I'd float away into oblivion.

The problem with falling asleep so early, though, was that I'd often wake up in the middle of the night. If I was hungry, I'd get out of bed and microwave some leftovers as quietly as I could. If I wasn't hungry, I was just plain bored. I would watch the red digits on my alarm clock flicker into each other, waiting for the sun to come up so I could go out into the world and get another day over with.

One of those nights, a few weeks into the school year, I shoved away the crap on my nightstand to look at the clock. 3:51 AM. I sighed at how early I'd awoken and looked down at the papers my drowsy arm had scattered onto the floor. Resting on top of my class schedule was the cheap invitation we all found taped to our lockers the week before. The homecoming dance was on its way, and the whole school was making a huge deal about it because it would be the last dance of the century, as if the year 2000 would come along and there would never be another dance.

Sam begged me not to skip out. She insisted I join her and her new boyfriend, Joe. Reluctantly, I agreed. It would be the first year I wouldn't ask a girl to be my date. I'd always thought my life would be easier when I didn't have to attend dances with girls, but I was sorely mistaken. It was more embarrassing than ever. Before, I was the semi-cute nerdy guy who was nice enough to accompany some girl who recently broke her leg or wore headgear. Now, I was the school queer, third-wheeling it with his cousin and her date. It didn't feel like much of an upgrade.

I reached down and grabbed the invitation to throw it away, only to reveal an old picture of Michael and me underneath. We stood proudly under the tree in my front yard, showing off our new tuxedos right before prom. It was like a postcard from another world, a reminder of how much my life changed since that night, only four months before. I picked it up and crumpled it into a ball, just like the one Xavier tossed at my head on the first day of school. I even aimed for the trash, ready to shoot it right into the can.

But then I unraveled the glossy paper and stared at our smiles for a minute before I got out of bed and slipped it into a book on my desk.

Since life at school wasn't exactly grand, Saturday was always the best part of my week. I usually got to spend a quiet day at home alone while my mom worked the day shift at the hospital, and all the while, I knew school was at least a day away. Unfortunately, the morning of the homecoming dance was different. It was the one Saturday in recent history my mom didn't have to work.

"Are you still going to the dance with Sam and her date this evening?" I heard from behind as I poured myself a bowl of cereal. "Don't you think you should just ask a girl?"

Every time she asked something like that, it was so obvious she had some kind of hope I'd rehabilitated overnight, and suddenly I was the normal female-chasing young man she always dreamed of having for a son.

Unfortunately for her, I was no longer sorry for being a disappointment. That was one of the perks of all the therapy she made me go through over the summer. It almost made me wish I was still seeing Dr. Carver. "I'm not asking a girl," I reminded her. "I can't believe Aunt Cheryl and Uncle Carlos get it and you don't. I would've thought it would be the other way around."

"It's always different when it's not your kid," she sighed disapprovingly. "I just want you to think about what's best for you in the long run, Luke. Don't you think you could just ask a girl one last time? It's your last homecoming."

I didn't even answer. There was no point. I took my cereal into the living room and planted myself on the couch. An overly-made-up woman reported live from a hospital parking lot in California, where a man in some city was killed the night before by a group of gay bashers while he was walking home from a dance club. My stomach sunk into a familiar disappointment in the world, and I sat my cereal down next to me, looking for the remote. My mom stood behind me again, holding it out. I reached up and took it.

"I'll never understand why you'd want that for yourself,"

she exhaled, and then picked up her folded laundry and walked toward her room. "You think life will be different in the city, but no matter where you go, there are people who will hate it, Luke."

I rolled my eyes and flicked through the channels, not paying a second of attention to whatever I finally landed on. All I could think about was the warning my mom tacked on to the end of the news lady's report. And as irritated as it made me, I wondered if she was right.

Dr. Carver had convinced me if I could just make it through my senior year, maybe there'd be light at the end of the tunnel. I could jump on a bus, get the hell out of Santana, and start my own life in the city, where she told me magnificent personalities and modern places might be waiting for me. She made the city seem like some kind of fantasy world where I wouldn't be an angry ogre, but a lonely prince who might meet another lonely prince and live happily ever after.

A few hours later, I went over to Sam's to help her choose a dress. It was a nice day out, finally under 90 degrees, and I couldn't stand to be stuck at home with my mom's thwarted sighs following me all over the house. When I arrived, Sam grabbed me by the hand and yanked me up to her room. A red dress hung near the closet, and a blue one sprawled over the corner of her bed. "I just can't choose!" she cried desperately. "Which one?"

To my surprise, I didn't hate either of them. Usually, I disagreed with her when it came to clothes, but it seemed she finally took the advice I'd always given her: *Aim for class*.

I told her to go with the red one, because it was a rusty red, which would look nice with the golden treetops outside. "I swear, you gay guys always know what to do!" she beamed. She grabbed the dress and scurried to the bathroom. I rolled my eyes, both at her stereotyping me, and the stereotype's validity in that moment.

Taped to a mirror on the wall, a strip of photos we took

at the summer carnival gleamed at me. In the top photo, Sam hugged a stoic me. Below that, Sam gave a stoic me bunny ears. Under that, Sam flipped her hair next to a stoic me. And in the bottom photo, Sam sat alone, smiling wide after she pushed me out of the booth for being too stoic, which ironically caused me to laugh my ass off.

I grinned at the memory.

When she twirled back into the bedroom, she was draped in autumn-colored glory. "I'd say you picked the right one," she complimented.

"Glad I could help," I grinned in return. "I hope it makes up for me not going tonight."

Her smile dwindled into a frown. "What do you mean you're not going? I already made a dinner reservation for three! Joe doesn't mind. Seriously."

"*I mind*," I contested. "It's a school dance, Sam. Even if Joe said he doesn't care, he's got to. And he should! You're supposed to go with your date, not your date and her gay cousin. Trust me. If I go, it won't be fun for any of us."

Her frown persisted.

"Besides," I added, "I don't feel like seeing Michael and his meathead friends when I have the option not to. I really don't want to go. I promise. Just do me a favor and don't tell our parents. We can take pictures in the front yard, and then I'll go catch a movie or something."

Her frown curved into a defeated smile and she held out her pinky finger. I hooked it with mine and thanked her for understanding with a relieved smile.

That evening, after our parents had their fill of snapping their disposable cameras and finally excused us to be on our way, I asked Joe to drop me off at the movie theater at the edge of town so I could easily burn a couple hours before going home. Sam made one last-ditch effort to convince me to join them, but I assured her the dance was the last place I wanted to be.

I strolled up to the theater in full homecoming attire as

the sky faded into a tangerine glow and the matching street lights below flickered on.

When I pulled open the building's glass door, I scoffed at how ridiculous I looked. But I also knew if I needed to fake going to the dance to keep my mom from threatening my reenlistment in therapy, it was a small price to pay. I asked the lady at the admissions booth for a ticket to the newest slasher flick, and she gave me a pitying stare and slid me a stub under the neon light, chewing meekly on a piece of gum and motioning for me not to pay.

Once inside, I took a seat in the back of the empty room. When it's homecoming night in a small town, there aren't too many people lined up for the movies. Somehow, though, as the previews began to roll and I loosened my tie, a familiar figure did walk in front of the screen, and sat down in the middle of the front row. I sunk into my chair, hoping when he looked around, the projector blinded him and he didn't see me.

It was Ray Melendez.

He was nineteen, worked on cars for a living, and was apparently molded by God himself, with his broody gray eyes and a jawline plenty of people would die for. He appeared in Santana a year earlier and got himself a job as a mechanic at the place Michael's dad worked. He was quiet everywhere he went, and he always seemed to be watching everyone else like a hawk. Once, I saw him at the grocery store and he scared me when he caught me staring; he grabbed me with his eyes for a good minute before he let go. Ever since then, I tried not to look at him.

Beside the fact that he was built from his work and a handsome copper from the sun, he also seemingly walked everywhere in town wearing a different rumor about him. There was plenty of gossip around town about Ray, the most popular being that he once put a guy on life support. People joked that he had come to town on the run, and that's why he kept to himself. In fact, the only reason anyone even knew he was nineteen was because he got busted trying to buy whiskey from the liquor store, and the owner told everyone and their mother about it. As the movie started, I watched his silhouette, ready to duck if he looked around.

Either the movie was boring or my sleeping pills from the night before were still kicking my ass, because two hours later, a nudge on my arm woke me up. I felt myself slumped over to the side, jabbed by the armrest next to me. I lifted up my head and opened my eyes and the lights had come up, and the credits were rolling, and Ray Melendez was looking down on me. I thought I was dreaming.

"Movie's over," he said with an oddly soft confidence, slipping his hands into his black jean pockets. It was only then I realized I'd never heard his voice before. It was lower than I would've guessed. It was also a lot less serial-killer-sounding than I thought it would be, based on all the rumors.

"Thanks," I mumbled, frozen in my seat.

He nodded before he turned and walked away, and only after he disappeared from the theater did my heart remember to beat. The face of my watch glowed on my wrist. It was ten o'clock. Late enough to go home.

The next afternoon, my mom was in a shitty mood after work. Clearly frustrated, she didn't even bother asking about homecoming before she sat at the dining table and sighed a breath of relief to be home from another day.

She asked me to get her a glass of water, and while I did, she began to tell me the hospital was reducing spending, which meant she'd have to take a pay cut, which meant it was time for me to get a job, because I needed to learn some responsibility, and coming home after school and sleeping until it was dark wouldn't teach me anything but laziness. That might have all been true, but I knew the bigger truth was that ever since my dad had taken off, my mom struggled to scrape together enough money for the mortgage, and this

17

looming pay cut wouldn't help.

When I called and told Sam, she brought over a newspaper so I could look for jobs in town, and she could fill me in on everything I'd missed at the dance. As my eyes jumped through the ads and I realized how many jobs in Santana were *not* for me, Sam reported on the latest scandals in detail: the dress choice tragedies, the huge cheerleader catfight, the two house party arrests, and so on. I half-listened, nodding my head as I read.

By the time she was done gossiping, I'd gone over the entire *Help Wanted* section five times, and had one listing circled in red ink.

A woman with the longest pearl necklace I'd ever seen sat across from me at the coffee shop on Main Street the next day after school. I recognized her immediately from around town. She stuck out because in addition to her statuesque beauty, she was one of maybe three Black people in all of Santana. She was tall, composed, and striking, like a classy model for a department store commercial, or one of those ex-movie stars fortunate enough to age well without a ton of plastic surgery. Although she could pass for forty, I guessed she was in her fifties. Her lips were painted a bright red, matching the polish on her fingernails, and her smile was as bright as it was relaxed and graceful.

"You are absolutely adorable," she smirked, in a deep and yet feminine drawl. "My name is Zondra Devereux, but you, my dear, may call me Zondra. This is my café. I own it, I run it." She took out a thin folder of papers and opened it up. With her reading glasses pulled down to the tip of her nose, she asked if I'd ever worked in food services before.

"No."

Had I ever been convicted of a felony?

"No."

Had I ever been fired from a job?

"No."

"Honey, have you ever *had* a job?"

"No," I answered again, hoping it wouldn't mean the end of the interview.

But she only put down her pen for her eyes to widen joyously. "You're looking for your first job?" she gleamed, "Oh, I remember my first job. It was 1952 and my father had me in the back of the family tobacco shop rolling cigars at the age of ten. I used to make ten cents a day and I couldn't have been happier. Of course, you'll make more than ten cents a day if you work here. That was years ago." Looking past me, she could feel herself digressing and glanced back down to her questionnaire. "What makes you interested in working here, Lukas?"

"Honestly?" I asked.

She nodded.

"I need a job to help my mom pay the bills, and this is the only place hiring in town that doesn't require me to change tires or donate sperm."

She burst into a glamorous laughter. I was thankful she found my joke amusing. "I love a man with a sense of humor," she smiled. After scribbling some notes onto her paper, she looked back up and whisked off her glasses, squinting her eyes. "Are you a responsible young man, Lukas?"

"Yes."

"Good. Do you promise to work hard?"

"Of course."

"Then you're hired. You can start next week."

And that was that.

It almost seemed too easy.

Telling my mom I scored a job on my first interview was less of an occasion than I'd expected. She nodded with a pleased smile over her dinner and reiterated everything she'd said before about how beneficial the experience would be for me. It clearly made her feel better to say that my working after school was really about me at the end of the day, and whatever she needed to do to lift her mood before my next news was fine by me.

"Also... we got our progress reports today. I need you to sign mine."

She looked up from her stew. She knew progress reports only had to be signed when there was, in fact, no progress to report. "You better be keeping those grades up," she warned. Despite her obligatory display of concern, I could tell the only thing she felt was tired.

I stood up and pulled the folded paper from my pocket. I handed it over and she opened it up. Predictably, her face morphed into that familiar disenchantment she should have patented by that point. "Three C's and a D?" she asked, seemingly more puzzled than angry. "Why are these so low, Lukas? It's not even October and you're already this far behind?" I always knew she was frustrated when she called me Lukas and not Luke. I shrugged. She went on: "You've always been an honor student. Straight A's. First the whole... *not liking girls thing*, and now this? What am I doing wrong?"

My mouth opened on its own as if words were about to shoot out, but nothing came because I didn't know what to say. I couldn't think of a possible way to reason with a statement like that. I was lucky enough to genuinely understand there were things about me that my mom just didn't get, and I knew I didn't have the energy to try changing her mind. On top of that, I was annoyed. I hated that she turned everything happening in my life into a sad tale of a woman abandoned with a teenage son she couldn't understand, and the unfathomable strife she faced as an unwillingly-single mother.

She picked up her bowl, walked over to the sink, and dropped it in carelessly before her attempt at having the last word: "I work my ass off every day, Lukas. All you have to do is stay out of trouble and get some decent grades so if you want to go to college, it won't break us! Why do you make everything so hard?"

"I make everything hard?" I asked. Suddenly I didn't feel

speechless anymore. "All you do is remind me that people are going to want me dead for existing, Mom. Why should I even think about college? Don't you think it's pointless if someone's going to beat me and tie me to the back of a pickup truck halfway through?"

She seemed stunned at the image I'd painted. "You're the one who wants to live that way, Lukas! Father Bernie says homosexuality might be something you're born with – I told you that, and I agree with that – but you make the choice to tell people."

"What do you want me to do?" I yelled. I could tell she wasn't done; I'd interrupted her, but I didn't care. I said it again: "I would love to know. What do you want me to do? Do you want me to find myself a nice girlfriend and lie to her? Do you want me to go around town and pretend I'm like Michael, and never shut up about girls, even though I wouldn't mean any of it? I already tried that for seventeen years and I hated every second of it."

"Right now what I want you to do is keep your mouth shut and go to your room," she growled angrily. I could tell I struck a nerve, and I felt nothing less than satisfied, even though she'd made it clear once again that she wasn't.

TWO

When the bell ended third period that Monday, I stayed put while the rest of the class shuffled out of Mr. King's room. I figured if I was going to fix the mess my grades had become, I'd start at the bottom and climb my way out. King slumped in his chair and sloppily shuffled through a stack of quizzes. "Yes, Mr. Bradley?" he inquired, looking up as I stepped closer.

I hated when King called me that. Mr. Bradley was my dad, who was a dick. My first instinct was to tell him never to say it again, but I quickly decided against it. It wouldn't be productive. It probably wouldn't be a good idea to tell him he had a tiny piece of food stuck in his front teeth, either, which he did. I couldn't help but keep looking at it, trying to figure out what it was.

"I was wondering what I can do to raise my grade in your class. My mom saw my progress report and kind of freaked out. I guess I've been a little off this semester." I hesitated for a second. I wasn't used to having to ask teachers for extra help, and the fact that King was so creepy only made it feel more awkward. "I was thinking maybe I could write a paper about the unit we just finished for some extra credit?"

He sighed. "Please close the door and have a seat."

I got up and quietly shut the door, and as I sat down in one of the desks in the front row, he got up and came around to the front of his own desk, folding his arms. "Mr. Bradley, I know you've been struggling this year." King always seemed to talk just a little too slow and stare without blinking for a little too long. I felt even more uncomfortable as his dark blue eyes peered at me, somehow making the whole room seem colder. "I want you to know I understand. I really do," he nodded. "Being different from everyone else is difficult. And it's difficult for everybody."

I nodded back patiently. What did he mean *difficult for everybody*?

"This world can be harsh, and cruelty from others can make motivation hard to find. But you've got to find it, for your own sake, Mr. Bradley. What you can do to raise your grade in this class is try harder. You were in my class a couple of years ago, and you were a star student. I know you're an intelligent young man."

I couldn't land on whether I was more offended at his condescending indifference toward my life being a shit show, or squeamish at the way he stared down at my shirt while he talked to me.

"So you're saying it's my fault this year sucks?" I spurted out. That was what it sounded like he was saying. I knew I sounded defensive, but I couldn't help the way I felt. And King didn't seem to have a clue what it was like to have an entire school against him. For crying out loud, he thought everyone liked him, when in reality, people were nice to him because they knew he was the biggest pushover in the whole school. The truth was that everyone thought he was creepy, and there were rumors he was a pervert. I was so angry, listing off everything horrible about him was on the tip of my tongue, but I bit it for the sake of not making my situation even worse.

"I'm not saying it's your fault. I'm saying it's your responsibility to cope with it, and to rise above it. I believe you can do that."

After saying all he had to say, he went back to his seat and began looking through the papers on his desk again. I knew if I sat in front of him for another second I was going to lose it and say something I'd regret, so I grabbed my backpack and sarcastically thanked him for his time before I left the classroom.

I was excited to get to work after school. My first few days at the café had gone well and I was learning everything quickly. As I walked into the coffee shop, Zondra praised me for my punctuality and with her ever-glowing smile, motioned for me to join her behind the counter. She handed me a red apron and said it was the perfect time to train because afternoons were the slower half of the day.

She was right. Only a few people came in while she showed me how to make the new cinnamon caramel concoctions she'd created that morning, all while telling me about her childhood in Louisiana. Most of the stories were tailed with lessons, like parables from some imaginary Southern bible, but I didn't mind. I liked the way she talked. Something about her voice was comforting in the way listening to a grandmother is, and even though she didn't know much of anything about me, she looked at me as if she'd seen me grow up.

By the time we both knew it, it was seven o'clock. The day was done. We cleaned up and then slipped into our coats, and Zondra asked if I'd like to go to her house for dinner. I remembered my mom was working late at the hospital that night, and I was sure whatever Zondra would make for dinner would be better than the canned ravioli I'd been eating for the past three nights.

"Definitely yes," I smiled politely.

Zondra lived in a house much nicer than the average Santana home, on the outskirts of town near the golf course. That was where the more wealthy people lived, and ironically, it was known as the "white neighborhood." I wondered how the owner of one little coffee shop could afford to live among the people who owned multiple and bigger companies in town, especially alone. Or at least I assumed she lived alone. She didn't wear a wedding ring and she hadn't mentioned a man in any of her stories.

As we walked into her living room and its warmth enveloped the both of us, she took my jacket and led me around a corner. Her kitchen was light and spacious and decorated in an array of bright colors. And it smelled like a feast had been waiting for us. Zondra must have noticed I was savoring the smell. "If you think it smells good, just wait until we eat. Laura's a wonderful cook," she smiled.

Laura?

Did her sister live with her? Did she have a housekeeper?

She pulled out a chair and told me to have a seat.

"You're home!" another woman gleamed, joining us at the kitchen table. She walked with the same subtle elegance as Zondra. She stood a bit shorter but equally sure of herself, and had a comparable sense of joy in her voice.

"I'm sorry we're later than I expected. It was another day of training Lukas. But it's going so well and he's getting the hang of everything so quickly!" She turned to me next, and draped her arm around Laura's shoulder. "Lukas, this is Laura. My wife."

On the outside I smiled, "Nice to meet you, Laura."

On the inside I screamed, "Zondra's a lesbian?!"

Zondra and Laura insisted I make myself at home, and they served me food as if I were their child and this were family dinner. They asked about how senior year was going and just like Zondra had done all day, Laura told me all the things she could remember from when she was my age. I watched both of the women while I ate and listened to them, noticing every move they made. I saw the way they caught each other's eyes, and I saw the light in one's face when the other recognized the story she was beginning to tell, and I saw the way their hands would sneak back to one another's on the tablecloth every so often.

Laura asked me what I wanted to do after graduation, and I told her I'd always dreamed of going to the city, much to her delight. "I don't know if Zondra's told you, but we were city women in our past lives," she reminisced.

"But when it was time for a change, Santana was just what we needed. Maybe the opposite is true for you, Lukas," Zondra added.

"Maybe so," I nodded, and then asked about their lives before Santana.

They met a million years ago, fell in love, and it seemed like they might have even had kids. It was hard to tell, because of how many times they'd fall from the middle of one story onto the beginning of another. They didn't even say how they ended up in Santana, and I didn't ask. I didn't need to. Honestly, I was distracted. My mind was so consumed with the idea of them, together, as wife and wife, and it was okay, and everything was fine, and they were happier than any married people I'd ever met.

When I said I needed to get home after dinner, they both put on their coats to drive me. They must have wondered why I was so quiet, because as much as I tried to engage in the conversation, I couldn't do much other than admire the silhouettes of their faces when they glanced at each other in the moonlight streaming through the windshield. They were in love, and I couldn't look away.

I could only think about all the times I'd been awake at three in the morning and let my mind wander in the dark, to the depths of the desires I had for what was now sitting right in front of me. I thought of all the times I'd told myself that to wish for something like what Zondra and Laura had found in each other was a waste of time – nothing but a fantasy. I thought of how mistaken I'd been for so long in convincing myself it didn't exist.

Of course, I'd accidentally left some door open and doubt, the universal enemy of hope, spilled onto my newfound epiphanies. *Just because they found it doesn't mean you will,* a voice echoed between my ears. *What makes you think you deserve anything they have? And who would that person even be? This town isn't big enough for lightning to strike twice. Be happy for them and quit there. It's not for you. It's not for you. It's not for you.*

"Lukas, is this your house?" Zondra said, pointing out the window and snapping me back into reality.

I nodded and got out of the car. "Thanks for dinner."

They waved goodbye, and as they drove off into the night, I stood there in front of my house and I breathed in the cool autumn night air, and somehow, I found myself feeling hope again.

Doubt be damned.

As much as it made me a horrible cousin, it's true that misery loves company, and I was comforted in knowing Sam was constantly in a state of romantic turmoil. Unlike me, she had no problem finding a boyfriend. Her problem was keeping them, for one reason or another. Like most of her relationships, her brief affair with her boyfriend Joe ended after a total of four weeks. They were only one day away from their monthiversary when she found out he cheated on her with some junior.

She called to tell me the news one otherwise-calm evening, and in a familiar vengeful tone, instructed me to put on some dark clothes and come over to her house. When she answered the front door, she was swathed in my uncle's camouflage hunting gear. Before I could even say a word about it, she put her hand up to preemptively hush any questions, instead unpacking a carton of eggs from a grocery bag and handing it to me.

We approached Joe's house, and I told her she was acting crazy. "I don't know if this is such a good idea," I whispered to Sam, surprised she wasn't more worried herself. Uncle Carlos always joked he was waiting for the day that he would throw one of us in jail. I remembered thinking since I was a little boy that I really, really, never wanted it to be me.

"Here." She handed me an egg when we finally got to Joe's house, ignoring my concern. "I already know you won't go first, so I will. Then you throw yours. Got it?"

I sighed and nodded.

She took a deep breath and launched her egg toward the house. We heard a thud and peeked out from the bushes to see a shiny slime running down the paneling next to the front door. I couldn't help but smile and she tried not to laugh.

"See? It's easy. Now throw yours."

I pitched my egg toward the house as hard as I could, and a second later, glass shattered. My hastily thrown egg somehow broke through the living room window. My jaw dropped and I turned to Sam, waiting for her plan. Her eyes were wide open and it was clear she was caught off guard. "Shit!" she yelled, and grabbed the carton. She threw one more egg toward the house and took off down the street, expecting me to follow.

We only made it to the next block before she jogged over to a stop sign and grabbed hold of it, trying to catch her breath.

"We have to hurry!" I said nervously, looking back and noticing the lights in the house illuminating, one by one. "Why are you just standing here?" She looked down to the ground and put her hand to her stomach. I rolled my eyes. "Sam. This is not the time to cry! You can cry at your house. Let's go!"

And then out of nowhere, the most disgusting hurl I'd ever heard broke the quietness of the quaint street as Sam's dinner fell onto the sidewalk. The sound alone made me want to throw up right along with her, and seeing that my shoes had fallen victim to her regurgitated tacos didn't help.

Suddenly, though, it didn't matter. The screech of Joe's front door flying open pierced the air, and his dad ran out into the lawn. "Goddamn kids!" he roared, shooting a rifle up at the sky. I grabbed Sam's hand and we dashed into the night.

The next day at school, I had to keep myself from falling asleep in every class. I was practically a zombie by the time Chemistry came along. Thankfully, my teacher was peppier than normal, which made it easier to keep my eyes open.

"Well, it's about that time! We're close to starting our very own experiments with the chemistry sets," Ms. Pacheco announced after the bell rang. She gleamed as if we made it to the Olympics. "Are you ready to find out who your partners will be?"

Most other kids hooted and hollered. They were excited because Ms. Pacheco had spent the last six weeks telling us once we'd read enough, we could start the "fun" part of the class. I couldn't have cared less about any of it.

But as Ms. Pacheco started down her list, I did feel anxious knowing I'd have to work closely with someone else.

A couple names in, she got to mine. It's funny how many thoughts can go through your head in the two seconds it takes someone to say, "Luke Bradley." As soon as I heard my name, my body froze up, preparing to find out whose would follow. I prayed for Sam's. It was the one class we had together, and we had planned on being partners if the teacher let us choose. Across the room, she crossed her fingers, staring at Ms. Pacheco intensely.

Of course, it was not Sam's name that followed mine.

"Your science partner will be... Michael Medina."

Michael shot up from his seat like a firework. "Miss, I need you to change that." Hunched in the seat next to him, Xavier chuckled like a jackass.

I let my face sink down into my hands, and prayed I was dreaming. This wasn't happening. It couldn't be. I couldn't work with Michael. For the longest time after he shunned me, I wanted nothing more than to speak to him, but now the thought of it horrified me. It made me feel sick.

I could tell Ms. Pacheco didn't know what to say in response to Michael's request. She looked down to the list, and then back to Michael. "This list is final. I'm not changing it."

I raised my hand, and before she even looked my way, I pleaded like my life depended on it. "We really can't work together. Can I work alone? I'll do all the work by myself if you let me."

Michael wore the same desperate face, but she put up her hand to signal we were both wasting our time. "Find a way to make it work for the sake of your grades, or don't. Either way, it's not my problem. You're seniors. You cannot let whatever personal problem you have get in the way of passing this class. Not if you'd like to graduate, anyway. I'm moving on now."

As she continued down her list, I turned around and glanced at Michael, just like I did on the first day of school. He glared back angrily. It was the same glare he gave me when we were kids and I accidentally drove his remote-control car into the street, right into the path of somebody's big truck. *This isn't my fault so don't look at me like that*, I grunted in my head, since I couldn't yell it at him across the room. And as if he heard me, he looked away. He looked as defeated as I felt.

Even though she already knew we wouldn't be partners, Sam looked just as disappointed as me when her name was called with someone else's. She scribbled a sad face on her notebook and flashed it across the room.

Usually when I came home after work, Mom already had dinner waiting on the table. That evening, however, the house was silent; everything sat still in the same dark blue as outside. As I tossed my backpack onto the couch, I noticed there was light coming from inside her bedroom. I walked down the hall and quietly pushed the cracked door open. She was sleeping on her bed, with a familiar photo album resting in her arms.

It was the album I made for her a couple Christmases ago. I worked on it for three weeks, and when she unwrapped it, she almost cried as she flipped through the colorful pages. "I wish you were this little boy again," she grinned solemnly, grazing the glued-on pictures with her fingertips.

Once, my mom had the most incredible smile I'd ever seen on a woman; it was warm and joyful and reassuring. It seemed to have left with my dad, though. Now, all that remained in its place was a cold sorrow, and with every day since he'd left, it only became more and more permanent. All the time, I wondered if there was anything that might make her feel alive again, or at least make her realize she had always been too good for him. She didn't understand with his absence came the opportunity to be better than before, when she was constantly overcome with paranoia that he'd leave. She was too preoccupied by her heartbreak to realize that the day he packed his shit and took off was probably the best day of our lives. You can't worry about someone leaving after they've already gone.

I gently pulled the album from her arms and set it down on the nightstand next to her bed before I covered her up, turned off her light, and softly closed the door behind me as I stepped back into the hallway, standing still to admire the dark quiet of the house once more.

Then it was time for a pill. An early night's sleep sounded better than ever.

Later that night, I walked into the school locker room. The smell of steam and skin rushed into me, and I felt more awake than I had in quite a while. Strangely, I wasn't sure how I'd gotten there, and even stranger, although there wasn't a window in sight, I knew it was late. Probably past midnight.

As the door slowly swung shut behind me, I made my way over to my locker and dialed it open. There was a note inside.

Meet me in the shower.

Somehow, I knew the handwriting. How was this

31

happening? I shut the door and looked down. When had I taken off my clothes? Only a towel was wrapped around my waist, which would normally make me more than uncomfortable. But for some reason, in the moment, I liked it. It felt good.

My chest began to move slower and I could feel my breathing deepen as I slowly stepped toward the spanking sound of the shower at the other end of the room. The air was thick and warm. It was a welcome feeling, compared to the chilly wet tile underneath my feet.

I neared the one shower stall with a closed curtain and running water, peeling off my towel and dropping it onto the floor.

As my heartbeat bolstered, I touched the end of the curtain and slowly drew it open. A cloud of steam warmed my whole front side, and standing before me was Ray Melendez. He looked me straight in the eye as the hot water spraying from the shower head hit the side of his neck and fell from his broad shoulders, down to his pumped up chest, and then to his chiseled stomach, until suddenly my eyes snapped opened and I darted up from my pillow. It might as well have been on fire, I was awake so fast.

I lifted up my sheets and looked down, catching my breath.

Goddammit.

More than a week passed before Zondra said anything about her big lesbian reveal. I wondered if she thought I shouldn't be surprised, since I was gay, too. I hadn't told her about me, but I figured maybe she knew, in the way people just seem to sometimes.

Well, of course I was surprised. She was an old lady! Were old ladies even allowed to be lesbians?

Of course they were. My brain *knew* that, but I didn't seem to *get it.*

She just didn't seem like a lesbian to me. I put a mental picture of Zondra next to that one Ellen DeGeneres magazine cover. Nope, it didn't make any sense.

Jesus Christ, Lukas, stop it, I finally told myself.

Just because she was a lesbian didn't mean she had to be a walking stereotype, and what a hypocrite I'd been for ignoring that. I was awfully gay, and I didn't flip my wrists or have a lisp or wear tight pink shirts (although I did wear out my Jennifer Lopez tape over the summer).

I tied my apron strings behind me one afternoon, watching her put on her coat to leave, and I noticed the café was empty and we were alone. "Can I ask you something?" I said, as she picked up her scarf and threw it around her shoulders.

"Of course you can, Lukas," Zondra smiled. She came over to the bar and sat down.

"Why didn't you tell me that you're...? Well, you know... About Laura."

"Should I have? I didn't know it was an issue." She seemed confused.

"It's not. In fact, I'm... like you. I just didn't expect it, that's all. I guess... I don't know. I've never met another person like me before."

"A gay person? Oh, honey, yes you have. Believe me."

"Okay, well I definitely haven't met two, who are married to each other. I mean, I was thinking about it, and is that even legal?"

Her smile faded a bit.

She touched the pearls on her necklace and behind her glasses, a thoughtful squint revealed she was trying to construct an appropriate response to my question. "Luke," she sighed, "Marriage is not a piece of paper you receive from the government. Marriage is Laura being a part of my life since I was twenty. It's us, staying together through multiple foster children, hateful people trying to tear us apart, and her battle with cancer a couple years ago. It's our commitment to loving each other."

Her grin returned at the satisfaction her answer had clearly given her, and as for me, I didn't know what to say.

I just stood there, wiping the same cup I'd been wiping for minutes, as she gleefully told me she'd see me the next day and left.

When I set the mug onto the counter, I found myself wearing the same grin as Zondra. Since she was twenty. That was like a hundred years. That was love.

As much as I liked working at the café, I had at least three school days off every week because Zondra didn't believe "kids" should work more than half-time. At first I contested, telling her I didn't mind working every school day and on weekends, if it meant getting out of my house. But she didn't relent. "You have the rest of your life to work like that," she said. "Right now is when you should be able to stop and smell the flowers."

As the first week of October ushered out the summer weather and replaced it with a cooler calm, it was easier than ever for me to admire the world. Fall was always my favorite time of the year.

On my way home from school one day, flaky leaves slid and tumbled down the sidewalk and reminded me of the years before. When we were kids, Michael and I used to rake together the most colossal heaps of amber leaves, just to throw ourselves into them. We'd lay in the crunchy piles and talk, sometimes for hours. In fact, it was only the same time last year that we stared at the sky from under the tree in my front yard and I listened to Michael go on about some girl in his math class. He loved her red lipstick because he felt like it made her look innocent and crazy at the same time. I told him I couldn't imagine putting that much thought into someone's mouth, and we both laughed. The memory made me chuckle.

Then, as I reached my front door and instinctively slid my key into the lock, Michael's voice suddenly appeared. When he said my name, I jumped and grabbed my chest. "You scared the shit out of me."

He stopped himself from laughing. "Sorry," he said,

shoving his hands into his letter jacket. "Look, I know you're mad, but I came here to call a truce."

I wondered if I should pinch myself to make sure this was happening. Was Michael Medina really telling me there would be no more cafeteria food flung at my back, or books smacked out of my hands, or profanities yelled at me on the way to school first thing in the morning?

"A truce, huh?"

He rolled his eyes, just like he always did before calling me a drama queen when I'd freak out about forgetting to do a homework assignment, or wearing socks that didn't match. "Believe it or not, this sucks just as much for me as it does for you," he muttered, his eyes looking past me. I could tell it was hard for him to say that, as wrong as he was. His dad's voice had to be swirling inside his head, telling him to quit acting like a little girl. "We were best friends for like... our whole lives," he added.

"*Were*," I repeated after him, setting down my backpack and crossing my arms. "Why do I feel like this is a trick?" I could feel my eyebrows interrogating him. "You've had no problem with the way your buddies have treated me all year, but now you give a shit? Why? Because we have to work together? Don't want your grades to go down because your football life will be over?"

He shook his head. "Of course you're overthinking this." He sighed and contemplated what to say next. Apologizing was foreign to him. "I don't blame you for being mad, okay? I guess some of the guys gave you a hard time for being... *confused* or whatever, and I didn't stop them, and that was messed up. But I came here to say I'm willing to forget anything ever happened. Things can go back to the way they were before prom. I'll tell everyone to forget about it and lay off."

I was so struck by the sheer falsehood of being called *confused* that I barely absorbed anything else he just said. "I'm not confused. I know who I am – I know *what* I am – and you have a problem with it." My heart was still pounding so hard I could feel it in my head, same as the day I blew up at Xavier. "And if 'things going back to the way they used to be' means I have to act like I'm someone else just so you don't think I'm disgusting, then fuck you." I picked up my backpack. My face was warm with fury. "I hope you realize that for twelve years you were best friends with a faggot, and it didn't matter until the faggot told you the truth about it."

He stood still, speechless and clearly dumbfounded.

When I went inside and slammed the door behind me, I closed my eyes and took a deep breath, hoping to let my heart calm down. Then I kicked off my shoes and went to my room, yanking the tuxedo picture from prom out of the book on my desk. Something tumultuous began to pump through my veins as I stared at Michael smiling next to me. An inexplicable level of rage I hadn't felt in months. I tore the picture to shreds before I even realized I was doing it, and when it was gone, I found myself sitting in the corner of my room, keys in hand. I rolled up my sleeve.

I was upset but I wasn't crying. It was like there was no room for crying. My body was in autopilot mode, possessed by something dark and terrible.

I pressed my house key onto the tender skin under my forearm, and suddenly, before I could drag it anywhere, I heard Dr. Carver's voice in my head. "Lukas, I want you to take a deep breath. Count backwards from ten." I pulled all the air I could into my lungs and held it for a second before I blew it out slowly.

Ten... nine... eight... seven... six... five... four... three... two... one.

Sure enough, when I opened my eyes, everything was less of a blur.

My keys dropped onto the floor and I pushed myself up, taking another deep breath before moving to my dresser and unscrewing the lid from the orange bottle inside. I swallowed a pill, fell back onto my bed, and within moments, I disappeared.

THREE

The day after Michael's appearance at my house, Sam listened to me complain about it in the cafeteria. I could see her frustration at every detail as she chewed her lunch.

"He's such an ass!" she grunted, displaying mashed up turkey sandwich between words. She took a second to swallow. "He needs to get over himself and stop acting like he's better than you."

I sighed. "All I know is, I'm not excited to see him in class later. I don't know what to say to him now. We should have kept doing what we were doing, just talking enough to get our work done."

She nodded, finishing up her lunch and then eyeing mine. "Are you eating that coleslaw?"

I looked down at the paper cup of watery mush. "You can have it," I said.

She took the cup from my tray, and I remembered she had done the same thing the day before, and the day before that, too.

"Don't jump across the table and scratch my eyes out or anything," I said, "But why have you been eating so much lately?"

"I don't know. It's really weird," she answered, "I've

been starving ever since I got to school, and I ate breakfast right before I left."

Sam returned her attention to the food in front of her, and my eyes couldn't help but wander toward the STOP TEENAGE PREGNANCY poster next to the vending machines. Suddenly, it might have all made sense: the eating, the moodiness, the throwing up on my brand-new shoes that night we egged Joe's house. "Have you taken a pregnancy test?" I asked.

She halted mid-chew, only allowing enough movement to swallow her coleslaw. "What?" she uttered quickly. "That's impossible." She put down her spoon and her hands clasped together under her chin. "We only had sex twice. And the last time was after homecoming. That was almost a month ago." As she realized maybe it wasn't so impossible after all, she took a deep breath. "I would know by now, wouldn't I?"

I shrugged. "Maybe you do."

Toward the end of every month, Mrs. Morales broke my math class into pairs and assigned a project for us to complete over the weekend. For September's project, I'd been lucky enough to be absent. When I came back, I was told to do it alone. When October's assignment came around, I wasn't so lucky. My name was called with Nissa Delfino's.

She had just started at Santana that Monday. She was from the city, and she was all anyone at school could talk about. Throughout the hallways, girls either called her their new best friend or murmured that she seemed like a skank, and seemingly every guy gazed like a hungry dog, each of them preemptively bragging behind locker doors they'd be first to get her number.

On this particular day, Nissa wore lime green pumps with tight blue jeans and a pink pleather jacket. Her nails were plum, and they matched the headband keeping her shimmering dark hair in place. She looked like she woke up in a Mattel box that morning. When I glanced over after Morales called her name with mine, she didn't even look up from the *Cosmo* magazine she studied on her desk. I rolled my eyes and asked myself what I could have done to make the universe loathe me as much as it obviously did.

In the last few minutes of class, Morales told us to get together with our partners to plan for the project. Nissa still didn't look up, so I walked over to her desk, dropping my math book onto her *Cosmo*. "Oops," I grinned.

"Oh, hi!" Nissa smiled genuinely, handing my book up to me, as if I'd made a sincere mistake. She closed her magazine. "What's happening? I was totally distracted. Something about partners, right? I'm guessing you're my partner. Oh, this is going to be so much fun. I actually *love* math!"

I wondered if her head was full of glitter.

"Look, if you want, I can do the project and put your name on it. I mean, unless you want to do it. That's fine, too."

The bell rang. Class was over.

Nissa hurriedly shoved the *Cosmo* into an oversized yellow bag and giggled. "This is a *partner* project, silly. We can work on it together. How about after school? Meet me at the flagpole when we get out. We can work at my house. I don't live far. I'm Nissa, by the way. You're Lukas, right?"

She plucked an unmarked orange envelope from her bag and handed it to me. Before I could even open it, she told me I was a gem and her heels clicked on the floor as she left. I wasn't sure what to think. I didn't know if I could possibly like her; she was horrifically giddy. But she knew my name. The most popular girl in school was just nice to me.

I tore the top of the envelope and pulled out a pumpkin-shaped invitation from inside. Tiny silver ghost confetti tumbled out. *If you received one of these invitations from me*, the card read, *I better see you (IN COSTUME!) at my Halloween house party this Saturday!* A bold giant heart was drawn underneath, followed by an eloquent signature.

Instinct told me to throw the invitation right into the trash since going to any party in Santana felt off limits, but instead, I opened my bag and slipped it between my books.

I never liked to hate anything. I always preferred to dislike things, because *hating* seemed to require too much effort. Generally speaking, I never had the energy for it. If there was anything in the world that I always found the strength to hate, though, it was waiting. Like that day after school, in front of the flagpole. As I anxiously scanned for Nissa, everyone coming out of the school looked at me as if I had a ticking bomb strapped to my chest.

I wished I did.

Finally, my name pierced the air as Nissa let the world know I was waiting for her. I looked down and began walking toward Main Street, and she hustled in her heels to catch up. "Lukas? Lukas, wait a second! A girl can't run in six-inchers!"

She proceeded to talk my ear off all the way to her house, and when we got to her doorstep, she took a key from her purse and let us both in. The interior looked like some kind of soap opera set. Everything was lavish. For a second, I forgot we were in Santana.

"It's practically all mine," she bragged, "My parents are seriously never home. We just got here and they're already leaving town this weekend. Wait. You're coming to my party, right?"

I tried to change the subject. "I know how you feel. My mom doesn't ever leave town but she's always at work. There's only one hospital in Santana and they need all the help they can get."

Nissa's eyes widened. "Oh my gosh, this town is so small. Luke, you've got to tell me everything about Santana. I need to run this place. We both can. It'll be so much fun."

"You must not know very much about me if you think I could ever run any part of this town," I answered. I reached out my hand, pretending to introduce myself for the first time. "I'm Lukas, the town fag."

She gasped, clutching her charm necklace. "Take that back."

I must have seemed confused.

"That word, I mean. It's atrocious. I find that extremely offensive. Why would you talk about yourself like that?"

I couldn't help but smile. It was nice of her to say. And to be honest with even myself, I didn't know why I said things like that.

Dr. Carver said it was because I had my own issues to work out.

Nissa tossed her purse down and we sat at her long, fancy dinner table to work on the project. "Lukas, don't be so hard on yourself. Other people treat you the way you let them, you know. If you want to be the king, or *queen*, of Santana, well then you simply... need to be it."

"I don't want to be the king or *queen* of anything," I told her. "If I had it my way, I'd be invisible."

"That's not right," she said before I even finished, shaking her head disapprovingly, "It's just not. You don't have to be royalty if you don't want to, but you definitely can't be invisible. How does an invisible person find love?"

"Gross," I answered instinctively. "Quit being such a girl."

She laughed, opening her math book. "You know, you're not invisible, but I still see right through you, mister."

"Is that so?" I asked.

She nodded. "I suspect you might be human. And I think one day, you'll tell the world to screw off. And I believe that even you, Lukas Bradley, are meant to be someone's someone."

The automatic reflex to deny everything about her optimism tingled through me, but I stopped myself from shutting it out. Instead, I smiled, and she smiled, and I wondered if Nissa Delfino might be onto something. For just a moment, I sat with the prospect of being someone's someone, and admittedly, it felt good.

41

That evening, I walked home from Nissa's house after sunset, in that very particular time when the sun is gone, but people still haven't turned on their lights, and all the buildings in town seem as if they've been slathered in the same cobalt paint. Everything was blue and calm.

Nissa wasn't lying about living close to the school. The ranch she lived on was only two blocks away. Audrey Hernandez used to live there, but her family moved away the summer before because her mother died from cancer and her father couldn't bear to stay in town. It was apparent Nissa's family had a lot of money because they'd taken the mess Audrey's family left and had begun to make the entire estate look like new.

I was sure her Halloween party would be one of the biggest parties of the year.

Even I would be there, thanks to a post-studying guilt trip, in which she reminded me she was new and didn't know anyone. It was hard to decline her invitation after she'd been so nice to me all day. And it also didn't hurt when she mentioned there would be booze. How could I argue with that? I hadn't been to a party with alcohol since before my great exile. I told her I'd be there, as long as I could wear a mask. It wasn't like I had plans that didn't involve solitude and a rented video anyway.

I stepped on the brown leaves pushed into my path by the chill. The sky became darker and a few lights in the park began to blink on. The basketball court illuminated beside me and a familiar hypnosis hijacked my brain, as a shirtless Ray Melendez appeared, shooting hoops from the center of the court. He wasn't even facing me, but I knew it was him. I could see the scar everyone talked about running down his back. It was thick, and it ran all the way from his neck to the elastic of his shorts.

As much as I felt like a stalker, staring from the shadows of the sidelines, I couldn't take my eyes off of him. He dashed rapidly around the court, and beyond the sound of his sneakers, I could hear him breathing hard. His muscles flexed and relaxed. The band of his underwear peeked out from his basketball shorts. His hands moved effortlessly as he pushed the ball into the air and it swooshed through the net.

It had been over a month since that night at the theater, and I couldn't put into words how pathetic I felt that the moment he nudged me awake after that stupid movie unexpectedly became a highlight of my whole year. As he moved before me, I felt the same flutter in my stomach.

Suddenly, the basketball smacked the backboard and I snapped out of my daze as it bounced toward my feet.

Before Ray saw me, I turned and hastily continued home in the dark, hearing the plank of the basketball growing more distant behind me.

I woke up that Saturday morning to the faint resonance of humming. I thought I was dreaming at first. I hadn't heard that hum in years. But when I slid out of bed and slowly made my way into the kitchen, I found my mom standing on a stool, dusting above the window curtains. She was already dressed for the day.

"Someone's in a good mood," I teased.

She jumped. "You just about scared the life right out of me, Luke." She stepped down and set the duster on the counter, and I noticed she wore some kind of strange grin.

"What's going on?"

"What do you mean?"

"I think the last time I saw you in this good of a mood, I was still learning how to color inside the lines."

"Don't be silly," she said, beginning to wipe the counter. "It's just a beautiful morning. That's all."

I nodded slowly, and she began to hum again as I poured myself a bowl of cereal. When I sat down at the kitchen table, I figured it was the perfect time to cover my tracks in advance for Nissa's party. "I'm going to Sam's later. I might spend the night," I lied. I knew any party where there might be alcohol would be out of the question.

"Sure," my mom smiled without taking her eyes off the counter. No further questions. Whatever was on her mind was welcome to stay there, as far as I was concerned.

"Maybe she finally got laid," Sam shrugged.

"Gross!" I pretended to gag, lying on her bedroom floor, watching her carefully brush bleach into her hair. "Also, do you really think you should breathe in those chemicals? Just in case you really are…"

Sam turned around and interrupted me, bleach brush still in place. "Stop it right there." She faced the mirror again and turned up her radio. "I'm not."

I could have told her, for the millionth time, she should take a pregnancy test just to make sure, but I knew I'd be wasting my time. She would only tell me, for the millionth time, she'd take a pregnancy test when she wanted to. "Well, if you really think you're not… then you should come to the party with me tonight. We can tell your parents you're sleeping at my house."

She shook her head. "I already told you, I'm not going to that party. For one, I don't want to see Joe, and for two, after the week I've had, I need a drink. But I'd better not. You know, just in case."

I rolled my eyes. The girl made no sense.

Just then, there was a knock at the door and without waiting for a reply, my Aunt Cheryl came into the room, hands on her hips. She waved hello to me before walking over to inspect Sam's hair. "You'll end up bald with all these chemicals, girl," she laughed, and looked my way. "Luke, are you staying for dinner?"

"Oh, I'll probably head home. Don't want my mom to eat alone," I lied, looking at my watch. It was almost time to head to Nissa's and help her decorate.

"You're such a good boy," my Aunt Cheryl smiled at me. "Sam, why can't you be as thoughtful as your cousin?"

Sam chuckled. "Luke really is such an angel, isn't he?"

A few hours later, I watched Nissa's Halloween party bustle around me through the eyeholes in my mask, and I wondered how the Zorro version of myself could still be such a wallflower. All I'd done since the beginning of the party was watch Nissa float around socializing, admiring my work with the décor and wishing Sam had come with me.

After a while, I somehow ended up at a table outside with some random kids from my art class. Tito Gomez was a cowboy. Katie Roberts was a cat. They were clearly too drunk to care who was behind my mask, and they offered me a shot of tequila. When I took it and thanked them, they realized it was me. For a moment, I thought they were about to tell me to scram, but instead, they laughed in solidarity, and patted me on the shoulder as we all cringed from the shot. The burn was equal parts horrible and relaxing. We all recovered and then downed another. And another. Before long, it was a contest of who could stomach the most.

By the time I swallowed six overpoured shots, I quit. I was feeling good but I knew if I kept going, I'd end up sick. Art Kids understood. They weren't half bad. We laughed and made fun of our teacher's German accent, and eventually, I even took off my mask. Would we be friends once we went back to school? Probably not, but it didn't matter to any of us in the world of this Halloween party. Everything slowly seemed to warm up, in a good way. I found Nissa in the kitchen and she kissed me on the cheek. "See? Aren't you so glad you came?" she gleamed.

Naturally, at the height of my hope, I heard cheering coming from outside the kitchen. I followed Nissa into the living room to find out what the fuss was for, only to see it was because Michael and his football friends arrived, all decked out in their varsity jackets and stupidity.

They actually came to the Halloween party as jocks.

It was like I couldn't escape from him. I'd been nervous all day about what would happen if he were to show up, and when he didn't come for the first couple of hours, I was so relieved. Now I just felt like I was going to throw up, and I was forty or fifty percent sure it wasn't because of the tequila.

Before I knew it, I was walking away from the party. Did I even say goodbye to the kids from my art class? Or Nissa? I wasn't sure. I could tell the tequila had begun to kick in because I felt like I wasn't walking straight, as much as I tried. My arms and chest and legs felt warm, and I just wanted to lay myself down on the ground. When I got to Main Street, a car honked at me because I was wandering off the sidewalk and onto the road. I squinted and breathed deep and told myself to just get home.

And then I was suddenly terrified. I couldn't go home. I knew my mom would wonder why I wasn't at Sam's, and she'd definitely know I was drunk. For a minute I thought about going to Sam's, since I was supposed to be there, but when I imagined the hell my Uncle Carlos would raise if he took one look at me, I stopped walking and sat down on the sidewalk in front of some store. The orange lights along the streets seemed too bright and then not bright enough, and I could smell chimney smoke. Was it already that time of the year?

I sat there for a few minutes before a black car slowed down as it passed me. It stopped a little way down the road and then backed up. The passenger window rolled down and a voice from inside called out. "You alright?"

I lifted up my head, realizing I was either falling asleep or already there. I grabbed onto the brick wall of the store and tried getting onto my feet. It took a minute, but I did it. "I'm fine. You can keep driving now."

"I don't know. You look pretty wasted. Need a ride?"

I started laughing. I didn't even know why.

I said something about not needing a ride because I had nowhere to be.

The next thing I knew, the car was parked and the driver's door opened. *Oh God*, I thought to myself, *I'm definitely going to die now.*

The news story about the guy in Wyoming flashed through my mind, and I only became more scared when the dark figure stepped onto the sidewalk in front of me and came into the light. It was Ray Melendez, and the glow falling onto him from above made his face look angry.

He must have been able to tell I was petrified.

"You don't look okay."

I told him I would be, if he didn't kill me.

"Kill you?" he laughed. He reached out his hand to help me up. Somehow, I was sitting on the ground again. "You're wasted. Let me take you home."

I pushed his hand away. Now I *knew* I was drunk. I told him I didn't want to go home. I told him I wanted to stay right there, on the sidewalk in front of Sally's Antiques. I told him to get in his car, and leave me there. Because that sidewalk was a nice sidewalk and it was exactly where I wanted to be.

FOUR

Fingertips nudged my arm.

"I need to go soon," a voice said.

It felt like I'd been lifeless for seven years; it was a struggle just to open my eyes, and it happened slowly. But it only took a second to realize the sheets covering me weren't my own. The bed I was in wasn't mine. This wasn't my room. I sat up to find Ray standing before me. Was this even my life?

He wasn't wearing a shirt, just like that night at the basketball court, and he looked as surprised to see me as I was to see him. "Damn, you had a rough night," he said, eyebrows raised.

I said nothing in return. I just grunted like a dying animal, trying my hardest to remember how this could be possible. Maybe I was dreaming. Was this his place? It was just one big cement room with the basics: a table, a lamp, a wood stove, a bed, and an old couch, where I guessed he had slept, by the pillow and blanket thrown over it. There was a small kitchen and a bathroom, and that was the extent of the whole place. It was the smallest apartment I'd ever seen.

"I'm guessing you don't remember anything," he said,

walking to the table and picking up an iron, only to press it down flat on the shirt laying in front of him.

"I remember leaving the party," I yawned, rubbing my eyes and still trying to think.

"Let's just say you made it to that store by the school that sells all the old shit, and then you were done. Didn't look like anyone else was coming for you, so I picked you up. I was going to take you home, but you begged me not to because your mom would freak if you walked in drunk. So I brought you here."

I buried my face into my hands. "I remember now. Not all of it, but I remember you stopping. Kind of." I pushed the sheets off me and realized I was wearing sweats and a hoodie that weren't mine. "Where are my clothes?"

He grabbed a tied up grocery bag from the floor by the bathroom door and tossed it at me. "In there. But you might not want to open that. You were pretty sick."

I wanted to curl up and die. Cause of death: humiliation.

"Well, thanks for helping me out." I reached for my shoes and put them on. "I don't normally do that," I added, like some kind of disclaimer. "I mean, not that you care, but I just thought I would tell you."

"You already did," he answered without looking up from his ironing, "Last night. All night. Probably thirty times."

"Oh." I stood up and grabbed the grocery bag.

It was strange. He seemed almost as nervous as me. And I was definitely as nervous as I was embarrassed.

"I'm not trying to kick you out or anything," he said, "I just have work in half an hour and I have to be there."

"Don't worry about it," I answered quickly, "It was nice of you to let me stay here in the first place. Embarrassing for me, but nice of you."

"No problem." He still didn't look up from his ironing, but I could see him smile. "Lay off the tequila next time."

I couldn't help but smile, too. It was a stupid smile – an exposing smile – and I tried to conceal it. "Will do," I said, and turned to the door to leave.

I heard a jingle behind me, and Ray held out my keys and wallet, and as horrendously cliché as it may have been, when I grabbed them, our eyes met somewhere between him looking down and me looking away at some imaginary thing on the wall.

It was only for a split second, but it was enough to make me feel a way I couldn't remember feeling before: like there was finally this person who was much more like me than anyone else I'd ever known. And surprisingly enough, it was this person who I knew next to nothing about.

"And then I left," I told Sam the next day.

"That's crazy," she replied without looking at me, impatiently keeping her gaze set across the room. She eyed the pregnancy test sitting on her dresser as if it were about to run away. "I can't believe he took you to his house without gutting you or something. I thought you said he was a serial killer."

"Well, I heard that. But I don't think it's true now. I think he's just a loner."

"Wow," she said, her eyes still fixated on the stick. "That's really interesting and all, but has it been three minutes yet?" She stood up, clearly anxious to read the result.

I looked down at my watch. "It's been one."

She sat down and sighed reluctantly.

"Have you thought about what you'll do if it's positive?" I asked.

"Well, I'm guessing I'll get really fat and then have a baby, Luke."

"There are other options."

"In New Mexico? Without my parents finding out? Get real."

"What about adoption?"

"I don't know, Luke. Hopefully I'm not even pregnant. I don't think I can make that kind of decision. I'm seventeen." She turned to her window for a second before

50

rising back onto her feet. "Maybe it's done early."

She walked over to the dresser and looked down at the stick. I couldn't see her face at first, but I heard the gasp. And if I didn't know then, I knew as soon as she turned around. Her face said it all.

My eyes asked if it said what I thought it did.

And without saying a word, she nodded.

Later that week, Michael wrote our names on our worksheet as we finished up our latest experiment and I picked up the beakers we hadn't used. Since his random effort to patch things up with me, I'd noticed the harassment I received at school decrease at a bizarre rate, but he hadn't mentioned anything about our conversation. We'd gone back to speaking strictly about science. Chloride this, seventy-three milliliters that. When I came back to the table, Michael set down his pen.

"You know, when I said I wanted things to go back to the way they used to be, I didn't mean you going back to being... you know."

I pretended not to hear him and began jostling books into my bag as the bell rang. We had a weird schedule for midterms. Science was our last class for the day, and I was beyond ready to go home and sleep for a while before I had to go into the café.

My indifference got the best of him. "Seriously? You're ignoring me? Are we five years old?"

"I love that you've decided to talk about this now, on the one day your buddy isn't at school." I motioned to Xavier's empty seat and then turned around and threw on my backpack, walking straight out of the classroom. I didn't even stop at my locker in the hallway before I headed straight toward the school's back door.

It was only seconds later that I heard Michael jogging out behind me, and I had a flashback of him coming out the same doors at prom. It was too much for me not to be flustered. I couldn't even muster up the words to tell him to fuck off. Instead, I continued on my way and he followed closely behind.

"Luke. I told you, I'm done being a dick, okay?" He felt like a little girl again and it made him uncomfortable. It was clear he didn't want to be having the very conversation he was starting, and it baffled me that he was. "Haven't you noticed the guys quit messing with you? I told them to cut it out. I wasn't kidding when I told you I want to be your friend again."

I let out a dramatic laugh as I turned onto the sidewalk. "Friends? I think we both know that's not going to happen. You made that perfectly clear when you just left to Albuquerque after I told you the biggest thing I ever told you, and then ignored me when you came back home. And then you ignored all the shitty things your friends did to me." I looked back to make sure he was listening. He was. "If you think I could ever just believe you woke up one day and decided not to be an asshole, you're out of your mind. It doesn't make any sense. I wouldn't be surprised if you were following me right now so you could take out a pocketknife and shove it into my back."

I heard him groan behind me in frustration. "Why do you always have to be such a fucking drama queen? Quit being so suspicious! It was Sam. She told me off. Okay? She told me everything."

I turned around. He finally caught enough of my attention for me to stop walking.

"I was stupid to quit being friends with you over what you told me. I should have been a better friend to you than I was. And I know how you can get. I should have known better." He looked away, watching the traffic pass by. Maybe he was nervous about being seen with me. Or maybe he was just nervous because he was having an actual conversation, which he probably hadn't done in the past six months.

As uncomfortable as he may have been, I didn't like any of it either. Even though I wore long sleeves, my arms felt exposed, just knowing he knew about the cutting. A part of me was furious with Sam for telling him everything, and at the same time, something else in me felt full knowing he cared. There had been a part of me wondering all along if it would even bother him if he knew. This did change things.

I turned and watched the cars whoosh by, too. Suddenly, I wanted to believe him, but it was still hard to trust he was serious. For crying out loud, it was only earlier in the year that the tables were turned and I was begging him to talk to me, but he told me I was dead to him, and those words scorched so badly, I nearly turned his metaphor into a reality. You don't just forget those things. "No," I felt myself saying. It was happening again. The autopilot.

He turned away from the street. "What?"

"No. Forget I exist. I'm dead to you now."

A car full of jocks drove by us just then, shouting a bunch of shit from the windows as they passed by, and it was enough to keep me going.

"Did it ever occur to you that you're dead to me now, too? You are such a piece of shit. Seriously. Don't fucking follow me, and don't fucking talk to me again."

The whole thing came out angrier than I meant it to, but I couldn't help it. I didn't even hear what I was saying until it was already said.

Michael turned his focus back to the street, and he left it there as I turned and walked away.

My backpack hit the kitchen floor as soon as I got home. I went straight for the phone in the kitchen, to call the café and tell Zondra I needed a sick day. Work was the last place I wanted to be after what happened with Michael. All I would do is mess everything up. Luckily, Zondra told me to take the afternoon for myself.

My stomach felt like it was upside-down, and even I was baffled at the anger that just possessed me. I went into my room and headed for my dresser's top drawer. I needed to sleep everything off. It was only 1:12, and as I strolled over to my bed and threw myself onto it, I sighed in relief that I had another three hours before my mom would come home from work.

When the front door open and closed in the living room, I sat up and squinted at the clock again. Somehow, it was already 4:51.

Another sound traveled down the hall. My mom was laughing.

Then, another sound. A man's voice.

Yawning, I staggered into the living room. My mom jumped as if I'd just risen from the dead. "What are you doing here? I thought you worked tonight."

"Zondra called. I didn't need to come in because it was dead today," I lied, wondering why she looked so concerned. I figured it had something to do with the man standing next to her, friendly-faced and clutching onto a couple grocery bags. A police officer. He towered above her, which wasn't hard to do with my mom, and he had salt-and-pepper hair with a matching goatee. He was well-built and extremely good-looking. If this was what I thought it was, she didn't do half bad.

The stranger in my kitchen could tell I was examining him and extended his hand. When I reached out my own, he took it and shook it firmly. "Richard Velasco. Call me Richie."

"I invited Richie over for dinner," my mom smiled nervously.

Whether or not it was because Richie saw the surprise in my eyes, he walked over to the counter and set his two grocery bags down before moving back toward the front door. "I'll grab the rest of the food from the car," he said, and walked out of the house.

"I didn't know you were going to be home," my mom said defensively.

I was still putting everything together in my head, but it was instantly clear she felt guilty. And I figured she should.

"You know, it's interesting that your Catholic intuition tells you your gay kid's a huge sinner, but you're over here dating Officer Richie when your husband hasn't even signed divorce papers."

"We both know that marriage is over. He's been gone a long time," she argued, "And for the record, I'm not dating anyone. Richie's a friend. Did you know his wife passed away last year? God knows the last time he had a good meal."

"Right," I muttered, sitting on the couch and pushing my feet into my shoes.

"And where do you think you're going?"

"I don't know. But you can have the house all to yourself."

Groceries in hand, Richie stepped back as I grunted past him outside.

Sam's house was typically my default destination, but that would be the first place my mom might look for me. So the café seemed like a better place to go, until I thought maybe it wasn't, since I'd called in sick earlier. I walked aimlessly until I found myself in the playground behind the elementary school, and gravitating toward the swing set. Thankful I remembered a jacket, I zipped up and sat on the old rubber seat, pushing myself ahead and pumping my legs to take me as high as I could go. Then I let myself soar forward and backward, staring into the sky and breathing in the fall sunset.

I couldn't help but remember the last time I was there. It was about a year and a half earlier, right after my mom and I came home from a weekend with my grandparents to find my dad had packed up and left. My mom never did tell me what was on the note he left. She just took it in and then tore it to shreds, retreating to her room and leaving me with my own thoughts to assess the situation. More than I was hurt by his leaving, I was scared for my mom. Her nightmare had come true. I called Michael and told him to meet me at the playground behind the elementary school, and within fifteen minutes, we were both there, swinging in a silence only broken up by the occasional thoughts that came into my head, as I pieced together what my new life might look like.

Michael mainly listened and nodded and looked at me. He worried for me the way I worried for my mom. I could see it on him. And I loved him for it. Because in a world where Sam hadn't yet begun to double as my cousin *and* my friend, his reassuring watch was the one thing that made me feel like everything would be okay.

Suddenly, something snapped me out of my nostalgia and as the world once again melted from gold to blue, guilt filled my guts. I wondered if it was selfish of me not to be happy for my mom after seeing her drown in sadness for so long, and I asked myself if I'd been too harsh on Michael when he tried apologizing to me earlier in the day. What if I'd put a bullet in my last chance of fixing things with him?

The darkness surrounding me seemed like it was seeping into my head. I took in one more full chest of air before jumping off the swing and heading back home.

At school the next day, I teetered between feeling guilty about my mom and feeling guilty about Michael. I couldn't focus on anything, and blamed the clouds for my trance. Every time I looked outside, they covered the sky and the sun was nowhere to be found. It felt like every decent feeling was hiding with it.

Luckily, by the end of the day, the light found its way out from behind the grayness, and as I walked down the street after school and finally felt its bright warmth on my face, I heard my name from behind. I turned around to find Nissa jostling toward me, clacking in her black heels. "We haven't talked in like, three years! Did you have fun at my Halloween party? I feel like I barely saw you."

"Too much fun. I think I should lay off tequila for the rest of my life," I grinned as she caught up to me. "But thanks for inviting me. It was definitely an interesting night."

She laughed and threw her arm around me as we walked into the café. "First of all, you can never have too much tequila in your life. Second of all, you are invited to any parties you help me decorate for, because it was marvelously spooky." As I tied my apron strings behind my back, Nissa sat down at the bar and her voice lowered. "Third… I've decided to find you a boyfriend."

"That's adorable!" Zondra gleamed, coming out of the back with a new bag of espresso beans for the machine and startling us. "I think you should find him one quick. Lord knows he needs a life outside of school and this café."

"Good luck with that," I told both of them, but mostly Nissa. "I don't know who you're going to find for me in Santana. Not that I even want a boyfriend. My life's miserable enough, thank you."

"Isn't he charming?" Zondra grinned sarcastically, slipping into her coat to leave for the day. She told Nissa it was nice to see I had friends like her, and ordered me to make her a drink on the house before the door jingled shut behind her.

"I'll take a latte for me, and an extra hot change of attitude for you," Nissa smiled. "Lukas, don't you want a boyfriend? Don't you get lonely? I mean, your cousin seems great, but wouldn't it be nice to hang out with someone you have more in common with?"

I rolled my eyes and turned away to steam the milk for her latte. And as I poured a couple shots of espresso into her mug a few seconds later, I heard Nissa say my name. Not for an answer to her question, but as if there was something I needed to see. I turned around from the espresso machine to find Ray standing next to her, and he could tell I felt almost as confused as the morning after Nissa's Halloween party.

"You still need your car looked at?" he asked, seemingly expecting me to catch on.

But I had no idea what he was talking about, and my face must have been more bewildered than Nissa's.

He sighed. "Don't tell me you were so drunk you don't remember."

"No, no... I remember...," I interjected. I must have told him about the rattling sound my mom's car had been making. Why would I have told him that? I wasn't sure. But I couldn't think of any other reason he would have to look at the car.

"I told you I could look at it for you and you said you'd bring it by sometime," he added.

I nodded.

"Do you remember where my house is?" he asked.

"Yeah, I think so." Another lie. Of course I remembered where his house was.

"Can you come over on Saturday? I work that morning, but I'll be done by four."

I nodded.

"Cool," he said, and ordered a black coffee to go. I filled a paper cup and noticed Nissa examining him from head to toe, subtle as ever, before I snapped on a lid and handed it to him.

He thanked me, smiled at Nissa, and left.

Nissa's confusion lingered. "That's Ray Melendez, isn't it? I've heard about him." She turned and looked out the window, making sure he was really gone. "And people are not lying, he really is hot. And kind of terrifying at the same time. Don't you think?"

"I didn't notice," I lied, wiping the counter.

She replayed the conversation in her head, trying to piece everything together. "Okay, first of all, when did you ever talk to Ray Melendez while you were drunk? I know he wasn't at my party because I would definitely remember. Second of all, Lukas, this is perfect."

"It's a long story," I said, still wiping. There was no way I was about to tell her how pathetic everything went after her party. "And what's perfect? Ray Melendez? I hardly think he's going to be my new boyfriend," I added, hoping she might think otherwise.

Instead, she laughed. "Your new boyfriend? No. *My* new boyfriend! Did you see the way he looked at me when, he first came in?"

I shook my head. I didn't see when he first came in. But it made total sense. Nissa was the most gorgeous girl in town, and if he wanted to get her attention, helping me was probably all strategy.

"He came in here and obviously he was looking for you, but he definitely stopped and looked at me. I got *the vibe*. Can you imagine? The most talked-about guy in town and *me*? Amazing. And my parents would flip, which is even better."

Her voice faded and I watched her go on, nodding and smiling and wondering how I could have expected anything but this to happen.

When I was a kid, I loved watching those old family sitcoms on TV, the ones with the housewife moms and the bread-winning dads and the kids who couldn't help but learn a life lesson every week. Compared to my parents, my Uncle Carlos and Aunt Cheryl always seemed like the parents on those reruns, and I envied Sam for it most of the time. The night she decided to tell them she was pregnant, however, I wasn't sure what I was thinking when I said I'd be there. They always had so many dreams for her, and I knew they'd never see this news coming. They didn't even know she wasn't a virgin.

"Lukas! What a nice surprise," Aunt Cheryl gleamed, standing at the front door that night, "Sam's up in her room."

With a smile of my own, I thanked her and stepped into the house, taking off my shoes at the door. When I tapped on her doorframe, Sam stopped pacing back and forth and looked up from the carpet. "This would be so much easier if I could take a shot of whiskey first."

I laughed and threw my arm around her shoulders. "You'll be fine. You've got the best parents in the world."

I held her hand as we returned to the main floor to find both of her parents in the kitchen. Her mom was putting plates away from the drying rack, and her dad was reading the paper at the table.

"I need to talk to you," Sam said quietly. Aunt Cheryl closed the dishwasher and Uncle Carlos put his paper down onto the dining table, motioning for Sam to take a seat. Both of them looked concerned.

Sam sat and I stood behind her, mirroring my aunt standing behind my uncle on the other side of the table. My stomach turned for her; I couldn't imagine what she felt. "I don't know how to tell you this, so I'm just going to say it." She spoke quickly, crossing her arms and resting them on the table as if she were about to cut them a deal. "I'm pregnant."

Both of her parents' eyes widened and I put my hand on Sam's shoulder in solidarity. Neither of them knew what to say. They looked at her, looked at me, and looked at each other in shock before either of them said a word.

Uncle Carlos broke the silence. "Who's the father?" he asked sternly.

"Joe Armenta," Sam answered.

She might as well have confessed to killing a priest. Aunt Cheryl covered her mouth, and Uncle Carlos clenched the newspaper in his fist. "Joe Armenta who got busted for stealing beer last year? You better be joking, Samantha!" I hadn't seen him yell like that in years. My heart was pounding and I looked down at Sam to make sure she was okay.

Her face was turning as red as my uncle's and tears started to flood into her eyes. "Before you say you're going to kill Joe or you're so disappointed in me, let me just say I'm more upset than you are. I'm so scared! And I don't know what to do, and I'm sorry, and I just need you both to be my parents right now." She folded into a frown and began to cry hysterically, burying her face in her hands. I was pretty sure she amplified it all for effect, but I played along, kneeling down to console her.

Sam always knew how to work her parents. She was their only child, and she knew there was nothing and nobody more important to either of them. I could already see her performance was a success when my aunt and uncle rushed over to join me in holding her. "Of course we'll be here for you," my Aunt Cheryl said. "We love you no matter what. We'll always be your parents!"

"We'll always be here for you, *mija*," my Uncle Carlos muttered. He was clearly still furious and I could see the instinctual calculation in his eyes as he imagined himself strangling the life out of Joe, but nonetheless, he bent down and kissed Sam's forehead.

Neither of them were happy about it, but it didn't matter. My aunt and uncle were going to be there for Sam because they were her parents, and they loved her, no matter what.

Another problem solved in thirty minutes or less.

When I got home, my mom pointed at the coffee table and told me I had mail. I picked up the long white envelope and looked it over. It was from a college up in Colorado.

I'd forgotten I even applied, not only to get into the school, but for a scholarship, too. Images of a new life flooded into my head out of nowhere. Visions of mountains and campuses and strangers and a blank slate. I shook myself out of it and took the letter to my room and set it on my dresser. I had to look at it and imagine all the possibilities one more time before I tore it open, just in case they all got shot down like a bunch of hunted birds as soon as I read it.

To my surprise, when I finally mustered up the courage to look at what was inside, it was good news. The college wanted me. My heart started beating faster with every word in the letter. They said my essay was satisfactory, and they were impressed with my grades, which were much better before the year of hell I was currently living in. They'd given me the scholarship, too. I wouldn't have to pay for school, or room and board.

So why did I feel weird about it? Something felt off. What was pumping through my veins seemed less like hope and more like an uncertain anxiety. Sure, everything would be brand new – the people and the places – but I would still be the same me. And I had no plans other than leaving Santana. I didn't know what I wanted to study. I didn't know what I wanted to be when I grew up. Even though it was the most important time to figure out the answers to those questions, they were the last things on my mind over the past six months.

I tossed the letter back down to my dresser and crawled into bed, pulling the covers over me. And as I laid there, tangled in my sheets, I began to second guess everything. I wondered if I even wanted to go to the city. After all, it really seemed no safer than Santana, and if everyone in the city was like Nissa Delfino, I might not be able to keep up.

Or maybe I was doubting myself. Maybe I would be fine there, and I would keep up, and I would find friends who were like me, and I would find someplace I could belong to. Maybe I'd even find someone I could belong to.

Suddenly, my future was too overwhelming to think about, especially after helping deal with the crisis that was Sam's future only an hour before.

I rolled over and pulled the cord on my lamp.

Lights out.

That weekend, Ray tinkered under the hood of my mom's car in the small dirt parking space outside his apartment. I sat on his stoop, watching every meticulous move he made. The undershirt he wore left every inch of his arms out for the world to see, and naturally, I wasn't mad. In fact, I was more grateful than ever for the unseasonably warm day interrupting Santana's cloudy fall.

"It's not a big problem," he sighed, pulling the hood shut. "I think I took care of it. If it starts acting up again, bring it back." He pulled a rag out of his back pocket to clean his hands and I thanked him for the millionth time, nervously looking down at my watch. It was almost time for me to get to work. I wasn't sure if I was more eager or disappointed to get going.

"So, are you one of those straight-A students?" he asked.

"What gave you that impression? When I was dozed off in the movie theater or when I was drunk on the side of the road?" I joked.

"You just seem smart. Something about you, I guess."

"I used to be pretty smart. Maybe not anymore. I don't know."

"Well, maybe one of these days you could help me out. I didn't finish high school back home. I'm thinking about getting one of those… diplomas for people like me."

"A GED?"

He nodded.

"Yeah, maybe I could sneak you some books from our school library," I said. "It's much better than the library in town." As I zipped up my jacket, I remembered what Nissa told me earlier in the week: "*When you see Ray this weekend, you have one job, Lukas. Get me a DATE!*"

I told her I'd try my best.

"My friend Nissa likes you," I told him.

He seemed taken back. "That girl with all the bright clothes?"

"Yep."

"She thinks I'm cute?"

"She does."

"I see."

"Anyway, I thought I'd tell you. She was hoping that maybe…"

"And what do you think?" he uttered suddenly.

Everything in my brain came to a screeching halt and I could feel the confusion showing on my face. "What do I think about what?"

He didn't answer me, though, except for a quick

"Nevermind," as he pulled a sweater on.

By instinct, I looked back down at my watch. "Thanks again for looking at this old thing," I told him. "I owe you one."

"I'll remember you said that," he replied as I got into the car, and in the pit of my stomach, I felt the same flicker I felt the last time I left his house.

The café was dead that evening, so I took out a box of Thanksgiving decorations from the back to hang on the walls. Another sea of night swallowed the world whole, and the smell of coffee intertwined with the jazz tape Zondra played throughout the day. It made for a soft peace, but I was unsettled.

The stillness of everything only gave my ever-wandering mind the opportunity to overthink every word Ray said earlier that day, and what it all might have meant. There was a part of me that was convinced he was flirting with me. But that made no sense. Not if Nissa was right about him eyeing her at the café. And the truth, I kept reminding myself, was that I didn't know anything about Ray, except that he had a bad reputation, lived in a rat hole, and for some unknown reason, fascinated me. Even if he was flirting with me, how pathetic was I to care?

Zondra dramatically barged into the café, dropping a giant cardboard box onto the first table in her path, and smashing my train of thought to pieces. "Lukas, dear, do you have any homework that you *must* finish before tomorrow?" She batted her long lashes between breaths. I shrugged, reminding her it was Saturday. "Oh good!" she beamed, "How would you like to help me with a project?"

"Sure," I answered. "What's in the box?"

Her grin widened as if she'd been waiting for me to ask. "They're old photos of me, and Laura, and our friends and family through the years. I'd like to make an album. Christmas is next month and Laura's always wanted a big book with all these photos organized by year." She opened the box flaps and breathed in the dusty nostalgia. "I haven't gone through these photos in ages."

Her smile softened as she sorted through some of the pictures. There must have been faces she hadn't seen in a while, some of which she missed. She lit back up and picked out one photo to flaunt it at me. "Look at this one. Was I not simply gorgeous?"

"You still are and you know it," I said without hesitation, coming out from behind the counter to get a better look. I picked another one out of the box. "You look like a movie star here," I told her truthfully. From the black-and-white photograph, Young Zondra stared glamorously into my soul, dressed in a silky gown and draped in pearls only outshone by her eyes.

I reached into the box to pick out whichever photo my hand landed on next. At first glance, I recognized the woman in this picture. Young Laura had the same serenity in her eyes as the woman I met in Zondra's dining room. She stood proudly in an elegant black dress, and judging by her hair and makeup, I guessed the photo was from the sixties. I flashed it at Zondra and she melted into a grin.

"I love that one. Laura gave it to me in college. We'd just met at some party the week before and had gotten along instantly. Both of us were in the writing program but had never seen each other. Wasn't she something? Look at the back."

I flipped the photo and read the slanted cursive aloud: "Zondra, I know we've only just met, but I've got a feeling we shall write each other's stories. Best to you. Laura."

Zondra sighed, still gleaming. "I can't believe how quickly the time's gone by. One day, it will be you telling some hopeful young person about the wonders of your first love."

"I'm not hopeful," I said immediately. Almost defensively. "I don't believe in all that. It's for some people, but not everyone. Definitely not for me."

She stopped and examined me, trying to determine

whether or not I was serious. Then she laughed. "For a second, I almost believed you." She got up and went to her purse on the counter, rifling through it until she pulled out a stack of cards. "You know, there's a way to find out for sure, Lukas. I'm willing to bet a great love story is just around the corner for you, if you'd accept it, anyway."

My mom always warned me to stay away from tarot cards. But she was also a hardcore Catholic and I couldn't be bothered with all that. Not if Zondra could tell me what might happen with Ray.

"Now, you don't have to tell me anything you don't want to," she smirked, taking a seat across from me and shuffling the deck. "I have a feeling there's a boy who has captured your interest, but that's none of my business." She fanned out the cards in front of me and added: "You just think about him, *if there is a him*, and draw a card. The card won't predict the future, but it will give a sign of what you should consider."

I was wary to feel hopeful, but Zondra's optimism intrigued me. I summoned a vision of Ray in my mind and slipped out a card, setting it down on the table. I had no clue what it was or what it meant. It looked like some kind of strange animal.

Zondra's lips opened slowly and concern seemed to flush the excitement from her face.

"What is it?" I asked.

"The Devil," she said, keeping her eyes on the card. "Were you thinking of a boy you know?"

I nodded.

She sighed. "This card indicates he could be harmful. Something about him could lead you somewhere you don't want to be, whether it be temptation, or violence, or something else."

My eyes widened; it felt like someone had drained everything from inside me. Suddenly, all those times my mom told me to stay away from these cards seemed legitimate. I should have listened. "What should I do?" I asked. "Never see this guy again?"

"Look, Lukas. I told you, these cards don't tell the future. They just tell us what to keep in mind. Be wise. If you're very mindful of your actions, everything will be all right." She could tell I was anxious and grabbed my hand. "You're a smart kid, Lukas. Just watch yourself."

FIVE

When the time came for the next round of progress reports, I noticed my grade had only gone from a D to a C- in King's class. I thought it would be higher. I'd gotten all my other grades under control, but everything I turned in for King had a bunch of trivial red notes on it when he handed it back. Nothing I turned in was good enough for him.

As the class shuffled out of his room, I felt pathetic for having to go back a second time to ask if there was anything I could do. Before I went up to his desk, I took a deep breath and reminded myself that if it would save me from another one of my mom's rants, it would be worth it.

Just like the first time, King seemed to be waiting for me to go up to his desk. He looked away from his papers and picked off his thick glasses, setting them down on a stack. He was wearing too much cologne. Old people cologne. "Allow me to guess. You saw your progress report, Mr. Bradley," he lamented.

"Yes," I said, trying to breathe through my mouth. "I thought my grade would be higher. I've brought every other one up to at least a B, but this class just isn't going well for me. I know if I get a good grade on the final, I'll end up with a B, but I'm worried about the test, because I'm never good with finals. I get nervous."

He brought his hands together as if he were brainstorming.

"I'm sure it seems like I'm not interested, but that's not the case," I continued, trying to convince him it was true. "I'm really trying."

"I've noticed the tests are where you struggle. If you'd like, perhaps we could set up a time for me to help you prepare, one-on-one."

"Yeah, sure," I said quickly. I figured that even if the tutoring didn't help, going through the motions might at least earn me some pity at the end of the semester.

"Wonderful." King tossed his glasses back on. "Before finals, we'll set up some time to study, all right?" He moved his stack of tests into a brown leather bag, revealing a green folder lying underneath. On its label, the word KEYS was written in bold black marker. The answer keys to all of King's tests. The power contained in that thin little file was mesmerizing. It was so close, yet so unattainable.

As quickly as the folder had appeared, King picked it up and slipped it into the top drawer of his desk. I thanked him for his time and left the classroom, refocusing my thoughts on having to study with him, and hoping more than anything he'd run out of his toilet water cologne before it happened.

"Luke! There's a girl here to see you," I heard Mom call from the front door. It was Nissa. As soon as I came out of my room, she ran over and threw her arms around my shoulders, kissing me on the cheek. Never having experienced Nissa's jubilance before, my mom was puzzled.

"She gets excited. Don't worry, I'm still a queer," I clarified.

My mom rolled her eyes and went back into the kitchen.

Nissa nudged my arm. "You are absolutely *rotten*, Lukas."

She followed me into my room and looked around, fascinated by everything on my walls. "Museum of Lukas," she joked, looking through the small stack of cassettes on my desk. When she remembered what she came for, she set a bag down on my bed. Of course, it was bright and glittery, complete with pink tissue paper sticking out from the top. "It's a present to say thank you. You can open it now, if you want. I was going to wait until Christmas to give it to you, but I thought you might want it for Thanksgiving Break, so I decided to stop by on my way out of town. My parents have summoned me to the city for Turkey Day."

I smiled. I couldn't remember the last time I got a gift from anyone other than my mom. I reached into the bag and tossed the paper onto my bed. There was a book at the bottom, and when I pulled it out, I was struck by the cover: two men holding each other romantically, on a rooftop overlooking some sparkling city. "What's this?" I asked, my eyes glued to the picture.

Nissa scoffed like I'd forgotten my own name. "It's a love story! One of my favorites. Like, ever."

"But these are two guys," I said. "Is this a thing?"

She laughed. "The gay boy is asking me if gay love is a *thing*. Priceless!"

I set the book down on my nightstand and gave her a hug. Normally, I wasn't a fan of hugging anybody, but I realized how thoughtful she was and my heart got the best of me in the moment, until my brain took over again and I pulled away in confusion. "Wait. What's the *thank you* for?"

"I was waiting for you to ask," she gleamed. "The other day I went to the café looking for you and you weren't there. Well coincidentally, as I was walking out, Ray was walking in. So I started talking to him, and one thing led to another, and BANG! He asked me out!"

I felt my eyebrows raise on their own.

"I owe it all to you, Lukas! I don't know what you said to him the other day, but it totally worked."

All I had said was that she liked him. But I guess that

70

was all he needed to know. I smiled at Nissa. "Wow. This is great!" I lied. It wasn't great. It meant the logical Luke in my head was right. I never stood a chance with any guy like Ray. And why should I have? Nissa was so flawless that even I could see the appeal. I looked down again at the book she brought me. "I'm happy for you," I added.

That part wasn't a lie.

The heat went out at the café on the first snowy morning of the season. When I first walked in, I muttered a few bad words to myself, realizing I wouldn't be working without a jacket. As I took a look around, though, eventually it didn't seem so bad. The whole frozen-over thing kind of worked. Somehow, the chill made everything more crisp, and the smell of espresso lingering in the air made everything cozier. Looking at the bright side seemed like the best thing to do. Besides, I was on Thanksgiving Break, which meant I probably didn't have to see anyone from school for almost a week.

At least that's what I tried to convince myself.

About an hour in, the door bells jingled and I looked up to find Michael stomping the snow from his shoes onto the welcome mat. "Looks dead in here," he noticed.

"Heat's out. Everyone's taken their coffee to go." I looked back down to my book from Nissa, trying to find where I was before he came in. "You should probably take yours and leave, too. Wouldn't want you to get frostbite."

"Hey. Let's play a game," Michael said, coming over to the bar and taking a seat. As he began to take off his jacket, only to zip it right back up when he felt the cold I'd just warned him about, he explained the game in greater detail: "It's a fun one. It's called DON'T BE A DICK."

My eyes widened and I closed my book. He was not in the mood.

"Figured I'd come here this time. If you're on the clock, you can't leave."

He looked me in the eyes and it felt like he wouldn't let

me look anywhere but back at him. I didn't know what to say without setting him off, so I kept my mouth shut. He was edgy again, like when he followed me out of the school. I clinked a mug down in front of him and watched the steam billow from inside as I filled it to the top with decaf.

He sighed. "Look. I have to tell you something. It's important. It's embarrassing, too. But I'm telling you anyway. And I don't care if you still hate me; if you tell anyone else, I'll fucking kill you."

I nodded, too wary to even agree with him verbally.

"Do you remember my Uncle Jack?" Michael asked.

"How could I forget?" I answered without hesitation. When we were in the fourth grade, Michael's uncle came to Santana to live with his family. Everything was great for a few months. Jack helped Michael's dad start his own mechanic shop, and Michael wanted to be just like Jack. He talked about him all the time. One night, though, Michael's dad caught Jack stealing from the business and kicked him out. Jack moved back to where he came from, and a few months later, he shot himself. Michael was devastated after Jack left, and it was only worse after the suicide. He was always quiet about everything, though. He never wanted to talk about it. "That seems like it was a million years ago," I said.

"Maybe to you," Michael replied quietly, sipping his coffee. He cringed. "Got any sugar? This shit's nasty by itself."

I grabbed a few packets from behind the counter and tossed them down in front of him.

"Anyway," he continued, "I lied to you about him."

"He's not dead?"

"That part's true."

"You're confusing me."

Another sigh. He was hesitating.

"Michael, whatever it is, just say it."

"He didn't steal from my dad," Michael blurted out. "My dad kicked him out because of something else he caught

72

him doing." He stared at his mug and then looked at me, realizing I still wasn't sure what he was trying to say. "Something he caught him doing to me."

It took a moment to register, but then it did. And I couldn't believe I didn't realize it before, and I sure as hell didn't know what to say. I was frozen. Struck still as the night I told Michael about me at prom. If I didn't know him as well as I did, I would have wanted nothing more than to grab the kid and tell him I was sorry for not knowing, and that I couldn't imagine what he'd carried around with him for the past eight years, keeping that kind of secret from everyone. But I knew it wouldn't do any good. Not for Michael.

"Why are you telling me this?" I asked, still cautious with my words.

He shrugged. "You told me your biggest secret. Now I'm telling you mine." His eyes were red like he was trying not to cry, and he stopped looking at me. He pushed his coffee forward, accepting he couldn't stomach it. "I guess I just want you to know I'm sorry, and this is the reason why it scared me when you told me what you did. It's stupid, but it just scared me that you could be like him. I mean, I know you're nothing *like him*, but I guess it was just my reaction. And then, once I left for the summer, it was weird. And when I came back, you were so mad."

"Michael, stop," I interrupted. I scratched the back of my head as I searched for the right words, as if there were right words to be said. I took a deep breath and decided on only what was important: "It's okay."

Michael sat at the bar all day. We talked and talked until I finally kicked him out so I could close up. To my own surprise, by the end of the day, I was starting to believe things could go back to the way they used to be between us. He talked about what a hard-ass his dad was, asked if I could get Nissa's number for him, and scowled when I told him it was never going to happen. He even asked me when I thought I would get a boyfriend, which was plainly not easy for him to ask, but he did it anyway. I was glad he was there. No one else stayed long since it was so cold, and his company made the day go by quicker.

By the end of my shift, I was so ready to go home. It had been as exhausting as any other eight hours on my feet, or maybe more exhausting, and I smelled like stale coffee and warm milk. I put on my coat and pulled the cord dangling from the OPEN sign. As it flickered off, I saw a silhouette standing out the window.

When I stepped outside, I pulled the door shut and locked it. "You scared the shit out of me. What are you doing here?"

Ray grinned. "Am I really that scary?"

I remembered Zondra's warning about him and shrugged. "Maybe."

He chuckled. "Well, don't forget, you still owe me for checking out your mom's car." He raised his eyebrows a little, and I noticed his dimples seemed darker in the pale light of the sky.

"So what do you want?" I asked.

But without answering, he turned and started walking toward his car, stopping halfway to make sure I was following.

Zondra's voice resounded through my head, telling me to be careful. But what did that mean? She herself said the cards didn't predict the future, they just showed me something to consider. So I considered it. "Fine, I'll go with you," I said, "But in the event that you don't murder me and leave my body somewhere, you'll have to bring me back later."

Ray laughed and got into the car, and when I opened the door and sat in the passenger seat, I had an odd sense of déjà vu from the night of Nissa's party. The smell of leather was familiar, and I could faintly remember him asking me if I was going to throw up. I shuttered.

Ray revved up the car, and as we pulled out of the café

parking lot, I asked where we were going. He didn't answer. Instead, he reached over and turned up the music. A few minutes after we turned onto Main Street, I realized we were leaving Santana. "Okay, I'm serious," I told him, feeling the nervousness in my voice. "Where are we going?"

He glanced over with a taunting smile, deciding whether or not to tell me. He liked that I was afraid. "You'll want to zip up that coat of yours," he teased like he was telling a scary story, "It'll be cold."

I looked away from him and out my window. We were heading toward the hills on the outskirts of town. How stupid could I have been to get into a car with a guy Zondra specifically warned me to stay away from? "Take me home," I demanded. But before I even looked back at him, he nudged my arm with his elbow.

"Calm down," he quipped. "We're almost there."

After the longest twenty minutes of my life, we pulled into a dark parking lot.

I looked around. We were at the head of a hiking trail. "Does this go to El Maldito? Why are we here?" I asked. "It's freezing. And that hike's a quarter-mile. You know that, right?" I was dumbfounded. El Maldito was one of the most scenic places anywhere near Santana. It was a huge waterfall that poured down into a cave from a gap in the earth above. But it wasn't a place anyone should want to be at night. For Christ's sake, I knew *El Maldito* was Spanish for *The Cursed*. My Uncle Carlos brought Sam and I when we were kids and told us it was named El Maldito because of how many people were drawn into the waterfall for its beauty, and then drowned unexpectedly because they underestimated its power after the winter snow melted and turned the water violent in the summer.

"Well, today I was thinking. And I want to know if the waterfall in the cave is really frozen," he answered. Clearly he'd heard too many stories from people who lived in Santana for too long. Instead of just saying it was cold outside, everyone's parents would tell their kids in Spanish,

It's so freezing, El Maldito is all ice!

The only time I asked my mom if it was really true, she shrugged.

"You wanted to know if the waterfall is frozen," I echoed. "You know, that is the dumbest thing I've ever heard." I thought about telling him to take me home again, but I hadn't seen El Maldito in a long time, and even I used to wonder if it really stiffened into a fifty foot icicle after summer. "You're lucky I have nothing better to do."

Ray reached back and grabbed a flashlight, clicking it on under his face. "Are you afraid of the dark?"

I took the flashlight from his hands and got out of the car, not waiting for him to follow as I started up the path.

After a few minutes of walking, I clicked the flashlight off. "How's this for afraid of the dark?" I whispered, and we both gazed out. The moon was full and the snow was well-lit. It was dreamlike, really. Santana was just a small cluster of lights glowing in the distance, and other than that, there was nothing but miles of indigo land.

We continued on the path without the flashlight, all the way until we reached the entrance of the cave. "I don't think we need to go in!" I yelled over the roar coming from inside, "It's obviously not frozen!"

There was a gusty wind blowing out from within the ominous hollow, and by the light of the moon, I could see Ray peering in. He wanted to see it for himself.

"If you think I'm about to go into a cave at night, you're out of your fucking mind! We weren't even supposed to come this far!" I turned on the flashlight and pointed it into the dark, but even with the added light, it looked like the water inside was crashing down out of nowhere. To me, it looked like a nightmare. There was no way I was going in.

"I bet you'd rather come in with me than stay out here by yourself!" His glance turned from the cave to me, and he grinned as he snatched the flashlight out of my hand and started trudging into the cave. I tried to let him go alone, but as soon as I felt remotely deserted outside, I ran through the snow behind him, careful not to step into the rushing flow leaving the cave.

Luckily, we only had to walk about twenty feet before we jumped and skipped and balanced on the rocks at the base of the waterfall, and when Ray clicked the flashlight off again, we could see only the slightest bit of moonlight falling into the cave with the gushing water. We stood there for a few seconds before my face felt like it was covered by a sheet of ice from all the mist. I started shivering, both at how cold it was and at how scary the loudness of the crashing water was in the dark. I turned around and wiped off my glasses, peering at Ray and trying to make out the silhouette of his face.

"You scared?" he leaned in and asked over the thunder of the water. Even though all the air around us was moving and thunderous, we were so close I could smell him and I could feel his breath on my cheek. My heart was beating in every part of myself.

"I'm cold!" I yelled, "Can we go back now?"

In the dark I could just barely see Ray nod, and only a second after we started to move back toward the opening of the cave, I heard a splash when he slipped on a rock and his feet plunged into the water. He splashed all over the place as he quickly stepped up onto another rock. I pointed the flashlight at the soaking bottom of his pantlegs and I couldn't stop laughing.

"Fuck, it's cold!" he shouted. "Let's go!"

We hurried out of the cave and raced back down the trail three times faster than we'd gone up. When we got to the car, I jumped into the passenger seat, and Ray went back to the trunk to look for a pair of sweatpants he hoped were still back there. He found them and changed behind the car, coming around afterward and tossing his wet shoes and jeans onto my lap as he hopped in.

I swatted them to the back. "Turn up the heat!" I yelled.

He scrambled for the dials on his dashboard. "Jesus Christ. My feet are freezing!"

I looked down and saw his toes curling up as warm air finally blasted out of the vents in front of us. We both shook in our seats, trying to warm up. "Don't pretend that wasn't awesome," he said a minute later, shifting the car into drive and pulling out of the lot. His teeth were chattering.

"Seeing you fall in was awesome," I laughed.

As we turned onto the road back to Santana, he let out a chuckle. "I can't believe you came with me." I looked at him and he was smiling straight ahead, eyes on the road. "You're all right."

"Well, like I said, I didn't have anything better to do." I looked out my window at the moonlight falling onto the hills by El Maldito, thinking of how stupid we were for going there in the dark. I could only imagine my mom's horror if she knew. And maybe that was the best part. I'd never done anything like that. In addition to thawing out from the freezing cold, some other warm feeling pumped through me and I felt a sense of invincibility, as if I'd beaten the danger Zondra warned Ray might bring into my life. "What do you say to round two?" I asked him, and in the green glow of his console, I could see his curiosity.

Ray drove us straight to Santana High's parking lot, and when he turned the car off, he reached into the back seat for his wet shoes. "You think there's a security guard or something?" he said, slipping them back on.

I shook my head. My school could barely afford books made after the 70's, much less security during Thanksgiving Break.

We ran around to the back of the building. I knew one of those doors would be janky enough to maneuver, even if it was locked. Sure enough, with the right jerks and pulls, it fell open and Ray followed me in. We snuck through the dark hallways and it was only a minute before we came up to King's classroom.

I pulled the door open slowly and quietly, as if Ray and I weren't the only two people in the building, and as we crept in, I could hear Zondra's voice in my head again, asking if I was sure I wanted to do this. Hiking into the darkness was stupid, but maybe stealing was a new level of bad decision-making.

Nonetheless, I took the flashlight from Ray and went over to King's desk, pulling open the drawer where I'd seen him put the folder. Sure enough, there it was. I picked it out and flipped through the pages inside, and the high I felt from earlier came back, even stronger than before.

On top of feeling invincible, I felt like I'd struck gold. Zondra's warning made less sense than ever now. We took the key to the final down to the school office, and as the copy machine scanned the sheet and spit out a duplicate for me to take home, I looked around at everything in the lifeless dark, admiring how big everything seemed when it was empty. The entire night was coming together in my head. I couldn't believe it wasn't a dream.

"And then you kissed, right?" Sam asked the next day as I filled her in, cross-legged in my regular spot on her bedroom floor.

"What? No. Then we left everything the way it was and got the hell out of there."

"Okay, wait a minute. Let me get this all straight," she said, piecing together my story, "Zondra's basically a fortune teller. And she tells you not to make a bad decision with Ray Melendez. So then you decide to make a *couple* bad decisions with Ray Melendez. And now you're freaking out, because you think maybe you're doomed."

"Pretty much," I nodded. That morning when I woke up, I had to look at the copy of the test key in my sock drawer to convince myself the night before really happened. The arousing high had completely vacated my body, and all that was left was a bunch of doubt telling me Zondra's cards would have the last word.

Sam went on. "Not to mention, you still think there's something there with Ray, but you're probably wrong, because he literally just asked Nissa Delfino to be his girlfriend. And on top of that, you've randomly decided that you can forgive Michael for all the shit he did to you, for no apparent reason. Does that sum it up?"

"Yeah, I guess," I answered. I held one of the pink pillows from her bed and stared at the butterfly light fixture she had since we were kids. Oh, how things had changed.

"All I have to say is, if there's a decision I would regret it would be forgiving Michael. But then again, I'm biased. I've hated the kid ever since he cheated on me with Heather Hernandez. Do you remember that? So disgusting. I'll never forgive him."

Sometimes, I forgot part of what brought Sam and I closer over the summer was our mutual distaste for Michael. "Will you still like me if I'm friends with him again?" I asked Sam.

She scoffed. "You think it would be that easy to get rid of me? We're literally bound by blood."

My Aunt Cheryl cleared her throat loudly at the doorway to announce her presence. "Good morning, kids! I didn't even hear you come in, Lukas."

"I hope it's okay that I came over," I said. "I've had a long week. I had to tell someone about it."

"Oh, you know you're always welcome. In fact, your Uncle Carlos and I were hoping you and your mom might join us for Thanksgiving dinner."

"Thanks, but she's cooking as we speak." I looked over at Sam's clock. "Actually, I think I'm supposed to help her with the mashed potatoes in about five minutes." I got up from the floor and grabbed my coat from Sam's bed.

My Aunt Cheryl said she'd walk me out, and followed me down the stairs. Right before I closed the front door behind me, she stopped me by gently pulling the door back open. I turned around. "Lukas, I just want to thank you," she said. "You've been a very good cousin to Sam, and your uncle and I are so glad she has someone who understands what she's going through." My face must have shown how puzzled I was by her comparison. "Not to be pregnant, of course. But to be different. I know the kids at school can be... *less than pleasant*. I'm glad you have each other. I hope you know we think the world of you."

I couldn't remember the last time someone had said something so nice. I melted a little, and I didn't even know what to say in return, other than to thank her, and to tell her I was lucky to have Sam, too.

It was the second Thanksgiving since my dad left us, but it was the first that my mom had decided to make dinner. The year before, she made me go with her to feed homeless people at the church, probably because she knew she'd break down making a feast for two. This year, however, it wouldn't just be the two of us.

"When he comes over, you need to act like a respectful young man, not some little punk," she said to me as I wandered through the kitchen, eyeing the food I'd starved myself for all day. "He's done absolutely nothing to you, and you better not treat him the way you did before."

"I don't have a problem with Officer Richie," I answered coyly, "In fact, I think he's pretty hot. Can I sit next to him?"

I looked over to see her response. Just as I suspected, she nearly dropped the whisk into the gravy. "Luke, stop it. And don't call him that. *Officer* is his occupation. His name is Richie."

"It was just an observation. If you can lust after Officer Richie as a married woman, how come I can't? Aren't you calling the kettle black?"

"I told you, I am not lusting after anyone. And if you talk like this at dinner, you're not using my car to drive to work for the rest of the winter. I'm serious, Lukas."

I rolled my eyes. She was good. She knew there were few things I hated more than walking to the café in the snow, especially for a 5:30-in-the-morning shift.

When the doorbell rang, I grinned. "I'll get it," I said, only to be met with a stare reminding me of her threat. I opened the front door and of course, Richie stood before the autumn leaves blowing around on top of the snow outside.

He carried a pumpkin pie in his hands and wore a friendly smile on his clean-shaven face. My mom came up from behind and reinforced herself by putting a hand on my shoulder.

"Nice to see you again, Richie," I said with a smile.

After dinner, Zondra called to invite me over to the café for dessert, because she and Laura had too much for two people. She told me to bring a friend, so I called Sam, who could never get enough food anymore.

"How was it, Lukas?" Zondra asked.

"Dinner with Officer Hottie Pants? Not as bad as I thought it would be," I admitted, staring into a nearly-empty mug of tea. "He's quiet. My mom did most of the talking, which is weird because she hasn't done much of that in a long time."

"Maybe he was nervous," Laura supposed, cutting into a fresh sweet potato pie and slipping slices onto plates. "Your mother probably was, too."

"You think your parents are weird?" Sam chimed in, cradling her cider, "My dad cried tonight when he cut the turkey because his *baby's having a baby*. Who does that?"

"Everyone copes in their own way," Zondra grinned from behind the bar.

"Being a parent's no easy job," added Laura. She refilled my cup and then looked up at Sam and me. "Both of you should cut your parents some slack. They're trying."

Sam and I looked at each other. We both knew she was right. In both of our situations, our parents were grieving dreams they had for us. They were learning what every parent probably has to learn at some point: that you can't map out your kids' lives forever. They had expectations for us that they may or may not have had the right to create, and now, they were paying the price for it.

As Zondra and Laura began to ask Sam about the names she was considering for the baby, a part of me suddenly felt guilty again. A familiar whisper told me I shouldn't expect my mom to be alone forever just because I thought I might be. Maybe she could be happy with Officer Richie. And after the way dinner went, I thought it might not be such a horrible thing. He really wasn't bad in any particular way, even when I told him I was a queer, just to see how he'd react.

"So, Officer Richie," I had announced across the table, "Did my mom tell you I'm a flamer?"

My mom's eyes darted toward me in horror to see if I was seriously bringing *that* up, and then shifted to Richie to see his response.

"No, she didn't," Richie answered. "But I don't know why she would. Doesn't make a difference to me. My uncle's gay, and he's the best man I know." I could tell he was uncomfortable by the way he looked at my mom before going on. "I'm not an ignorant guy, Lukas. I know it doesn't make you a bad person. In fact, I'm willing to bet you're a better kid than you want me to think you are."

And then he picked up a spoonful of mashed potatoes and took a bite. My mom patted him on the top of his hand, smiled, and continued with her dinner, too. I didn't know what to say, so I just took another bite of turkey and told my mom the food came out well.

Officer Richie had put me in my place, and somehow, I respected him for it.

After Thanksgiving Break, every teacher made sure to remind us finals were right around the corner. One would think I'd be relieved, because I had the answers to the scariest test, but it only made me more nervous. If I used the answers, would King know I cheated? And if I didn't, would I fail the class?

In the end, I figured the best way forward would be letting King think his tutoring was a success so he could feel good about himself when I aced his final.

"Where have you been all my life?" Nissa sighed dramatically. I looked up as she took a seat across from me, dropping her purse and books onto the library table. She looked gorgeous, as usual, her hair perfectly placed and her lipstick precise as ever. I could see in her glittery eyes she was genuinely happy to see me, despite the fact that she'd rather be anywhere but school.

"Me? I've been in the big city," I answered jokingly, referring to the book she gave me before leaving town. "I loved it, even though it was a love story. I felt like I wasn't in Santana the whole time I was reading it. I owe you big time."

"You don't owe me, silly. It was a gift. I'm glad you liked it, even though it was a love story." She laughed, pulling out a notebook. "Also, we're study buddies for math. Just FYI."

Then, like clockwork, my other *study buddy* appeared – the only person who could possibly ruin my reunion with Nissa. I could have been blind and his sharp old musk would have given him away. "Ah, Mr. Bradley. I forgot to ask you in class today, would you like to plan a tutoring session for this weekend? Finals are fast approaching."

Instantly, I was mortified. I could feel it showing on my face as I nodded.

"Good," he nodded back, and nodded to Nissa, too.

She nodded in return. It was like a conversation of head nods that only ended when he finally told us to hit the books and left us alone.

"What the hell was that?" Nissa winced. "He gives me the creeps."

"He's tutoring me so I can pass his stupid final and get the hell out of this school," I answered. "And I'll take any help I can get."

The night Michael came over to my house for the first time since the year before, a bunch of weird feelings floated through me. It was like a mix of embarrassment because I knew my mom would ask him a million questions, and bitterness because we seemed to be starting from scratch, and even a little sadness because the thought of being around him still felt foreign.

When he knocked on the front door, my mom looked at me and asked if I was expecting anyone. I hadn't told her he was coming. I shrugged, figuring I'd give her a good surprise for once. When she opened the door, there was Michael, standing in his maroon letter jacket with his old backpack draped over his shoulder.

It was always obvious to me that I would never have romantic feelings for Michael. I just couldn't imagine it, but even I sometimes couldn't help but wonder why. Michael had always been a good-looking guy. He was fit, he was charismatic, and girls went absolutely crazy over his dimples. I just couldn't imagine kissing him, though. The thought alone felt inherently wrong.

However, there was a different adoration I did feel for him that was never the same with anyone else. It resurfaced most strongly every time he was vulnerable about something, or every time we stood up for each other, or perhaps most of all, for every time I saw the way he loved and respected my mom as if she were his own.

And that feeling had always been mutual. My mom adored Michael in different ways than she could adore me, because he was so many things I wasn't. She reacted as happily as I knew she would when she found him at the door. She jumped up and brought him down into a hug that I myself hadn't gotten in a long time, and asked him everything I knew she would, from how his dad was doing to which colleges he was considering. A part of me was jealous; I couldn't remember the last time she was as interested in my life. But more than that, I was happy at how familiar everything finally felt.

When he followed me to my room, he threw his stuff down to the same place he did before, right next to my dresser. He looked around at everything that hadn't changed, and the few things that had. And that's when he saw my copy of the test key for King's final.

"What's this?" He held it up, seeming more confused than anything. "How'd you get your hands on this?"

I wished I was better at lying. "I took it," I shrugged nonchalantly. "I broke into the school over Thanksgiving Break. So what?"

"Alone?" he asked quickly. He knew it was already unlike me to do anything that might land me in trouble, but it would mean I was a whole different person if I were to do it alone.

I snatched the paper from his hand and put it in my sock drawer. "Yes, alone."

But it seemed like he somehow knew better. "I heard you're friends with Ray Melendez," he said. "What's up with that?"

"I'd hardly call us friends," I replied truthfully.

Ray and I weren't friends. I wasn't sure what we were, but calling Ray my friend didn't seem right. "He's dating Nissa, though, who is my friend. Didn't you want to date her? Are you jealous?" I smiled and patted him on the shoulder, hoping I changed the subject successfully.

He rolled his eyes. "Nah. I think I dodged a bullet with her. But I'm glad she's been a good friend to you. I was a dickhead," he said somberly. He threw himself onto my bed and rolled over to the side he used to sleep on. "Are you ready to be my therapist again?"

I sat cross-legged at the other end, the same as before, and he went on about three different girls with whom he may or may not have been in love (or at least *lust*). And just like before, they were all crushes based on not much more than the girls' eyes or perfume. I shook my head, and just like before, he laughed as I told him he was a dog and was going to die alone.

The next weekend, the time had come for my dreaded study session with King.

As the wind clipped at my ears, I knocked on King's front door. I knew I should have worn more than a sweater. December in Santana was practically an inverted Hell.

When he answered, it seemed like he hadn't been expecting me, which was strange, because the walk was longer than I thought it'd be. I was fifteen minutes late. "Mr. Bradley," King said at the door, signaling for me to come in.

I followed him through the living room, looking around. It wasn't as horrible of a place as I thought it'd be, and it didn't reek of his musky cologne. Instead, it smelled like old books and wood polish. Everything was old, but I wouldn't expect anything else. He led me into the dining room and told me I could set my book bag on the table, and picked up a glass of wine he'd apparently started before I arrived.

"What areas do you think we should focus on, Mr. Bradley?" he asked. He seemed different than usual, but I wasn't sure how. I opened my book to one of the pages I had marked, and I didn't even say anything before he flipped the book closed again.

A grin took over his face. "It was you, wasn't it?"

Immediately, I knew that he knew about the test key. But how? I froze, caught off guard. If I were Ray, I would have been able to deflect his suspicion without a flinch. But I wasn't Ray, and the fact that I'd been caught red-handed was undoubtedly written all over my face.

I tried to play dumb. "I don't know what you're talking about," I muttered, re-opening the book slowly.

This time, he slid it right off the table, still wearing his nasty grin as it smacked the hardwood floor. "You left them out of order and you left them upside down. I'm quite particular, Mr. Bradley." His breathing became heavier, as if he'd been waiting for years to bust me.

By then, I knew there was no point in lying. "Fine," I told him. "Yes, I took it. I went into the school over Thanksgiving Break. That's how bad I need this. And I'm telling you the truth about it. Doesn't that count for anything?"

He scoffed, swirling the wine in his glass slowly. "Normally, I'd say the satisfaction of catching you in your tracks is enough," he answered. "But I think in this case, I'll have to give you a failing grade as well."

I imagined an F on my report card, and I could barely stomach the thought of missing graduation. I leaned down to pick the book up from my feet and set it back on the table. "Mr. King, I know I messed up, but please don't do that. I'll write an extra paper. I'll do detention for the rest of the year. I'll do just about anything, but please don't fail me. I cannot be stuck in this town."

His grin faded, and as he stared past me, at the leaves blowing around outside, I could tell he was considering what I'd said. He seemed to be calculating. "It would do more harm than good if I failed you," he answered softly, "But you tried to make a fool out of me, Mr. Bradley, and you need to be disciplined."

My stomach sunk and in an instant, every murder story I ever watched on *Dateline* with my mom flashed through my head. I felt all but sure that this unrecognizable clone of my teacher was about to kill me and leave my body wrapped up in tarp downstairs in the basement. "I swear, I wasn't trying to make a fool out of anyone. I was just trying to pass your class."

"Stand up," he said. His teeth were red from the wine, as if he hadn't already seemed enough like some kind of monster before.

I wasn't sure I heard him right.

I leaned in and he was clearly annoyed that he had to repeat himself. "Stand up, Lukas."

It was weird to hear him call me Lukas. It gave me the chills. He called everyone in my class by their last name. I'd been *Mr. Bradley* to him ever since I could remember.

As the wind howled outside, I pushed myself out from the dining table and rose to my feet. His eyes traveled down my shirt, and the momentary confusion passed immediately.

88

As disturbing as it was, there was no denying his intentions. Before it even happened, I knew.

He reached forward and put his hand on my pants, and instinctively, I grabbed his hand and my eyes threatened to do *something*.

Kill him, maybe. Or leave, at the very least. But then he looked up and angrily answered my stare, and in my head, I could hear his old, pathetic voice: *You tried to make a fool out of me. You need to be disciplined.*

I pulled my hand back and pushed my eyes away from his, looking up to the painting on the wall behind him. It was a print, actually, of *The Last Supper*. I could feel my jeans coming undone as I realized how peaceful Jesus looked in that print, for knowing he was about to be killed. I could feel King's dry, cold hands take a hold of me, and then a warm slickness, and I remembered when I was a boy and I learned that Jesus predicted Judas would betray him, and then Judas did. Humans can be so repulsively predictable. God could have struck all the men dead to save Jesus, but Jesus knew that wasn't going to happen. He had to let Judas hurt him for the greater good. And so he did.

King was clinging to my hips like a leach. It didn't hurt, but it killed every part of me. I was like a tree, burning silently and miles away from civilization. I felt a nothingness take over every one of my senses.

I'd never done anything like it before, and as much as I was disgusted and felt some barbaric urge to grab my pen and stab King's neck and then knee his face in, I was suspended in disbelief. I tasted the salt of a stray tear escaping my cheek and everything seemed surreal, like a blurry nightmare. I felt so morbidly fascinated by what he was doing to me. I was powerless and heavier than marble, but at the same time, when reality began to seep into my head, an unreal sense of victory rushed over me as I looked down to see him on his knees in front of me, like a peasant begging for dinner. My hands moved to grab his hair and pulled his mouth off me. His hungry eyes looked up, and in that moment, he made a deal with the same possessed version of me that used to drag keys down my arm. The autopilot had taken control again.

I felt myself smacking King's hungry face with my hand before I fed myself to him again, bewildered and nauseous and cold.

SIX

My bones shook tightly under my skin as I turned onto my block from Main Street not even an hour later, holding myself and trying to muster up some kind of warmth from my sweater. Snow started to drift down, covering the world. When I walked into the house, the dry living room heat engulfed my whole body, and I breathed in a defrosting heap of air. My mom stood on a chair, singing along to some holiday concert on TV and hooking an ornament onto the Christmas tree. Richie held out another for her to hang next, waving hello as I kicked off my shoes.

"Doesn't it look great?" he asked, showcasing the tree like a new car.

"We've been working on it for hours," my mom added. "How was tutoring?"

I felt my stomach knot, like someone had stuck a fork in me and started twisting my guts like spaghetti, and the next thing I knew, I was on my knees in the bathroom, hurling into the toilet. My hands were shuddering as if I'd never come inside. "Luke, what's wrong with you?" my mom yelled from outside the door. She tapped a few times. "Are you okay?"

"I'm fine. I think I'm just sick. I need a shower," I

answered hurriedly, and caught my breath.

I squeaked on the water and pulled off all my clothes in a rush. When I stepped into the tub, my body coiled. My skin was so cold, the water felt like it was boiling. But I didn't let myself back away. I lathered soap into my burning hands and started scrubbing myself clean. I needed to wash him off. His mouth was lingering on me. I could feel it everywhere.

I scrubbed every part of me, rinsed out my mouth, and even knelt down under the falling water to try throwing up again, but there was nothing left to get out.

There was nothing left in me.

I ran track from seventh grade to eleventh. When I joined, it was because Michael said to do it with him, and so I did. And I happened to be good at it, and I also happened to love running. It made me feel okay when I had too much pent-up anxiety, or when I'd get nervous about a test, or even when my dad left. It also made me feel okay when I would worry about telling Michael who I was; I'm not sure why it didn't work after I did tell him. Probably because the pills replaced the need to run. They gave me the same sense of relaxation without nearly as much effort.

Something sparked the running machine in me again the week after I went to King's house. I'd been a melancholy robot, on autopilot for much longer than usual. Everything was so numb, I couldn't stand it. Honestly, I couldn't say what I even did during the days after, because it was like I wasn't recording memory.

After so long, I needed to feel something.

My old gym shoes felt like I'd never taken them off, and the hot sting in my legs was a welcome familiarity. The cold air outside scraped my throat, but it felt good. The sun was out and had melted a lot of the snow. I didn't even mind that the track was muddy. Little brown specks splattered my legs like freckles after summer, and I knew my mom would have a conniption when she saw me, but I didn't care.

I just felt so fucking good for the first time in what seemed like forever. The world was mine again, if only for a minute. The sound of my falling shoes and the pushing and pulling of my breath was a song I'd missed. It was like I'd found a tool in the shed that was exactly what I'd needed and forgot I had all along. It was like I'd taken three of my pills at once. The cloudiness seemed a little warmer. Finals didn't seem like a scary battle so much as a well-deserved end to a shitty semester. I was almost halfway done with my garbage senior year.

I felt completely weightless, until a fist bumped my shoulder. My eyes opened and I turned my head, still keeping on.

Ray jogged beside me. "Didn't know you ran."

"Yeah," I said, noticing the sweat streaming down my forehead. A drop fell off my nose. I stopped to catch my breath, wiping my face with my shirt.

"Don't quit because I'm here!" he smiled, and nudged my arm again, taking off in front of me. I tracked after him, watching the back of his arms and the definition of his shoulder blades through his shirt. I wasn't sure if I was more jealous of his body, or turned on. Maybe both.

I followed him around the track four times, until he finally shouted back, "I'll race you home!" He was about as breathless as I was. I pushed myself into turbo mode and caught up with him.

"My home or yours?" I asked, trying not to wheeze.

"Yours," he panted back.

I pushed and pushed, and thanked the heavens I only lived a few blocks away. Our shoes smacked the mud and sidewalk and pavement all the way there. He passed me at one point, but I passed him back, and finally, when we got to my front porch, I collapsed onto the paint-chipped wood, holding my stomach and heaving.

"I'm dead," I gasped. "Dying. Deceased. Passed away."

Ray laughed, but he was so winded, it turned into a cough. I threw myself up to my hands and knees and then

93

my feet, telling him to follow me. We walked through the living room and into the kitchen, and I pulled two glasses from the cupboard.

"Nice house," Ray noticed, observing the pictures on the wall leading back into the living room. He picked up one of the frames from an end table by the couch. "Is this you?" he asked, holding it up. I was six in the picture, smiling through an incomplete set of teeth and underneath a haircut quite indicative of the time.

"Shut up," I laughed. "It was 1988, okay? I'm sure your kid pictures aren't any better."

"I don't have kid pictures," he grinned coyly, and I couldn't tell if that was a good thing or not. He set the frame back down on the table and crossed his arms, staring into the Christmas tree. "This is nice," he admired.

I nodded, trying not to stare at him.

Suddenly, he grabbed his own attention and looked over at me. "I want to see your room."

"Nope," I answered immediately. My indifferent robot life had definitely included ignoring the mess it had become.

He pushed right past me. "Come on. You saw my place, and I wasn't exactly prepared for guests either." He strutted down the hall and put his hand on one of the doorknobs. I shook my head. It was my mom's room. He tried another, but it was the bathroom. He didn't even wait for my response to the last one. He walked right in.

I hurried after him, reaching for everything I could put in the right place. He looked at the few pictures I had on the walls, and then down at my desk, picking up the Halloween party invitation from Nissa. He opened up the pumpkin-shaped card, and his fingers traced the loopy handwriting and the heart by her name.

"She's something else," I grinned, picturing Nissa's exuberant gleam. "How are things going with... that whole thing?" I felt inclined to ask.

"It's good. I've been at her house almost every day," he answered.

I nodded, imagining that while I'd been zoned out over the past week, they'd been getting to know each other more than ever. When he was done examining the invitation, he tossed it down and looked up at me. "So what about you?" he asked.

I couldn't tell what he meant.

"When are you going to get a girlfriend?"

"I'm... I don't like girls," I replied, correcting him without a second thought. I caught the defensiveness in my own voice and suddenly, I was nervous. He knew about me already. What was he doing?

"I was kidding," he grinned. "How about a boyfriend then?"

I rolled my eyes. "Never."

"Why not?" He stepped closer. He was right in front of me, and I'd never noticed before, but we were exactly the same height. His eyes were directly across from mine, and his shoulders, and his everything. Mischief was scribbled in his slate-colored eyes, and in the back of my mind, I still wondered if he was actually as crazy as everyone said.

I almost forgot he'd asked me a question. "I don't want that," I answered. I hated myself for it, but I could smell his sweat, and the sweetness of his cologne, and it was exciting to me. I tried to think of anything else.

"Have you ever kissed a guy?" he asked, and looked down from my eyes to my mouth. My heart started to feel like it was growing inside my chest. But as much as I'd literally dreamt about this happening, I then began to feel the spaghetti fork in my stomach. Everything suddenly felt wrong. Ray leaned in and my palms pushed his chest away.

"You have to leave." When did my hands start shaking? He looked at me like he wanted to ask if I was okay, but I hastily pushed him out of my room, and then out of the living room.

I slammed the door shut behind him. It all happened so fast, even I wondered if I was okay. Outside, he zipped up his windbreaker, and I peeked between the blinds as he walked into the evening.

The next Tuesday, I tapped my foot, anxiously waiting for Alan Gurule to finish the history final. King wouldn't let anyone leave until all the tests were turned in. I'd been finished for over twenty minutes, and King's final was my last for the day and the semester. I was ready to go home.

Finally, Alan completed his test and turned it in.

King inspected the room to make sure everyone's desk was cleared, and then quietly announced that class was dismissed. Everybody broke into a flutter and only paused as King added: "Mr. Bradley, please stay."

His voice rippled through me and I had to close my eyes to tell myself everything was fine. It was almost over. Disgust crept up my throat and I swallowed it as King sat on his desk with his arms crossed, lying to myself for the millionth time: *You're in control. Show him you're in control.*

"What do you want?" I asked when the room was free.

"I just want to assure you that you'll be rewarded for your discretion, Mr. Bradley. You've done a fine job in the class and your grade appears to have improved greatly." His empty eyes travelled to my waistline, and I felt as naked as the day I stood in his dining room. It made me want to shiver and throw up and break his neck.

I couldn't even say anything. I just left.

When I stepped into the hallway, a hand grabbed me from the side and pulled me over to my locker. "Is there something you want to tell me?" Michael asked.

"You scared the shit out of me," I said, pushing his arm away and reaching for the dial on my locker. I felt his stare from the corner of my eye, and in my mind I was filing through all the excuses I could use if he'd just overheard my conversation with King.

"Xavier saw you running the other day," Michael accused, his voice shifting into a more quiet tone, "...with Ray Melendez."

I grabbed the books I needed for break and buried them

into my backpack, half relieved he wasn't referring to King, and half surprised he cared whether or not I hung out with Ray. "First of all, do your stupid football friends not have anything better to do than talk about me? And second of all, so what?"

"So what the hell?" Michael answered, "You know he works with my dad, right? I heard he has a record. He almost killed a guy. He's trouble, Luke."

"He hasn't been trouble to me." I snapped my locker shut. "Actually, I've probably been more trouble to him. Did you know I was so drunk after Nissa's Halloween party that I passed out in town? Ray's the one who picked me up and made sure I was okay." I started toward the doors to leave, as surprised at my defensiveness as Michael must have been.

He followed behind me. "Are you in love with him or something?"

"Oh, I'm a raging faggot, so I must be in love with any guy who talks to me, right? Give me a break, you idiot. He's been a decent friend. I don't care what he did before he came here."

Michael clutched my shoulder, stopping me again. "If you think being friends with that guy is a good idea, you're the idiot."

"Maybe I was better off without your opinions for the past six months," I flared. "I forgot how nosey you are. It's annoying."

He took his hand off my shoulder and almost said something, but stopped himself. He just turned and walked away. I didn't really mean what I said about being better off without him, and a part of me felt like I should say so, but if it were to get him off my back for a while, I also felt like maybe it was worth leaving there.

I sat on the couch, staring at Sam as she stood in front of me, turned to the side. "You can't tell yet. I swear."

"You can totally tell!" she insisted, rubbing her skinny

belly. "I'm already turning into a whale. My life's ruined." She plunged down onto the other side of the couch as my mom came in, stomping the snow off her boots.

"Looks like you got something in the mail from your father," she said, trying to sound happy about it. She tossed the card onto my lap before going into the kitchen. I took one glance before slinging it onto the coffee table.

"Don't you want to read it?" Sam asked.

"Not really," I shrugged, "It's not even from my dad."

Last year, there was a Christmas card in the mail for me, and it wasn't addressed in my dad's small, boxy chicken-scratch; it was a bold, curvy cursive. Marlice the Mistress had clearly sent it. What I didn't understand was *why* she sent it. My guess was that it was either out of guilt or spite. Regardless of the reason, it was gross.

"Oh shit!" Sam jumped up and slipped into her coat. "I have an appointment in fifteen minutes. My mom's going to kill me." She pulled on her gloves. "Let's hang out soon, okay? I heard the world might end on New Year's Eve because the millennium's changing, and I need to see you before the world ends!" She laughed at her own melodrama as scurried out the door.

When she was gone, I reached over and picked up the envelope from the coffee table. I slit the top and split the opening of the card just enough to snatch the twenty dollar bill from inside.

"Merry Christmas, Marlice."

Nissa's doorbell was so loud I could always hear it from inside when I pressed the button. I stood at her doorstep holding my Christmas present for her, and as usual, her eyes lit up when she answered and found me there. She threw her arms around my shoulders. "I knew you'd come to see me before I leave for break!" she squealed. It seemed like she'd just returned to Santana after Thanksgiving, and she was already on her way to another family trip for the holidays. As much as she begged her parents all week to let her stay home, it was no use. She'd be in the city by the same time tomorrow.

"Not only am I here to see you," I answered, "But I come bearing a gift." I handed her the newspaper-wrapped book of love poems I found at the antique shop the week before. "Merry Christmas."

She ripped it open and gasped at the cover, immediately giving me an encore hug. "Luke, I love it. You know I *love* LOVE!" She turned around and picked up a merrily decorated bag from the floor. She gave it to me, and before I even took it from her completely, gushed that it was a blanket. "I made it for you myself, Lukas Bradley. So the next time you're cold and lonely… put it on and you can just be lonely." She laughed at her own joke. "I'm kidding, I'm kidding!"

I opened the bag and pulled out the blanket. It was soft and thick, and my favorite dark shade of blue, and it smelled like her perfume. "You didn't have to do this," I told her, "I thought the book you gave me before Thanksgiving was my gift."

She rolled her eyes playfully. "That was a *thank you* gift. This is for *Christmas*."

I nodded and began to put the blanket back into the bag, but before it was all the way in, she pulled me into the living room and onto the couch. I sat, and across from me, she climbed into a giant leather chair. I imagined it was her father's chair. I hadn't met him and had only seen one photo, but I could easily picture the tall, suave man sitting there firmly, stern as Nissa was now. "You look serious," I told her.

"I want to talk to you about Ray," she said.

Suddenly, I felt like I was under a microscope. "What's up?" I asked warily.

"There are plenty of rumors about him, right?"

I nodded.

"Some people say he beat the hell out of a kid and left him paralyzed, some people say he was a huge thief. But nobody knows for sure why he came here. So I asked him the other night."

I sat up straight. On one hand, I couldn't believe she asked him. I wouldn't have ever asked him. Even though I was no longer afraid he was going to kill me, I was still intimidated by him. On the other hand, I was not surprised at all that she asked him, because she was Nissa Delfino, and she was about as reserved as Barbara Walters when she was curious about anything. "What did he say?" I asked.

"He said it's irrelevant," she sighed, and I could tell it was bugging the hell out of her. "Other than the fact that he's really hot, the whole reason I went after him was because he's so mysterious. I want to know everything about him. But you know what I've learned? I've learned that he is always busy and doesn't want me to know anything about him. I haven't even seen where he lives! He always wants to come here."

"You're not missing much," I told her, "It's a little apartment and he doesn't have anything there. He's probably embarrassed because he's seen how nice your house is."

"That's not the point, Luke. I want to see where he lives because it's a part of him. Whenever we hang out, I do all the talking. The times he's come here, all he wants to do is kiss, and then he always has to leave for some reason or another. We haven't even had sex yet."

As much as I felt sorry that she was frustrated, I couldn't help but feel a spark of selfish delight.

"Do you think we should break up?" she asked.

"YES!" I screamed in my head. But I caught myself before it made its way out. "I don't know why you'd do that," I said instead.

"It's hard having a boyfriend and feeling like you don't know him. I guess when I come back from Colorado after New Year's, I'll just have to work extra hard to crack that shell."

"If the world's still here," I added, pointing at yet

another story about the big New Year's panic on TV.

"The world is not going to end," Zondra proclaimed, pouring hot water over the tea bags in my mug at the café. "The news people just need a story to sell. That's all this *Y2K* thing is: a story. The computers might do something crazy, but that's got nothing to do with the world ending, Lukas. There's a lot more to the world than computers." She set down the teapot, and handed me a pack of sugar. "Everything will be just fine."

It was a relief to hear someone so confident that everyone was blowing New Year's out of proportion. And as I looked around the café, I believed Zondra was right. The world was definitely much more than just computers, otherwise it might not be so complicated.

It was the last day the café would be open until New Year's Eve, and the last time I would see Zondra before then. She and Laura were going out of town for Christmas, and she decided to close the café until their return. I told her I could hold down the fort for the week, but she shook her head and said I needed to have some *Lukas time*, whatever that meant.

After Zondra wiped down the counters, she took out a mug, poured herself some coffee, and brought it over to where I sat. She pulled out a chair and sat next to me, lifting a necklace out of her apron pocket and laying it out on the tabletop. It was a shiny black stone latched to a thin silver chain, and for as simple as it seemed, it was oddly striking. "Put it on," she instructed, and so I did. The stone rested over my heart. "This is going to protect you."

"From what?" I asked. Suddenly, the warm assurance that just filled me up drained back out of my chest.

"I had a dream last night, Lukas. I think it was a premonition." She lowered her voice. "I don't know what was happening, only that you had just done something terrible, and the boy was with you. You were running, and there was snow and it was dark."

It sounded like bits and pieces from the night we hiked up El Maldito and broke into King's room. "I don't think you were seeing the future," I told her. "I think what you saw already happened."

"I'm not so sure." Zondra took my hand and gazed sorrowfully into my eyes. I could tell she was genuinely concerned, and with each passing second, I felt more and more concerned myself. For a moment, I thought about telling her everything, but the idea of springing it all on her before Christmas felt wrong, so I told her I was fine.

But she peered into me and could see I was still unsettled. "Look, tomorrow's Christmas Eve. And if you promise to make good choices, I'll promise not to worry about you." She reached into her purse and took out a red envelope. "Here's part two of your Christmas present, dear. A little bonus for being so wonderful. You have yourself some fun this week and keep out of trouble. Do you hear me?"

I nodded, dreading the thought of spending the rest of the year Zondraless.

Every Christmas Eve, my family opened presents as soon as the sun went down. My mom found some cheesy holiday special on TV and organized my gifts under the tree so nothing would be missed. Unsurprisingly, this year Richie joined us, but it didn't bother me nearly as much as I thought it would. I was just happy to see my mom in a much better mood than the year before. There was a restored joy in her eyes, and if Richie was the reason for it, then I was happy to have him.

I opened my presents to find new clothes – a jacket, some jeans, new socks with no holes, and some new boxers. When I was younger, I would have hated it. Now, I was just glad it would save me some of the money I made at the café.

I got my mom a pair of earrings and a new rosary I found at the antique store. I'd thought I would only be able to get one thing, but when Sally, the owner of the store, saw me trying to pick which one to buy, she let me have both for the price of one and told me to have a happy Christmas. Since I knew Richie was coming over, I got him a pair of cufflinks. When I went shopping, I found myself unaware of the traditional gift for your mother's boyfriend whom you barely know. Sally suggested the cufflinks and threw them in the bag for free with my mom's gifts.

"They're great," Richie said, holding them out to show my mom, as she tried on her earrings. "I got you something, too," he added, and picked up the last gift from under the tree, handing it over to me.

It felt like a book. I peeled the shiny paper off and the bold letters of the title peeked through: ALEXANDER THE GREAT.

"I hope you like it," Richie told me. "I think you'll identify with him."

"Why? Because they say he was a homo?"

"Because he was a fighter," he answered quickly, before my mom could tell me to shut up. "I think you're a fighter, too, Lukas. And I think you're going to learn how to use your powers for good one day."

My mom grinned at Richie and I could see her satisfaction at his answer. Yet again, he took what I slung at him and let me have it back. I surrendered with a grin of my own, and thanked him for the book.

As soon as I carried my pile of gifts into my room, I could feel that the window had been open. It was freezing. I dropped my presents onto the bed, shut the door, and flipped the light switch to see that not only was the pane cracked open, but there was a small envelope taped onto the inside. I peeled it off.

The envelope said my name, and I knew it was from Ray. I stuck my head out to make sure he wasn't still there. He wasn't. I slid the window closed and turned the blinds, taking the card to my bed. I didn't know if I even wanted to open it. I could just see Zondra shaking her head. I could hear her telling me to toss it.

Of course, I didn't.

When I took out a card from inside, a picture of Rudolph the Red-Nosed Reindeer appeared and underneath, it said *Merry Christmas!* in bright red letters, louder than I could picture Ray even talking. I opened it up. Inside, he wrote:

Merry XMAS, Lukas with a K.

That was it. He didn't even sign his name. An ironically simple message, and yet, I sat there more confused than ever. Until I stared at his words long enough to spark a memory. From the night of the Halloween party.

Ray looked at me warily from the driver's seat as I reclined all the way back and held my stomach. "Are you sick?" he asked.

"I think I'm good," I lied. I knew I was going to hurl, I just didn't know when.

He could tell. "Talk to me," he said. "Tell me a story or something."

"A story?" All of a sudden I couldn't look out the window. The trees passing by were starting to make me dizzy. I closed my eyes.

"Tell me anything. Tell me your name."

"My name is Lukas," I said, still pressing my eyes shut. "Lukas with a K."

"*Lukas with a K,*" he repeated. I could feel him looking at me every couple seconds, hoping to the heavens I wasn't about to puke all over his car. "I've never heard of someone spelling Lukas with a K."

"Yeah, well. My mom says she wanted me to be different. Which is hilarious to think about now. Please don't take me home. She will kill me. Lukas with a K will be killed with a K."

"Calm down. I'm not taking you home," he reassured me. I felt us come to a stop and a few seconds later, my door opened and he pulled me up to help me out of the passenger seat. I stumbled with him into his house, and the next thing I knew, he was handing me clothes. "Can you change into these?" he asked, ushering me into his bathroom. I shrugged, only then looking down to see that at some point I'd thrown up all over my shirt. "I can help you."

I was mortified. "Nope." I put up my hand. "I'm good. No help needed."

"Cool. I'll come check on you if you're not out in a few minutes."

It took exactly one look at myself in his bathroom mirror for me to muster up enough sobriety to quickly get out of my black Zorro shirt and pants and into the sweats he lent me. When I opened the door and asked him what to do with my clothes, he pointed at the tub and told me to throw them in.

The next thing I knew, I was curling up in his bed, beginning to come to my senses and praying the worst was behind me. I looked over at Ray stretching out on the sofa as he stared at the ceiling, probably in disbelief at the turn his night had taken. "Are you so mad right now?" I asked, remembering how angry I had been when Sam threw up on my shoes.

He laughed and looked my way. "Nope, not mad. I think you're pretty cool, *Lukas with a K*."

12:14 AM.

It had been Christmas for only fourteen minutes, but the house had been quiet since Richie went home and my mom went to bed. My room still hadn't heated up from the window being open, and under my comforter, a quilt, and three blankets, my feet were still freezing. I knew I wasn't going to sleep anytime soon. My eyes had shifted from Ray's card to the numbers on my clock every few minutes for the past four hours, and I couldn't take it anymore.

I slipped out of bed and put on my glasses and some socks, and then went into the living room. By the light of the Christmas tree, I pushed my feet into my new boots and bundled up in the thickest coat I had. I opened the front door discreetly, making sure not to wake my mom, and squeezed out of the house, holding my finger to my lips and telling the moon to keep quiet.

It took about ten minutes to walk from my house to Ray's, but it seemed like five hours. It was so cold outside, my snot was freezing in my nose. I told myself at least seven times to go home, and reminded myself of all the reasons why, starting with the fact that I had no idea what I was even doing.

The moment I got to Ray's door, I paused. Zondra was in my head. I knew I could tell that voice to shut up time and time again, but just like in real life, she would never relent. "You're playing with fire," she whispered to me. "Go home, Lukas."

And just like in real life, I ignored her, knocking on Ray's front door. I didn't realize until I took my hand out of my pocket how badly I was shaking. Ray opened up and by the light of the moon and the snow, I could see how confused he was to see me there. "Luke?"

"Hi," was all I could mutter before he pulled me into the apartment and closed the door. Without even turning on a light, he grabbed a blanket from his bed and wrapped it around me. It felt hot compared to the biting cold out.

"What are you doing here? Did you walk?" He crossed his arms, covering his bare chest from the cold that I brought in.

I sat on his bed, feeling the heat from the house flush into my face. "Got your card," I said, not really knowing what to follow it with.

The mattress creaked as he sat down next to me. I looked over for just a second, but it was too dark to see him.

"I have to ask you something," I added.

I felt him looking at me. And I could feel that nauseatingly cliché heartbeat coming from my chest. The growing, pounding one I could feel in every part of my body.

"When you came to my house before Christmas break," I began to say, as if it were an answer rather than a question.

I could still feel him looking at me. And I could smell the warmness of his skin. "I feel like," I added. No, that wasn't it. "It seemed like," I tried again. "You were going to kiss me."

Suddenly I felt flustered and shaken, but I didn't want to take his blanket off me. It was my shield now. I felt oddly safe all wrapped up in it.

He was still looking at me, and still, he said nothing. I peered at him and I could see the faintest outline of his eyes in the darkness, and then the silhouette of his shoulders. I closed my eyes and felt the heat of his hand brushing down the side of my face, and finally, I felt his lips slowly touch mine. It was warm and wet and my whole body was still hammering from inside and I pressed my lips back against him and breathed him in.

But it only lasted a second before he pushed me back. "You have to leave."

"What?"

"You should go home. I gave you that card because we're friends. And I'm happy that we're friends. But I'm not like you, Luke." He got up and grabbed my arm, pulling me to the door. He took the blanket off me and tossed it onto the bed. "I can't…" he started, but then he stopped without finishing and I walked out. "I'm sorry," he said, looking at me before he closed the door, and I stood for a moment in disbelief, at both of us, as the cold covered me whole. Then I looked up to the moon in utter disappointment, and I shoved my hands into my pockets and went back home.

I snuck in by the quiet, colorful glow of the Christmas bulbs still illuminating the front porch, and slowly returned to my room, burying myself under my blankets in the moonlight. Between the freezing rattle in my bones and the shiver left over from being kicked out of Ray's house, I was restless. I closed my eyes and tried to make myself go to sleep, but to my surprise, an even older memory than before played, like a scratched-up VHS in my head.

The day after New Year's, 1995.

My thirteenth birthday.

"You two can make a pizza for dinner," my mom said to Michael and me, searching for her keys. She snatched them from under a pile of mail and added, "Your dad will be home tonight so keep the house clean. You can invite Jesse and Jasmine over, too, but that's it."

Jesse and Jasmine were twins in the same grade as Michael and me. When I was a kid, they used to come over all the time, and the four of us would play video games, or watch TV, or keep ourselves entertained outside. If I was the smart one, and Michael was the athletic one, Jesse was the artistic one, and Jasmine could give Michael a run for his money at any sport the boys would let her play. Like most kids, our differences somehow made us get along better instead of worse. We were a pack, until that day.

My mom kissed me on the forehead, and wished me a happy birthday one more time before she left the house.

It was another cloudy and cold day outside. We had gotten a few feet of snow earlier in the week, and like most kids on winter break, we spent the majority of our day sledding down the hill behind the junior high, or having snowball fights at the park. During one of those fights, Michael got a little too rough and tackled me like I was one of his football friends. I flew onto a patch of coarse ice, and as soon as I got up, I could feel the huge scrape spanning from my waist up to my ribs. I lifted up my shirt and pushed my fingers against the burn.

Michael just looked for a second and then picked up a snowball and threw it at Jasmine. He was girl crazy, and it was clear he liked her. There wasn't much that would distract him. I held my shirt away from me and hurried down the block to clean up and change at home.

I hadn't noticed Jesse followed me until I was pressing a wet washcloth onto my side in my bathroom. I jumped at his skinny frame standing in the doorway.

"Are you okay?" he said. He had always been even more

108

quiet than me. I may not have spoken much, but at least I was audible. More often than not, we had to tell Jesse to speak up.

"Yeah, I'm fine." I tossed the rag into the bathtub. "He got me good," I added, feeling around my shirt. Somehow, snow had snuck under my jacket and melted. I had a sweater hanging on my shower rack, so I took off the wet shirt to change. As soon as I slipped out of it, I noticed Jesse staring at me in the mirror. "What are you looking at?" I asked.

He glanced away quickly and I pulled the sweater over my head. I was self-conscious about my body, which had begun to change and was unrecognizable even to me, but more so, I was curious about his apparent curiosity.

He hadn't been looking at me, he had been looking at my chest. I knew there was a difference, but I wasn't sure what it was.

When I pulled the sweater on, I looked back at him, and for the first time in my life, I felt seen for something other than what most people saw when they looked at me. I almost felt as if I hadn't put a shirt on.

Still standing at the bathroom doorway, he didn't move when I walked toward him to leave, and we came face to face.

He and his sister both had the same dark hair. I'd always thought it was black, but up close, it seemed more like a dark brown. And I'd never noticed the little birthmark above one of his eyebrows. "Aren't you going to move?" I asked.

And he did. He stepped aside, and I walked past him. I started down the hall, and then for some reason unbeknownst even to me, I turned around again. He was still standing in the doorway of the bathroom, staring at me. "What are you looking at?" I asked again.

For a second, it seemed like he might say something, but then he didn't. I walked back toward him until we were face to face again. There was something in his stare I liked. He always looked at me like he was waiting for me to say something. That's the only way I could describe it. With Michael, I was always the sidekick and never the superhero, but with Jesse, *I* was the leader between the two of us. It felt nice. "Say something already," I told him. "You're weirding me out."

Instead of saying anything, though, he lunged forward and kissed me on the lips, and without thinking, I pushed him so hard, he stumbled backward onto the ground.

For a second, we both froze still. Just two thirteen-year-old idiots with no clue what to do. After a second, when the shock wore away, I waited to feel disgusted… and I found that I didn't. Then I realized he was still on the ground, and pulled his arm to help him up.

Neither of us said anything, still calculating in our heads what just happened and what it might have meant. I felt like I should be mad, or grossed out, or *something*, but all I could find within me was the urge to do it again. I pulled his arm and brought him over to me and I kissed him back. It was short and awkward, and we didn't even open our mouths.

But it was just enough to realize something I already knew.

Suddenly, I heard Michael's voice outside and the sheer horror of imagining him seeing what just happened sent panic through my every nerve. "Get out of my house," I told Jesse.

"What?" He looked confused more than anything else.

"Get out," I said again, grabbing the same sleeve I'd just pulled to kiss him, and trudging toward the door. He tried to pull away from me, but by the time he did, I'd already swung him out of the house and onto the porch. Michael and Jasmine looked over with the same bewildered expression as Jesse.

"He just kissed me!" I yelled without much thought, and immediately, Jesse looked more afraid than confused. Something in me knew he wouldn't say anything, and I pounced on the opportunity to save my own ass.

"What the fuck?" Michael said. He'd recently

incorporated curse words into his regular vocabulary, and the timing was horrible. It only made me more nervous. He ran up to Jesse and got up in his face. "Why'd you do that, freak?"

"Don't talk to my brother like that!" Jasmine yelled without missing a beat, and pushed herself in front of Jesse. She and Michael stared each other down for only a second before she took Jesse's hand and they went home.

That was the last day Michael and I ever hung out with Jesse and Jasmine.

For two weeks after that day, I made myself sick every other minute, thinking about what happened. But I couldn't make myself apologize to Jesse, or tell Michael the truth. Even after years of friendship with Jesse and Jasmine, I was so scared of what Michael would do that I kept my mouth shut.

Huddled under my sheets, trying to keep myself warm after my own rejection, I counted the time. It had been almost five years since my first kiss with Jesse. The only kiss I'd ever had until I went to Ray's and made a fool out of myself.

Karma, I thought. It was exactly what I deserved for embarrassing the shit out of Jesse for no reason other than fear, and then ignoring him to the point of pretending he never existed. We still went to the same school, and until that very moment, the thought of apologizing, or even acknowledging what happened that day, hadn't crossed my mind.

I wondered if the same thing would happen with Ray. I wondered if he would choose to forget I existed after our kiss, whether or not he felt the same way about me as I did about him.

SEVEN

On New Year's Eve, I woke up late. I wasn't sure how it happened, but I slept right through my alarm. I jumped up and hastily grabbed the closest clothes to my bed and threw them on as fast as I could.

When I walked into the café, Zondra frantically motioned for me to get behind the counter. The line was almost out the door. "Guess everyone needs to get caffeinated before their New Year's Eve parties tonight!" she chuckled.

I was just relieved she wasn't mad at me for being late.

Luckily for me, the day flew by. It was the first time since Christmas I'd done anything productive, and I was glad to finally escape the haze I sulked in all week at home. Before I knew it, Zondra and I were closing up. I wiped down the espresso machine while she dried the dishes. "You've been awfully quiet today," she observed without looking up from the mugs. "Didn't you have a nice week away from work?"

"Yeah, it was fine." I finished up the machine and began cleaning the counters. "I stayed in my room and read the whole time. Richie got me a book about Alexander the Great for Christmas. It was pretty good."

Zondra put the mugs away in silence, but once she was

done, she put her hands on the counter, peering at me inquisitively. "What are you not telling me? Something happened with that boy, didn't it?"

I shook my head. "His name's Ray, and I haven't seen him for the past week. I haven't seen anyone but my mother since Christmas."

"Oh?" Zondra replied, "Then something happened before Christmas."

As I tossed my rag into the sink, I looked over to see she was still studying me. "Alright, fine. I kissed him."

Her eyebrow arched. It was the same arch she'd give Mr. Salazar when he insisted we didn't make the coffee hot enough. "Lukas, I told you not to involve yourself with that boy, for your own good. The cards said…"

"Stop," I said without letting her finish. I'd never interrupted her before. "Sorry," I added quickly. "You don't need to worry. He made it clear he's not into me. He freaked out an told me to leave right after it happened."

Zondra frowned, and I could tell she genuinely pitied me. She tapped on the counter, signaling for me to take a seat at the bar, and sighed. "Well, that certainly explains why you didn't leave your room over the past week. Are you feeling okay? Safe with yourself, I mean."

"I won't kill myself over it, if that's what you're asking," I answered. "I just feel like an idiot."

"It's for the best that he rejected you, Lukas. I know you don't see that now, but you will. He and you would probably be poison together."

"I'll still have to see him when Nissa comes home after New Year's. I'm dreading it. It's all I've thought about this whole week."

She hesitated. "I don't think you should go into the new year dreading anything. If I were you, I'd go see him one last time, just to make it clear that beginning tomorrow, you won't have anything to do with him, whether he's dating your friend or not," Zondra said. "Leave him in 1999, Lukas. Leave him in the twentieth century. Leave him in this millennium!"

"I get it, I get it!" I laughed.

"Good," she said with a satisfied grin. "Now get out of here. You've got exactly four hours until midnight." She pointed up to the clock.

I pushed in my chair, walking around the bar to give her a hug. She squeezed me tightly and I kissed her on the cheek. "Happy New Year," I told her, before she pushed me toward the door, demanding I put on my coat and go.

I came home to an empty house. In my room, I spent a good twenty minutes sitting on the floor, looking at myself in the mirror. "I think we should stop hanging out," I nodded to my reflection, pretending it was Ray. "It'll be better for both of us. And for Nissa."

Suddenly, I was panged with guilt all over again. I wasn't sure how I'd face Nissa the next time I saw her. Even though I'd told myself over and over that it shouldn't really count because I wasn't a girl, most of me knew that was bullshit. At the end of the day, no matter which way I spun it in my head, I kissed her boyfriend.

I tried in the mirror again.

"It's not that I don't like you. The problem is, *I do like you*. And I like you too much, and it's awkward, and I don't like that I like you, because it's not right, you know?"

Nope, too much.

I kept looking at myself, willing the right words to come to mind, but there was too much going on in there. I couldn't think about Ray without considering the fact that I betrayed Nissa, or without seeing Zondra keeping an eye on me.

And even though it had been weeks, I still couldn't shake the nasty, twisting feeling in the pit of my stomach over what happened with King, either. By then I'd probably woken up from twenty nightmares about his hands, and his mouth, and the way he smelled, and even the sound of my zipper being pulled by his fingers. I cried a few times, mostly out of anger, and threw up over it twice. I felt like my body had been hijacked by my brain, and it was so dramatic, and yet there was nothing I could do to stop it. It was like there was a nightmare living inside my body, and it moved to different places, and it took over in different ways.

"Fuck you and fuck everyone else," I concluded to my reflection, and pushed myself up off the floor. It seemed like déjà vu as I pushed my feet into my boots next to the Christmas tree in the living room. As I slipped into my coat, I realized Ray might not even be home. But then I remembered he had no family in town, Nissa was gone, and I was practically his only friend.

The crunching of the snow beneath my feet was strangely calming. It kept me from turning around and going home every time the temptation came over me. I thought about how long my last walk to Ray's had seemed. This time, it felt like five seconds.

I walked up to Ray's apartment and I could see him through the window, shirtless again, standing in front of his couch ironing clothes. I felt nauseous as I tapped on the door. He looked up and saw me through the glass, and the same surprised expression from Christmas surfaced on his face. He set down the iron and pulled a shirt on before coming to the door.

"Luke…" he started, as if he had something important to say. Or maybe he was about to tell me to leave. I didn't know, because nothing followed.

"I don't want to see you anymore," I blurted out.

To my surprise, he only grinned. "Then why are you here?"

"To tell you I don't want to see you anymore."

"You're letting all the warm air out." He pulled me inside. "What if I want to be friends with you?" he asked, crossing his arms. "You don't want to be my friend just because I'm not… like you?"

"You're the one who kissed me," I answered quickly. "I kissed you back, sure, but you kissed me first."

115

"So?" He walked over to his small kitchen area and pulled two shot glasses out of the cabinet above the sink. "Maybe you take everything too seriously, dummy." He set the shot glasses down on the counter and then took out a big blue bottle from the freezer. "You need a drink. And don't worry. It's not tequila."

No, no, no, no, no, I could hear Zondra telling me from some dark corner of my mind, *That's not why you're here!*

He carefully poured vodka into each of the shot glasses, and then pulled a soda from the refrigerator. "You seem like the type who needs a chaser."

I knew I was standing in the moment where I should ask what part of *I don't want to see you anymore* sounded like *we should take shots.* But of course, I just took a shot glass with one hand, and the soda can with the other.

We clinked our glasses together and tossed them back, and that familiar burn going down my throat might as well have been Zondra's disappointment, or my own, for that matter. But within a few minutes, I didn't care. I didn't feel drunk, but I felt much better than when I'd arrived. I sat on his bed as he continued to iron, and he talked about some car he'd been working on.

Then we decided to take another shot.

I told him about the blanket Nissa made for me. He told me she made one for him, too. I realized it was the blanket draped over me when we kissed the week before.

Then we decided to take another shot.

I told him I didn't want to go back to school. He asked why. I told him I just hated everyone there.

Then we decided to take another shot.

He asked who the worst person at school was. I told him it was King.

Then we decided to take another shot.

I told him what King did to me.

Then I needed to pee.

One of the weirdest things about being drunk is when you pee, and it seems like you're peeing for hours. As I stood there, I thought about everything from Sam and the baby to what my mom and Richie were up to. I tried to guess what time it was. I wondered if Zondra knew where I was. After I peed, I zipped up and stood in front of the mirror, staring at myself. My head felt heavy, and it was so weird to me how I looked just like my regular self, but maybe a little more tired. I reached forward and ran my finger down the mirror.

Suddenly, I jumped as the door burst open behind me. Ray was dressed up in his coat and boots. "Let's go."

"What the hell are you doing?" I asked.

"We're going to your teacher's house to deliver a message," he answered, going back into the living room and stuffing a backpack with spray cans before throwing it over his shoulders. He tossed my coat at me and I put it on.

"Fine, but I'm not driving with you because we are definitely drunk and I am not going to jail today. My Uncle Carlos will kill both of us."

He peered around the kitchen, pushing papers around on the counter. "Where the fuck are my keys?"

It was only then that I remembered I told him about King. My face flushed with mortification, and I told him I didn't want to do whatever he was planning.

He found his keys and pulled me out the door.

"I always thought it was weird how drinking makes you warm," I said as we walked in the dark toward King's house. "I mean, that vodka literally came out of the freezer."

"Yeah, weird," Ray nodded from ahead of me.

"This is a stupid idea," I added.

He stopped and turned around. I walked right into him, and he put his hands on my shoulders.

"What he did to you was a stupid idea. He's a pig. Aren't you mad about it? Fuck that guy!"

All of a sudden, everything felt heavy again, like all the blood in my body had stopped. "I hate him," I said. "But what are you going to do? Tag his house? He'll just think it was me."

"You worry too much," Ray laughed, and I could smell the vodka on his breath, remembering he took shots twice as big as mine, and didn't even chase them.

When we came upon King's house, looming in the dark corner of his quiet neighborhood, that familiar spaghetti feeling twisted back into my stomach. I had to remember to breathe. The lights were all off, and the car I'd seen in the driveway last time was gone. The silhouette of the house alone was haunting. The cold began to creep back into my bones, and I felt like I was standing in a nightmare. "Please tell me you brought the vodka."

Ray unzipped his bag and pulled out the bottle. There was maybe an inch left. "Finish it off," he said. I uncapped the bottle and surprised myself by throwing it all back, no chaser necessary. Within seconds, I felt more warmth circulating from my stomach to everywhere else, and the world seemed a little calmer again. I took a deep breath as Ray snatched the bottle and smashed it onto the street. Then he tossed a can of spray paint to me and pulled out another one for himself.

I ran behind him over to King's garage door, and I watched him take a deep breath of his own before he looked at me. And in that moment I thought, *Wow, we're idiots*. I completely realized the stupidity that possessed me, and then I made the decision to ignore it.

I pushed him out of the way and sprayed a big "P" onto the garage, and then an "I", and then a "G." Ray roared with laughter. "Hell yeah! He's a fucking PIG!" He shook up his can and started spraying words of his own. "FUCK YOU!" he wrote, and then stood back to admire it. We both laughed, and we kept spraying and spraying until our cans ran out of paint.

Then Ray pulled a lighter out of his backpack and flicked it on. "Hey, watch this."

"What are you doing?" I asked, mesmerized by the little flame.

"Shh! Just watch." He held the flicker up to the letters, and suddenly the wet paint looked like a blue neon light. "PIG" glowed dimly on the garage door.

"I'll admit that's pretty cool," I chuckled, and turned toward him. He was already looking back at me, and the same suffocating heartbreak got me like a plastic bag over my head. Before I knew it, he kissed me, and I grabbed his jacket and pressed my mouth back onto his, and without taking himself away from me, he pulled me down into the snow, and I could taste his teeth, and his spit, and the vodka, and all of a sudden, I got why people did this. It felt good, and I felt whole in a way I never had. It felt like a piece of me I never knew I needed was finally there. I wanted every part of him.

And then all of a sudden, he stopped.

"Shit!" he whispered, and when I opened my eyes, I looked down and saw a faint orange glow on his face. I turned around and fear flooded my veins. Flames were crawling around the garage door. They'd spread from word to word, and the light was slithering its way toward the roof right before us. We both knew there was no way we'd be able to put it out. "Get the stuff! Get the stuff!"

We both scrambled up from the snow. Ray grabbed his backpack and I picked up the spray cans, and then we hauled ass to the end of the street. I looked back to see the flames were already dancing to the other side of the roof. "You go to your house and I'll go to mine," he told me hurriedly. "We were home *all night*. Got it?" I nodded and handed him the cans. He stuffed them into his bag and took out a pen. "Give me your arm." I reached out my hand, and on the bottom of my wrist, he wrote out his phone number. "Call me when you get home. We'll figure something out."

I agreed, and after we both looked back at the house one last time, we took off into the night.

I hustled home in the dark, trying not to slip on the ice, and forcing my brain to think about anything other than how cold it was. The more I sobered up, the more my body started to sting. The icy air pierced into my shoes and made my ears sore, and I kept realizing what just happened. The fire in Ray's eyes flashed before me when I blinked, and suddenly, I wasn't sure if the smell of smoke sneaking into my nose was coming from the neighborhood chimneys or my clothes.

Finally, I passed the last of the skeleton trees watching me hurry in the moonlight, and stepped onto my front porch, digging through my coat pockets for keys. I'd just yanked them out when headlights pulled up into the driveway and I heard my name shouted from behind the brightness. It scared the shit out of me until I realized who it was.

"Where the hell have you been? I've been calling all night."

"Why would you call my house this late? Did you wake up my mom?"

"What? She's not home, Luke."

I peered into the light, and could vaguely see Michael sitting in the driver's seat. "Get in!" he added.

Somehow, I knew not to argue. I shoved my keys back into my pockets and hurried into the Jeep. As I pulled the passenger buckle over my chest, I noticed it was past eleven.

Michael sniffed the air. "Jesus Christ. Were you drinking?"

At that, I unbuckled as quickly as I'd strapped in. "If you came here to question me, you can fuck off," I snapped, realizing I wasn't as sober as I thought. I reached for the door handle, but he stopped me.

"Wait. You need to come to the hospital."

My stomach sunk. "What?"

"There was an accident," he said.

My feet hit the pavement the second Michael parked in the hospital lot.

I burst through the waiting room doors, and before I

could even find Sam, my mom pulled me in. "Thank god you're okay," she cried. "We've been looking for you all night!" Over her shoulders, I could see Richie sitting next to Sam, his arm draped around her shoulder. "We don't know if they're going to make it," my mom sobbed. "It doesn't look good." Michael warned me before we arrived that my aunt and uncle were both in critical condition.

Sam stared blankly into the floor and Richie quietly assured her everything would be fine. "It was a patch of ice," my mom whispered to me, "They went right off that bridge by the church."

I hugged her back before moving over to Sam. Richie stood up to let me take his place. She threw her arms over my shoulders, and I held her as she broke down into tears. "What if they die, Luke? I can't do this by myself!" I stroked her hair, trying to ground myself in what was happening. Everything seemed like it was moving too fast.

I didn't know what to say, but I always hated when people would console other people by promising everything would be okay, as if somehow they knew it to be true. Maybe it wouldn't be okay. What did I know? "I'm here," I told her instead, and I held her as tight as I could until her cries calmed into whimpers.

Then the waiting room doors erupted open again. Paramedics wheeled a gurney in from outside, and pushed their way through the lobby, straight into the emergency room. For just a second, I caught a glimpse of the face, and my heart jumped into my throat.

"House fire," I heard one of the paramedics tell a doctor. "Third-degree burns all over his left side, and severe smoke inhalation." They disappeared into the ER behind the gurney.

Michael rushed over. "Did you see that? That was Mr. King!"

I could feel my jaw become heavy.

He was in the house.

I pulled Michael down to the chair and told him to sit

with Sam as I ran over to the courtesy phone. I pulled up my sleeve and punched Ray's number into the keypad. There was only one ring before he answered. "Did you make it home?"

"He was in the house," I whispered.

"What? Are you sure?"

"I'm at the hospital and they just brought him into the emergency room."

Then, a scream pierced the air.

I turned around, the receiver still pressed against my ear. Michael held Sam tightly as the doctor knelt down next to her, resting her hand on Sam's shoulder. My mom buried her face into Richie's chest on the other side of the room. This couldn't be happening. I felt myself hang up the phone, and as soon as I ran back over to Sam, she grabbed onto my shirt, shrieking hysterically as she pulled me down to her.

"How far along is she?" the doctor asked, brushing Sam's hair out of her face.

"Four months," I answered.

"We'll have to give her something to calm her down so nothing happens to the baby." She called for a nurse. Together, they picked Sam up and helped her into a wheelchair.

Only after she was rolled into another room and the door was closed behind her did I realize Michael stood beside me. He pulled me up. "I'm so sorry," he sighed.

I glanced up at the television in the corner of the waiting room. Fireworks sparkled on the screen.

It was midnight.

And the world may have ended after all.

EIGHT

"Did you see this?" I asked Ray, holding up the Sunday paper. I'd spent the last thirty-six hours at the hospital with Sam, until her mom's side of the family came into town and told me they would take her home to start planning her parents' funeral. I was reluctant to leave, but she shooed me out of her room, reiterating the doctor's assurance that she and the baby would be physically fine. The first thing I saw as I left the hospital was the newspaper, facing up on the reception desk and greeting me back into the world with the headline: HOUSE BURNS DOWN IN NEW YEAR'S FIRE.

Ray snatched the paper from my hands, staring at the photo of King's house, scorched from the bottom up. The words we'd painted onto the garage were blackened now, plain for the whole town to see. "Wow," he said, "Front page. That's a pretty long article."

"Let me summarize it for you," I offered, inviting myself in. "They have no idea who started the fire, but they found a smashed vodka bottle near the house, so thanks for that. Oh, and they can't make out the exact size of the footprints in the snow, but they think this was the work of two men."

"And what about your teacher?" he asked.

"Coma," I answered. "And hopefully it stays that way." Most of me felt wrong for saying it, but I imagined the second King woke up, the police would ask if he had any idea who might spray paint the words PIG and FUCK YOU! onto his garage. I couldn't think of anyone else who would have a better reason.

Ray tossed the newspaper onto the counter, letting out a sigh before his eyes wandered over to mine. I could still see the first flames of that fire when I looked back at him. "Are you okay?" he asked. "You look tired as hell. And isn't today your birthday?"

I calculated in my head. "Is today the second?" I'd been too preoccupied to keep track of time, between crying with Sam over my aunt and uncle, and worrying about what Ray and I had done. In my head, it was still the day before.

"Yes, today's the second," Ray smiled. "Happy birthday." He reached down and grabbed my hand.

"What are you doing?" I pulled myself away, remembering what led our attention elsewhere the night we let that fire get out of control. "We can't do this anymore. You're dating one of my best friends, and I cannot afford any more shitty karma. Neither can you."

"I know," he admitted, "You're right." He looked guilty and not sorry at the same time. I knew whether he called himself gay or not, he liked what had happened between us, and he wanted it to happen again. I wanted it to happen again, too, but I kept remembering Zondra's warning about him, and the fact that in less than a week, Nissa would return to Santana.

"It's not that I didn't like it," I said, anticipating to say more. But somehow, before I knew it, Ray's hand pulled me down onto his bed and I was on top of him, kissing him, and touching him, and throwing my coat onto the ground, and he was hard, and he was hot, and what the hell was I doing? No, no, no.

I pushed myself up from the sheets, but he stayed on the mattress, propped on his elbows and waiting for me to change my mind. Mischievously, he gazed right into me and triggered every part of my body to tingle with a demand for him, but I resisted, picking my coat up from the floor and slipping into it.

That's when I saw the necklace Zondra gave me before Christmas, resting on the small table next to Ray's bed. "Where'd you get this?" I grabbed it and felt around my chest, wondering how I didn't notice it was gone.

"You left it here on New Year's Eve. When I came home that night, I found it on my bed." He stood up and examined the chain with me. It must have fallen off while I was watching him iron that night, telling him how much I hated school, and what King had done to me. "The little connector was broken, but I fixed it yesterday." He smiled next to my face, expecting me to thank him with a kiss.

"We seriously can't do this anymore." I stepped back, and before he could say anything in return, I was out the door. Under the warm morning sun, I secured the onyx back into its rightful place over my chest, and I asked myself where this decisiveness about Ray had been two nights earlier.

When I got home, I pushed off my shoes and tossed them near the wood stove to dry. In the kitchen, I found my mom sitting at the table, having a cup of coffee with Richie. He stood up when I walked in. "How's Sam?"

"She's home with her mom's family," I answered. "I'm exhausted. If you need me, I'll be in bed until next year."

My mom put down her mug. "Wait. What do you want for dinner? It's your birthday. You name it, I'll make it. Green chili and tortillas maybe?" She looked at me with a mix of concern and friendliness on her face. If it were any other time, I might have jumped at the chance to keep a civil conversation going, but food was the last thing on my mind.

"I'm just tired," I told her, and she nodded. There was no doubt she could see the exhaustion under my eyes.

After soaking in the staleness of the hospital for two

days, I probably could have used a long shower, but once my bed came into view, I was too weary to care. I slipped out of my jeans and collapsed onto my sheets, my eyes closing out the world and my lungs pulling in all the air they could, only to push it all out again with the hope I might fall asleep quickly.

Everything became heavy and my mind finally began to drift off when King's beady eyes somehow snuck into the room. Suddenly, the memory of billowing flames burned through me, and the pierce of Sam's scream in the hospital jumpstarted my heart, and Zondra's hand on my shoulder sent chills down my spine. Ray's vodka-soaked tongue was on my lips. Nissa's ecstatic laugh was coming from the closet.

My chest pulled in another deep breath and my legs kicked my sheets off the bed. I didn't know where this stir had come from, but when I sat up, I realized it had come with a lot of sweat. My first instinct was to go to my dresser and pull out my pill bottle, but I realized my prescription hadn't been refilled. When I'd last run out, I convinced myself I didn't need to be medicated anymore.

I threw my head back down to my pillow, summoning Dr. Carver to tell me what to do, like she had over the summer. "Lukas, when everything suddenly becomes overwhelming and a little confusing, what you're feeling is panic. I need you to close your eyes and count in your head. Start at one, and visualize each number as it comes up." She paused for a moment before making sure I was counting.

I nodded.

"Good," she smiled quietly. Even with my eyes closed, I could always tell when she was smiling, which was most of the time. "Now, when you feel your body begin to relax, I need you to picture something that makes you feel happy."

Over the summer, I usually pictured myself running next to Michael on the track team. Actually, I pictured myself passing him and coming in first at a meet. It was ironic that I couldn't force myself to get out and go on a run at that time. But now, the thought alone made me want to get up and dash right out of the house. I told myself to imagine something else, but nothing came to mind. I wondered how I could be so tired and simultaneously forced out of bed by my own body.

"I thought you were taking a nap," my mom said as I pushed my feet back into my shoes and grabbed a jacket. She and Richie watched as if I were a dead man walking.

"I need to run off some steam," I answered. "It's been a crazy couple of days."

They both gave me the same look of understanding, and as soon as I closed the front door behind me, I sprinted onto the street. At first, I didn't know where I was going, but then I clutched the stone on my necklace.

Zondra seemed surprised when I staggered into the café, trying to catch my breath. She motioned for me to sit at the bar and pulled out a glass to pour me some water. "Honey, what are you doing here? I told you to take a few more days to be with Sam."

"I'm not here to work," I told her, glad to see the café was basically empty. "I need to talk to you. It's important."

"Well, I'm certainly glad to see you. I've been worried. You really loved your aunt and uncle. I can't imagine how you feel."

"Yeah," I muttered, and at that moment, something told me not to say a word about what happened at King's house. I'd come to the café sincerely believing I was about to tell Zondra everything, but as she looked me over with concern, I felt overcome with a rush of paranoia.

She could tell something was wrong. "Darling, are you all right? You look sick. Have you slept?" Zondra tried to catch eye contact with me, but I was zoned out. I came to the café to feel okay, but for some reason, every part of my body was telling me I'd come to the wrong place. My heart was racing and I couldn't figure out what my body was telling me to do. Suddenly, as if someone had thrown a blanket over the whole café, the air seemed thicker and everything seemed to darken.

"I have to go," I said, pushing myself up.

The anxiety possessing my body startled Zondra. "You said you needed to talk, Lukas. Let's talk over some tea. I'm worried about you!"

"I'm okay," I answered. I knew I was lying; she knew I was lying. It was clear I was miles from okay. "I thought I wanted to sit for a second, but I need to run."

She tried to get me to sit back down, but before either of us knew it, I was halfway down the street.

I stepped up to Michael's house and before I even knocked, the front door burst open. Michael's dad was on his way out. "Haven't seen you in a long time," he uttered in his deep, raspy voice.

Michael's dad never cared for me. Since we were kids, he wasn't thrilled when I'd come to spend the night, and I could always tell he never understood why Michael was friends with me. He always told me I needed to play more sports like Michael did, and he loved to wonder aloud why I never had a girlfriend, only to chuckle afterward and nudge me on the shoulder, saying he was just giving me a hard time. Nothing had changed over the years. In fact, I figured by that time he must have heard I was a queer. His distaste for me seemed stronger than ever.

"Is Michael home?" I asked.

"Michael!" his dad shouted without looking away from me. He smelled like engine oil and beer, as usual. "Your friend's here to see you!" Then he moved past me and threw some tools into his truck before revving the engine and taking off.

"Happy birthday," I heard Michael say. When I turned around, he melted from surprised to concerned. "What's wrong?"

"Everything," I answered honestly. My heart was still jumpy, my hands were clammy, and the nervousness in my throat made me feel like I was going to throw up. I felt my face becoming heavy. My eyes started to burn, and before I knew it, I was crying right there on the front porch.

Michael grabbed my shoulder and pulled me into the house. He led me to the living room and sat me down on the couch, making a seat of his own on the coffee table across from me. "Is it Sam?"

I shook my head, wiping the snot from my nose with my sleeve.

"Well, what is it then?"

I took a deep breath and looked at him. It was apparent he felt worried at the sight of me, just like Zondra. "I messed up," I said. "It's pretty bad. I don't know what to do." The exhaustion I'd felt earlier was back, yet my leg was shaking and my heartbeat was still going crazy in my chest. "I'm scared," I added, and started crying again. I knew I was a blubbering mess, but I couldn't control myself. It was like I couldn't get a grip of anything inside me.

"Luke, tell me what's going on. Did something happen before I picked you up on New Year's Eve?"

I nodded.

"Were you with Ray?"

I nodded again.

"Did he do something to you?"

I shook my head.

Michael was clearly at a loss, so I did the only thing I could think of doing. I told him the truth. The words quietly came out of me: "We set King's house on fire." And as soon as they were out, panic returned from every corner of my soul and pumped through me. I grabbed one of my hands with the other to calm myself down.

I could tell Michael was trying to piece together how it could be possible. "You were drunk when I picked you up…" he remembered.

"We were drunk and we just went there to tag his house, but then Ray lit the paint on fire, and the whole garage went up in flames, and we didn't know what to do, so we ran.

129

And we didn't think he was inside because we didn't see a car and all the lights were off. But then at the hospital when they brought him in…"

"Shit," Michael mouthed. That was always his go-to word when he couldn't think of anything else to say. And then he seemed curious. "Wait. Why'd you want to tag King's house in the first place?"

In that moment, I knew I had to pull myself together. I hadn't even thought about telling Michael what King had done to me. "It doesn't matter," I told him, drying my face. "Can I get some water?"

"Since when do you ask?" he said instinctively, and followed me into the kitchen. He watched as I pulled a glass off the drying rack by the sink and filled it up, trying to think of any way I could possibly change the subject. "I want to know, Luke," he said. "I saw what you guys painted on his garage. It was in the paper."

The air went dense again, and all of a sudden I was anxious about becoming anxious. I couldn't lie to Michael. I knew if I did, I'd start panicking. "I don't want to say it," I told him.

And I didn't have to say it. He knew. "You mean, he…?"

I nodded and turned away from him, trying to focus on anything outside so I wouldn't start crying again. I had never felt so embarrassed.

But as Michael's hand rested on my shoulder, I'd also never felt more relieved. He told me I needed to get some sleep and nudged me toward his room. He cleared off the bed, and as I put myself down, he pulled the curtains shut. "I'll call your mom and let her know you're staying over," he said, "Just go to sleep."

As the bedroom door closed behind him, so did my eyes.

"He's still here?" I heard a gruff voice ask in the hallway. "He needs to go home."

I sat up and squinted, staring at the clock for a few seconds before doing the math and realizing I'd slept almost an entire day. Michael's thick blue curtains mostly darkened the room, but the morning sun still sent in slivers of light.

"He was at the hospital with Sam for two days. He's just sleeping. Who cares?" Michael nearly whispered. I could tell he was trying not to wake me up.

"I care. He can sleep at his own house." Michael's dad clunked down the creaky hallway in his work boots and I could hear the front door screech. "He better be gone when I get home!"

By the time his dad left and Michael nudged his door open to see if I was awake, I'd thrown on my jacket and was standing right in front of him. "I know. I'm going."

"He's an ass, Luke," Michael uttered defensively.

"I know. He always has been." I sat on the bed to tie my shoes. He sighed, and I knew he felt bad. "I'm not mad," I told him. And it was true. I wasn't mad. If anything, I was somehow comforted in a way I hadn't been in a long time, hearing Michael defend me like that.

He followed me to the front door and asked if I was okay. I told him I was fine, thanked him for letting me crash at his house, and disappeared.

As soon as I got home, I went into the kitchen and called to check on Sam. Not much had changed since I'd left her the day before, and she didn't say much about how planning the funeral went. Somehow, I could hear the redness in her eyes and the paleness of her skin through the phone. I asked if she wanted me to come over, but she said she needed to be alone.

I stood at the phone in the kitchen, looking around and wondering why everything looked somewhat different in the house, even though nothing had changed for months. The Christmas decorations hadn't even been taken down yet. I sighed and went to my room to take a nap, and although I'd just slept longer than I ever had, I didn't wake up until four hours later, when my mom switched on the light. "You're finally home," she noticed. "Do you feel better? We were worried."

I said I was worn-out and asked her to turn off the light. She did, and within minutes, I was right back to where I wanted to be: the nowhere that is sleep.

That didn't change until the morning of the funeral. Even though only a week had passed since Uncle Carlos and Aunt Cheryl's accident, the small spaces of time I spent out of bed during those days seemed like an eternity. And when the funeral finally came, I was ready for it. I knew I had to be.

My alarm went off at six. I showered, put on my suit, and made a pot of coffee, all before my mom woke up and came to the kitchen to ask what I was doing. "Sorry I haven't been up much," I said, and handed her a mug, a truce for this one day to be dedicated solely to her brother and sister-in-law. "I didn't mean to leave you alone like that."

"No," she hushed me. "Don't worry about that. Yes, I'm very sad. Your Uncle Carlos was my rock." She sat down at the table and stared out the window for a moment before collecting her thoughts. "But Richie's been a good friend to me this week. I haven't been alone. And I'm glad you were there for Sam and got some rest. This is all so exhausting." Her tired smile assured me she had been honestly unoffended at my absence, and I felt better knowing Richie was around to keep her company.

When I let myself into Sam's house, her grandma looked up from vacuuming the living room and rushed over to hug me. Although she'd already gotten herself made up for the funeral, it was clear she'd spent the past week going back and forth between crying for her daughter and making sure Sam was okay. "I'm so happy to see you, *mijo*," she sighed, looking me over, and pointed upstairs. "Maybe you can get that girl up and dressed. Her aunts and I have been trying to get her out of bed, but she just won't do it. I need to meet everyone at the church to finish getting everything ready."

I kissed her on the cheek and told her to go ahead.

When I went up to Sam's room, there were empty chip bags on the floor. Clothes were scattered all over. Light blankets covered the windows to keep the morning sun out. She slept on her side, cocooned in covers. I almost wanted to leave her alone, but the funeral was in less than two hours.

I knelt down and brushed the hair from her face. I whispered her name a couple times, and slowly, her hazel eyes opened. She looked past me, at nothing in particular.

"What time is it?" she asked.

"A little after eight. We have to get you ready."

She nodded and sat up. "I feel like I don't have any tears left to cry," she said hollowly. "What if I don't cry, and everyone thinks I'm a bitch?"

"No one's going to think that."

She stared off for a second and then looked at me, her hair a big tangled mess. "I still feel like this isn't real."

I couldn't think of anything to say, so I put my hand on her shoulder. I knew there was nothing to tell her. I just needed to be there.

While she showered and slipped into her dress, I picked up the trash in her room. While she curled her hair, I made her bed. While she wearily applied her makeup, I drew the blinds open and let some light in. It felt good to take care of someone else. For the first time in the past week, ironically, I felt like I was okay. I was exactly where I was supposed to be, and even though everything was wrong, I could still do something right.

I held her hand firmly as we drove to the church, and I kept my arm around her shoulders as people shared their eulogies. It was hard for me not to cry while Richie and some other cops paid their final respects to Uncle Carlos, and some of the teachers who worked with my Aunt Cheryl did the same for her. I had to stop myself from weeping a few different times. As she had predicted, Sam remained stoic for most of the day, but when her parents were lowered into the ground, their final resting places only a few feet apart, we both burst into tears and held onto each other.

The day after the funeral, I went back to work, much to Zondra's delight, and to my own. I was hopeful that maybe my life would begin returning to normal. Everything that happened over winter break left me drained, and I was ready to get back into a routine, even if it involved sweeping up coffee grounds, doing dishes on a daily basis, and burning my hands with the milk steamer I still hadn't mastered. Zondra kept me company while I closed, even after she was finished working. "How's Sam?" she asked, as she dusted the windows near the door.

"She'll be okay, eventually," I answered, hoping it was true. I didn't know what Sam was going to do, and as much as I wished she could just move in with my mom and me, I knew money was tight as it was, and before much longer, Sam would have the baby. Her grandma decided to stay in Santana until everything could get sorted out with my aunt and uncle's house, but after that, she said Sam would probably have to move with her to Utah. "My plan is to be there for her as much as I can," I added. "That's all I can really do, I guess."

Zondra nodded. As I continued to sweep, I could feel her watching me. "Lukas, would you come here please?" She took a seat at one of the tables, tapping the chair next to her for me to come sit in. As I sat down, I noticed the concern in her eyes. "There's something I've been meaning to ask you." She seemed uncomfortable, and before she even said it, I knew where she was going. "Do you know the teacher whose house burned down?"

"Did your cards tell you that?" I asked, only half-joking. Her cards had become somewhat scary to me. I didn't know how much they could really predict after they were right about Ray. Somehow, the cards seemed to know I should have stayed away from him, and I couldn't help but wonder what else they might reveal.

She shook her head. "I don't ask my cards about other people unless I'm asked to. Consent is key. And besides, that's not really the way they work."

Relief ran through me. I trusted Zondra more than anyone else, but I felt it was best that she didn't know about what happened on New Year's Eve. "Yeah, I know him. He was my History teacher last semester. I don't really like him, but it's too bad what happened."

She cupped my hand with hers. "Some winter break it's been for you," she said, catching my eyes with hers. "I just want you to remember that Laura and I are here for you, Lukas. You can tell us anything. And we'll help you with anything you need. Please don't forget that."

Suddenly, it seemed she was anything but clueless. In fact, deep within me, I *knew* she knew, and I wanted to know how she knew, and what she was going to do about it, if anything. I contemplated asking, but instead I nodded appreciatively. I didn't have the energy for much else.

She winked and told me she had to get going. It was her night to make dinner, and she should have already been home. The bells on the door jingled as she disappeared into the night.

As I finished sweeping, for the first time in a while, I noticed a familiar pinch in my guts. It was the urge to see Ray, or at least to talk to him. I couldn't help wanting to know how he was. He probably kept busy working like always, but I still felt bad for ignoring him. His nerves about New Year's had to be as bad as mine.

I picked up the phone behind the counter and dialed his number. A moment later, he answered and I felt a rush of irony for calling Ray from the same place Zondra's cards first warned me to stay away from him.

I hung up.

By the time my alarm went off on the first day of school, I was already in the bathroom brushing my teeth. I'd been awake for an hour. My mom got up for work, stumbling out of her room in her robe to find me watching the news, already dressed and sitting next to my backpack. "Did you sleep at all?" she asked.

"Not really."

"Do you need me to refill your medication?"

"I'm fine," I told her, and clicked off the TV.

When I stepped outside, I breathed in the crisp cold January air, and wondered how I could possibly feel ready to go back to a place I detested so much.

Whether or not it was a horrible thing to feel, I knew a big part of it was the relief that King wouldn't be there. He was still in a coma, which I knew because after the world didn't crumble into pieces come New Year's Day, all Santana's sole newspaper seemed to cover was Mr. King.

They framed him as a teacher beloved by the whole school. They talked about the next basketball game scheduling a moment of silence and prayer for him. They interviewed his sister from Arizona by phone, quoting her as saying he was the "most caring man" she'd ever known and a "real-life hero" for devoting his life to nurturing our nation's youth. Unfortunately, she said, she wouldn't be able to visit anytime soon because she was on a winning streak in her weekly bowling league. They must have been very close.

As I neared the school, fuzzy mittens suddenly covered my eyes from behind, and if the scent of her sugary perfume didn't give her away, the giggle that followed did. "Lukas Bradley, did you miss me?" Nissa threw her arms around my neck and pulled me down. Before I knew it, I was smooshed into her chest.

When I was able to pull myself away, I realized just how much I really did miss her. The gloom I'd drowned in for the past week was way worse than it would have been if she were in town. And, maybe nothing would have happened on New Year's Eve if she'd been around to keep Ray all to herself that night.

"I'm so glad you're back," I told her. "It was the worst break ever."

"I heard. I hope Sam's doing alright," she said solemnly. "And I can't believe what happened to Mr. King. Isn't that crazy?"

Then, as we turned into the parking lot, a massive shove hit my side from out of nowhere and took me down. By the time I realized what happened, I was in the snow and looking up at Xavier, laughing on top of me. "You like this, Bradley?" he laughed. A few of the other football guys watched from behind him, and they all burst into their meathead laughter. Nissa swung her purse and hit Xavier in the face with it.

"What the hell is wrong with you?" she yelled. "Get off him!"

The buckle from Nissa's purse made a small cut under Xavier's eye. Touching it with his finger, he pushed himself off me and got up in her face. "Does little Luke Bradley need Nissa Delfino to be his bitch bodyguard?" he joked.

"She's not anyone's bodyguard," Ray said, stepping in front of Xavier. "But I can be, if you need your ass kicked." I felt my eyes widen, wondering what Ray was doing at school. Xavier peered at Ray, and for a second, I thought they were about to throw down right there in the parking lot, before the day had even begun. But instead, Xavier picked up his backpack from beside me without taking his eyes off Ray, and left, his football goons following behind. Nissa helped me to my feet and Ray dusted the snow off my backpack. "You alright?" he asked, taking hold of Nissa's hand.

"Yeah, thanks," I said, swatting the remaining snow out of my hair. "But what are you doing here?"

Nissa lit up. "I didn't even have the chance to tell you!" she gleamed. "He's coming to school with us!"

I was speechless.

"It's true," Ray said, "They have a program here. I can come in a couple days each week and get my GED by the

137

end of the semester."

"Isn't that fabulous?" Nissa nestled onto Ray's arm as we entered the school.

All I could do was nod with a smile plastered onto my face. I told them I needed to grab something from my locker, and as soon as they branched away from me, I pushed myself into the nearest bathroom, and darted into the closest stall. Suddenly, everything felt like it was closing in, and ironically, the reason for it all somehow seemed like it might be the remedy, too. If I'd built a mental fence to keep Ray out of my head, seeing him for just that brief moment blew it to smithereens. I inhaled a deep breath and pictured Dr. Carver's smile before I blew it out slowly. *Just get through this day and pray you don't have any classes with him*, I told myself.

For once, my prayers were answered.

By the time I walked into my last period of the day, I sighed at the relief of knowing I wouldn't share a single class with Ray. Even better was the fact that I also didn't share a single class with Xavier. I walked over and took the seat next to Michael in Study Hall.

The people who didn't know we'd made up seemed confused, but it only took Michael asking what they were looking at one time to cancel out all the curious stares.

"What the hell is Ray Melendez doing here?" Michael asked, "I saw him at lunch."

I told him about the GED program and he rolled his eyes. "I know," I said. "But on the bright side, he was able to get your stupid friend off me this morning. I'm sure you've heard about that."

"Yeah, I heard about it. Xavier's an idiot," Michael admitted. "Sorry. I'll tell him to knock it off."

At his desk, Mr. Garcia seemed nervous, looking up at the clock as the bell rang. After everyone still standing found a seat, he solemnly stood up in front of us. "There's no easy way to say this," he started, and began to choke up. "And I know some of you have already heard..."

I looked around the room. A few kids were staring off into space. Were they processing some kind of life-altering news or were they just bored? I couldn't tell. Mr. Garcia cleared his throat and took a deep breath before letting out the rest of what he had to say: "Mr. King passed away this morning."

It was as if an ocean of invisible water immediately filled the room. Everything became heavy. I couldn't breathe. The noise around me was muffled.

Michael nudged my leg with his, and I gasped for air. Suddenly, the roaring gossip of all the kids in my class came flooding into my head. "Don't panic," he whispered.

I nodded.

"We'll have an assembly in ten minutes," Mr. Garcia continued. "We'll remember Mr. King together. And the administration wants everyone to know, if you need to talk to a counselor one-on-one, that's always an option."

I didn't know what to think or feel. I hated it, but relief was once again one of the thousand emotions buzzing and whipping through me. It was bumping into the guilt and the fear and the sadness and the shock, but it was definitely there. *Everything's fine*, I promised myself in my head, but no matter how many deep breaths I took, my heartbeat felt like a jackhammer. Mr. Garcia took roll before we headed into the gym, and I tried to think of whatever I could to get it back down, wondering, along with a million other things, if Ray had heard the news.

As the school shuffled onto the gym bleachers, I looked around for Nissa. I knew she'd be easier to spot than Ray. She found me first, though, and loudly let everyone know the seats next to Michael and me were saved. Her heels clicked over, Ray following close behind.

My eyes scanned the crowd from left to right. Everyone was murmuring quietly, and it reminded me of the funeral service for my aunt and uncle the week before. I was glad

Sam hadn't come back to school yet. This was the last place she needed to be.

The mic squealed as our principal, Mr. Kramer, told everyone to be seated. Once the rumbling of the gym settled into a hum, he cleared his throat into the microphone until the room fell silent. As much as I tried not to, I looked over to Ray. He held Nissa's hand and when he looked over at me, I had no idea what he thought. I couldn't tell if a similar rollercoaster of emotions that had been ripping through my core made its way through his. He calmly turned his attention to the assembly. For all I could tell, he didn't feel much of anything, least of all anxiety or regret.

Mr. Kramer lamented dramatically. "We are all feeling so many things today. We might be angry, or sad, or reminiscent. We might be happy because of our memories with Mr. King, or frustrated, because we never got to say goodbye."

The main thing I felt at that moment was sick. I wanted to throw up, and I wasn't sure whether it was because of the nerves tingling in my stomach or the grossness of Mr. Kramer's sentiment. I couldn't think of one person who would wish to "say goodbye" to Mr. King.

"We all have so many good things to say about him, so why don't we begin? Who would like to start us off?" Mr. Kramer looked into the crowd and a couple of hands went up. He walked the microphone over to where they sat.

The first person cried that Mr. King once helped her pick up her books when she dropped them. The next person sighed that Mr. King gave him an extension on a paper when his dog died and he was too sad to finish it on time. Everyone sat on the bleachers looking like they were so concerned, when I'd seen most of them talk shit about King at some point. They all sat there, holding themselves as if it were cold. It wasn't cold. In fact, it seemed like someone had turned the heat up to a zillion degrees.

Suddenly, I saw a hand go up that belonged to someone I knew. It was Jasmine, my former neighbor, my former friend, and the twin sister of Jesse, my traumatic first kiss all those years ago. When Mr. Kramer reached out to give her the microphone, she took it and proclaimed without hesitation, "Mr. King was a pig, just like his garage said, and he got exactly what he had coming."

Gasps came from every part of the gym. "Holy shit," I heard Michael whisper next to me, as Mr. Kramer hastily grabbed the mic back from Jasmine, signaling for a teacher to escort her to the office.

"Wow," Nissa said, "I guess we know who set that fire!"

I looked over at Ray, and finally, I could see he felt at least one of the things I did: pure and utter confusion.

NINE

Michael and I went straight to my house after school to discuss what happened in the gym. I knew my mom wouldn't be home until late, and Michael said it was time to come up with a game plan.

"You haven't said anything for a while," he said as we walked toward my house, "Are you feeling better or worse?"

"I don't know," I answered. "I don't even know what to think right now." My head was still buzzing and I hadn't quite concreted the idea that King was really dead. I kept trying to connect my memory of that night to the fact that King was really gone forever. *King is… dead? King died. King's dead.*

No matter which way I said it, it didn't seem real, so it didn't feel like anything, really. The circus parading through my head earlier had slowly faded into nothing but a soft whoosh between my ears, the way wind might sound a thousand feet above the ground, reminding me my life was suspended midair.

When we got to my house, we went to my room. Even though no one was home, I closed the door behind us, and Michael threw his bag on the ground, sitting against the wall next to it. "Maybe this is a good thing?" he wondered.

"Which part?" I asked. "The part where King is dead, or the part where Jasmine stood up and basically made herself a suspect?"

He shrugged. "Both? I mean, you and I both know if he's dead, he's not talking... ever again. And if Jasmine turned all the attention on her, that takes all eyes off you." He looked pensive, as if he were realizing something else, too. "Plus, you didn't set that fire anyway. Ray did. If it comes down to it, you need to tell the truth, Luke. It wasn't your idea to go there, and you didn't set anything on fire."

That was true. But out of all the different things that had run through my head, and out of all the outcomes I pondered, there was no part of me that wanted Ray to get in trouble for what happened. He did it for me, after all. It was an act of vengeance for what King did. "Look, here's what I want." I stood up and started pacing as I planned, "I don't want anyone to get in trouble for this. Maybe it's fucked up, but King's dead. There's nothing anyone can do about that now, right? What if I just keep my head down, stay away from Ray, and save my money so I can still get the hell out of Santana after graduation?"

"What King did to you..." Michael looked perplexed. "Do you think he did that to Jasmine? Or..." It only took a short glance at him to realize Michael and I both knew Jasmine wasn't speaking for herself earlier in the gym. As long as we'd known them, Jasmine had been Jesse's combatant defender. "Maybe you should talk to Jesse," Michael suggested.

"Why?" I asked. "What difference does it make if the same thing happened to him? We know he didn't set the fire."

"But maybe you'll feel better about the whole thing if you know that fire did other people a favor." Michael stood up and faced me, his hands gripping my shoulders as if I were a football player and he were a coach. "Who knows how many people King did that to? And who knows how many *more* people he would have done it to? But now he won't ever do it again. It'll be easier for you to move on if you know this whole thing is bigger than you."

I was bewildered, and put my hands on his shoulders, too, mocking him. "Where's Michael Medina, and what have you done with him?" We both laughed. I knew this rare sighting of profound psychological analysis from Michael was right. I couldn't just forget what happened overnight, even if Ray and I never got caught. It was true that I could use all the help in the world to justify what happened.

I wasn't sure I was ready to talk to Jesse, though. "I have to tell you something else." I looked at Michael and asked if he remembered my thirteenth birthday, when I threw Jesse out of my house and accused him of coming onto me. He nodded. "I kissed him that day," I admitted. "I was just so afraid to say anything, I blamed everything on him."

"Damn," Michael muttered, staring out the window at Jesse and Jasmine's old house. I imagined he was feeling every sense of remorse I'd already experienced for how we removed them from our lives that day and never looked back. He took a deep breath and turned back to me. "Well, I guess you better start by telling him you're sorry."

The next day at school, I watched every move Jesse made, waiting for the right time to approach him. I'd been thinking since the night before of every different way to start a conversation, but every time I came across him in the halls or when I saw him eating lunch in the cafeteria, fear rattled through me and smothered my curiosity about what he knew. The whole day passed by before I knew it. I missed my chance. The next day, the same thing happened. And the next day. And the next.

I woke up frustrated with myself that Saturday, hating how many times I'd chickened out with Jesse that week, and my annoyance was only heightened by the fact that my mom and I had the same day off. By then, we'd been distanced enough from my aunt and uncle's funeral to start getting on each other's nerves again. Everything I did seemed less and less satisfactory, and every remark she made seemed more and more scathing. I spent the majority of the day in my room, but when it was time for lunch, I went into the kitchen to make a sandwich while she sat at the dining table looking at bills.

"I hope you plan on cleaning your room today," she said without looking up. When I didn't answer, she repeated herself. "You're not leaving this house again until that room is clean."

I didn't have the energy to argue. "Sure," I countered quickly, trying to finish making my sandwich so I could take it to my room. When I was done, I put everything away and started to walk out of the kitchen, but she looked up and took off her glasses. "No, Lukas," she said, "Eat in here. No more eating in your room. It's a pigsty in there."

There was nothing I wanted to do more in that moment than to tell her if she hadn't morphed back into such an unbearable bitch, I would have been happy to sit at the table with her. But I couldn't muster up the energy to venture into the catastrophe that would undoubtedly ensue. I had been running on empty for almost a month and was exhausted. Instead, I set my sandwich down on the table, went to my room, and changed into new clothes. I put my shoes on in the living room, and when I walked back into the kitchen, I took my sandwich.

"Where do you think you're going?" she yelled as I walked out the front door.

I just kept walking away from the house, inhaling the cool afternoon air. She yelled at me from the porch until I turned the corner at the end of the block, when she stormed back inside, slamming the screen door behind her so loudly I could hear it from a block away.

The first thing I felt was the instinctive fear she'd send my uncle after me; that had always been her looming response to my threats of running away in the past. It took me a moment to remember that wasn't a possibility anymore.

Since Zondra and Laura lived on the outskirts of town, it took me almost an hour to walk to their house. When I knocked, Zondra peeked out from the curtains before opening the door quickly and pulling me inside. "What are you doing here, Lukas? It's freezing out there." She looked out the curtains again. "Did you walk here?"

I nodded and she took me into the living room. There was a stand-up screen constructed in front of the couches, and reels of film sat in cardboard boxes on the coffee table. I'd clearly caught them in the middle of watching old home movies, but nevertheless, Laura looked happy to see me. She got up and gave me a hug while Zondra went to the kitchen to make some tea. I told her I was sorry for barging in. "Oh honey, don't worry about it," she smiled, "We were just reminiscing."

The movie lit up on the screen was paused on a summer scene, probably in the 1970's. It seemed like the sun was just about to set, coloring the city neighborhood orange. Young Zondra was surrounded by two boys and two girls. All of them held sparklers, their faces bright with smiles. Even though the scene was still, their eyes seemed so alive. "Were those your foster kids?" I asked.

"Yes," Laura gleamed proudly, and then pointed each of them out. "There's Tommy, Charlene, Julie, and the youngest is Sebastian." She clacked a button on the projector and the picture came to life. There was no sound other than the flickering of the film running through the machine, but somehow, I could hear what their laughter sounded like in the back of my mind. "They lived down the street from us, and when their parents were killed in an accident, they didn't have anywhere to go. They didn't have any other family. The state almost threw them into the system. Well, luckily, Zondra had a very close friend who worked with the city, and he arranged for them to come stay with us. It was only supposed to be for a few weeks, but in the end, they lived with us for four years."

"And then what?" I said.

"Well for one thing, even though Levenston's a big city, it was still the 70's," Laura explained. "Social services never liked the idea of two black women raising four white children."

Zondra came back into the room, carrying a tea tray. "And when the state found out we were lying to them, they took the kids away from us quicker than you can count to one," she answered.

I was confused. "What was the lie?"

"These people weren't about to work with a pair of lesbians, so we told them we were sisters." Laura sighed, pausing for a moment to blow the steam from her tea. "Once they were gone, that was it. There was nothing we could do. We were heartbroken."

Zondra grinned solemnly at the screen as little Sebastian made circles with his sparkler. I felt awful for interrupting their glance at the past, but I knew it was too late to leave when Laura realized I hadn't told them what brought me over in the first place. She asked if everything was okay. I nodded. "I'm fine," I told her. "I just needed to get out of my house. I hope it's okay I'm here."

"Of course it is," Zondra said, taking my hand. "You know you're always welcome."

"And we have a fabulous guest room if you'd like to stay," Laura added with a hopeful smile.

Then, like clockwork, there was a knock.

When Zondra opened the front door, Richie stood before her on the porch. He was dressed in his police uniform, and I realized she didn't know who he was. "Can I help you, officer?"

"I believe there may be a runaway boy here, ma'am," he grinned. His friendly dimples negated the intimidation of his cop garb. When I stepped into plain sight, he could tell I wasn't thrilled to see him. "Your mom's awfully worried about you," he said.

"Get real," I retorted. "I know she sent you here to come get me, and I'm not leaving. She's crazy. I'm going to lose my shit if I have to spend the rest of the day with her." Laura came up from behind me and put her hands on my shoulders.

"She just wanted to know where you went," Richie compromised. "I'm sure you can stay, if it's all right with these fine ladies," he nodded to Zondra. She smiled and said of course it was fine. "Great," he said, and then turned to me. "Luke, can I talk to you alone for a second?"

I told Zondra and Laura I'd be right back and stepped outside with Richie. I was fully prepared for him to try convincing me to go home and apologize to my mom, but every defense in me was locked and loaded.

"I need to ask you something about your History teacher," he said.

Suddenly, I felt hollow. "Okay…" I permitted.

"Have you seen the things that were sprayed onto his garage?"

"They were in the newspaper," I nodded.

"Right." He seemed uncomfortable. "Since he was your teacher, I was wondering if maybe you know of anyone at school who would feel that way about him. Maybe the girl who stood up at the assembly and said the guy got what he deserved?"

I shook my head. "Don't really know her," I said. "But a lot of people called King a creep. It could have been anyone who knew him, really." I was surprised at how calm and cool I was, focused on leading Richie anywhere but toward the truth.

"That's helpful, Lukas. Thanks," Richie said, and then peered off into the distance, as if he were taking a mental note. "I'll let your mom know you're safe," he added, making his way back to his patrol car. He got in, his headlights flared on, and within seconds, he was gone.

When I went back inside, Laura put the projector away and Zondra led me into the kitchen. She sat me at the counter and heated up some leftovers for me. When she set it in down for me to eat, the homemade plate made my mouth water. But I was only a few bites in when I became distracted by her stare at the other end of the table. "Now, I know you didn't just storm out of your house because your mom was frustrating you, Lukas," Zondra said inquisitively. "Your mom frustrates you all the time. What's really going on?"

I looked at my porkchops, contemplating how best to answer her question. "There are these people I know," I answered. "And I need to apologize to them, about something I did a long time ago. And I guess I just don't know how." I set down my fork and started thinking of the past few years, after Jesse and Jasmine had become people of the past. "I've spent so long trying not to be sorry about being gay, I feel like I don't know how to be sorry anymore. Is that crazy?"

Zondra listened silently as I spoke, and after I told her what had been on my mind, she looked from me to the other side of the room, filing through all the stories she undoubtedly housed in her head.

"It's not crazy," she said. "Sebastian was the little boy you saw in that film earlier. The youngest of the kids. He and I, we had a special connection." She got up and picked a photo off the refrigerator and brought it over to me. In the picture, Young Zondra held a toddler tightly in her arms, and they both gleamed for the camera. "He'd grown so attached to me by the time the state took him away, I knew he'd suffered greatly from our being separated." She sighed, taking the photo back from me and staring into their smiles. "But I knew there was nothing I could do. Laura and I had been found out, so to speak. The thought of taking the whole thing to court, and dragging the children into something that would grab so much attention, seemed like a bad idea at the time. So we accepted our defeat as quick as we could and tried our best to move on."

She took a moment to place the photo back under its

magnet on the fridge, searching her thoughts for the best way to continue her story. "Some years later, when Sebastian was a young man, he found us," she told me. The faintest trace of tears appeared in her eyes. "And for as happy as he was to reconnect with Laura and me, he harbored a sadness toward us, because we hadn't fought harder to keep him and his siblings when they were younger."

I was sorry for making her take this memory out of its box. "You did what you thought you had to do at the time," I offered, my best attempt to console her.

"You're right," she agreed. "And that was all I could tell Sebastian."

Suddenly, I understood why she'd picked this story in response to my dilemma. Her wisdom never ceased to amaze me.

"Lukas, we are all growing and learning our whole lives. When we've still got things to learn, we're all prone to making decisions we regret later on. It's human nature. I think giving yourself a break is where you need to start." She smiled at me and asked if that was any help at all.

I nodded, thinking back to who I was at thirteen. That day I pushed Jesse onto the ground and threw him under the bus for our kiss, there was so much I simply didn't know yet. Just like Zondra and Laura, I lived in a time and place where I had few options of how to react for my own sake. If Zondra could accept that about herself, I figured I could, too. When I finished eating, I thanked Zondra and Laura for having me over before letting them know I needed to go; there was something I needed to take care of.

As always, they understood, and after two tight hugs, I ventured off into the pink evening.

It wasn't long after Jesse and I kissed that his family moved to a new neighborhood. Like everything else in Santana, it still wasn't far from my house. Since I only remembered the name of their new street, I strolled until I saw the driveway sporting their mom's old van, which I noticed had since become the twins' to drive to school. By the time I reached their doorstep, the sun had disappeared, and I could see into their illuminated living room from the street. Jesse and Jasmine both sat in front of the TV, though only Jasmine was watching. Jesse's nose was buried in some book on the other end of the couch.

Jasmine answered the door when I knocked. It was clear I was the last person she expected to see. "I know," I said before she even spoke. "Weird."

"Um, yeah…" she responded, stepping out of the house and closing the door behind her. "What are you doing here?"

"What you said the other day in the assembly…"

"What about it?" she interrupted warily.

I hesitated to answer. Clearly, she didn't want Jesse to know I was there, or she wouldn't have shut the door. "It wasn't about you, was it?"

Her eyes squinted in suspicion. "What are you talking about?" she asked. But with her response, I knew it was true. For how much Jasmine had changed over the past five years, it was funny how much she had not. She could see my realization that I was right, and quickly added, "I assume you know about King then."

"I don't know who set that fire," I defended instinctively.

She shook her head. "But you know about *the reason* someone set that fire." There was no way around it. Just as I knew her tells, she knew mine. "So you came here to talk to Jesse, then. Is that right?" she inquired.

I nodded, and as she decided whether or not it would be permissible, she examined me from top to bottom, taking in the closest look she'd gotten in half a decade. I could tell she was about to conclude I didn't deserve to talk to Jesse ever again, but instead, she compromised. "I'll let him know you were here. If he wants to talk to you, he'll find you." I nodded my acceptance of her answer, because I knew it was fair, and as I turned to walk back toward the sidewalk, I heard her add one more thing before going inside: "I wouldn't hold my breath, Lukas."

On my way home, I wondered if I'd ever talk to Jesse. I knew Jasmine wasn't wrong for her approach to the whole thing. It made sense that he should decide when and where he'd talk to me again. He'd probably accepted long ago that we'd never have another conversation as long as we lived, and it was probably the way he preferred it. But the more time passed, the more I hoped he would talk to me.

Michael had been right. Ever since Jasmine's outburst in the assembly, when I first realized I might not be the only person King hurt, I found myself yearning more and more for the validation that he got what he had coming. Although I constantly asked myself why he wouldn't deserve what he got for taking advantage of me, regardless of what he did to anyone else, I didn't have an answer for that curious voice in my head. I didn't know why my own experience didn't seem like enough for his punishment to feel justified, but it didn't.

When I came home, I was relieved to find the lights off in the house. My mom had clearly gone to bed. I crept to my room as quietly as I could. Anything to keep from waking the beast, so to speak. I softly closed my door, and without turning on the lights, I went to my bed to take off my shoes. But I shot up as quickly as I sat down. Someone was under my covers.

I reached for the light switch, catching my breath as Sam sat up in a haze. "What are you doing here?" we both whispered at each other.

"I'm trying to sleep!" Sam grunted. She rubbed her eyes and explained that her grandma was driving her crazy. She called my house while I was gone, and sensing her distress, my mom told her to come sleep over.

"I don't know if I can move to Utah with her, Luke," she sighed, wearily gazing across the room at my dresser.

"She's too much. I just wish I could stay in Santana. This is my home."

I sat next to her on my bed and flashed back to only a handful of months before, when I was the one dreading the possibilities of my future, and she was the one person who assured me everything would be fine. The tables had turned. I knew I should provide the same insistence for her, and offer whatever support I could to keep her life from changing more than it already had. Besides, as selfish as it may have been, I hated the idea of her leaving Santana before me. She had become my rock and I couldn't imagine my life without her. In fact, I felt guilty that I'd been so consumed with my own drama over the past couple weeks, I'd largely left her in the care of her grandma, save for the calls I made every night to see if she needed anything.

The wheels in my head started to turn. The end of January had already snuck up, which meant there were only about four months left in the school year. I quickly calculated how much money I'd saved since I started work at the café, and how much more I could save if Zondra would give me some extra hours. There would be more than enough to supplement Sam living with my mom and me. The spare room we'd used as storage could easily be re-arranged to accommodate Sam for four months. Plus, getting her to finish school would be easiest if she were across the hall from me whenever she needed help catching up from what she'd missed. It seemed like the perfect idea for Sam to move in.

The only obstacle would be my mom. Maybe she'd be more open to it than I gave her credit for, I thought, considering the fact that Sam was sitting in my bed now. But I could also predict her mood every time bills were due. "We'll figure this out," I told Sam, "Get some sleep." I went to my dresser and picked out some clothes to sleep in before I turned the lights back off and left her in my room.

My mom sat at the kitchen table the next morning, her

brows raised when I walked in from the living room. "I noticed you slept on the couch last night."

I could tell from her voice she was in the mood to forget we'd fought the day before, which was good news for me. "Yeah," I said modestly. "I was surprised to find Sam in my room." I took out a bowl and poured some cereal before taking a seat at the table. "But I was glad to see her. I don't think it's working out with her grandma."

"Doesn't sound like it," my mom agreed, taking a sip of coffee. "I don't know if she'll like Salt Lake City, but she doesn't really have a choice now. The social security and life insurance policies from her parents are taking a long time to sort out, and her grandma's the only person who can afford to take her in the meantime."

I looked down at my cereal, unsure of whether I wanted to tread forward. It seemed like maybe she had already considered the possibility of Sam moving in with us and decided against it. On the other hand, I knew I owed it to Sam to at least try. "Well, I was thinking I could pick up some extra shifts at the café, and maybe then we'd be able to afford to keep her here."

It only took one look from my mom to know I had been right; it was nothing she hadn't already considered. "And then what?" she asked, clasping her hands over her mug and clearly expecting more from me. I wasn't sure what she meant. She explained further, careful not to let her voice carry: "So she moves in here, and you work more hours at the café to help me pay for food and the things she needs while she's pregnant with this baby. But then you graduate from high school in May, and what? You leave town, and Sam and her baby stay here with me?" Her voice was more inquisitive than accusing, but all the same, she made a point. I hadn't thought further out than the immediate future.

She watched as my brain started to sketch out life after May for Sam and me. All I ever planned was to leave my hometown as soon as I could. For as unsure as I felt about where in the world my life would go after high school, I knew I wanted it to be anywhere but Santana.

On the other hand, I was also sure the last thing Sam would want to do would be to pick up and leave town with a new baby. She'd just said the night before that she didn't want to leave Santana because it was her home. And after everything she'd already lost, I couldn't blame her for feeling that way. Besides, this town hadn't betrayed every good thing she'd felt about it the way it had me.

"If you let her stay with us, I won't leave after high school," I bargained. The abruptness of my decision took us both by surprise. My mom's mouth opened, and I couldn't tell whether it was because she was about to say something, or because she was shocked at my apparent change of heart. It must have been the latter, because no words escaped her. "If you let Sam move in with us, I'll stay here as long as she needs me," I repeated myself, awaiting her response.

She blinked out of her shock. "All right then," she said, visibly still trying to take in what I'd just committed. "If that's a sacrifice you're willing to make, Sam can move in." And with that, she got up from the table and went into the living room to watch TV.

I was frozen in my seat at the table, my gaze locked on the cereal floating in my bowl, and my mind as close to the edge of its own cliff as ever before.

TEN

"Stop right there, Lukas Bradley!" a spunky voice commanded from behind me. I turned away from my locker to find Nissa peering, her pretend anger pressing down her brows. "Have you been ignoring me?"

"What? No!" I answered quickly, fully aware that my vow to distance myself from Ray had resulted in only a few quick hellos between Nissa and me over the past month. "I've just been really busy. I picked up some more hours at the café, and Sam's been staying with me. Things are crazy."

"Well, do you work today?" she asked. It happened to be the one day I wasn't scheduled at the café that week. My only plans were to go home and watch *Wheel of Fortune* with Sam. When I shook my head no, she lit up. "Then I'm reserving you. You've been reserved! Come with me."

She pulled me out of the school behind her, and as she yanked me all the way to the sidewalk on Main Street, she spilled all the gossip to which she'd become privy since the beginning of the semester. She and Ray had become the most popular couple at school, mostly because everyone was so curious about both of them. She was a celebrity among Santana trash, and he was still the shady town enigma.

James Armenta got a blowjob from Carmen Hernandez. Heather Cordova thought she was pregnant. But the hottest rumor in the halls of Santana was that Jasmine Cortez was covering for her brother when she stood up in last month's memorial assembly for Mr. King and proclaimed he deserved his fiery death. At first, everyone thought her outburst meant she started the fire, but she was the life of Amber Taylor's Y2K party that night. Her alibi was airtight.

Jesse, on the other hand, was unaccounted for. He skipped that party and wouldn't tell anyone where he was between the sun going down for the last time in 1999 and coming up for the first time in the year 2000. Obviously, I knew he didn't set the fire at King's house, and that made me even more curious about where he was. What could he have possibly been doing that he'd rather keep a secret, when telling the truth could clear his name for the fire?

Nissa was still talking when I noticed we'd passed her house. I asked where we were going. "Mr. King lived a few blocks up from me," she said, "I want to show you something."

My stomach twisted and churned with every step away from Nissa's house and closer to Litchfield Road. When we turned the corner, the charred carcass of King's house stood out from the few other homes in his spaced-out neighborhood. The yellow police tape had been taken down, and all that stood between us and the house was a sign warning people to stay off the property.

I remembered Ray's dark silhouette leading me toward the garage that night, so confident he'd conjured up the perfect revenge for what King had done to me. Ever since the fire, the memory of that night had somehow become sharper and sharper, and I'd come to realize the smile on his face was mischievous and knowing. As much as it scared me, the only conclusion I kept reaching was that the fire was his intention all along. It was never an accident. My mind flashed back to the vodka kiss he planted on my mouth as the flames escaped the painted words, which could still be read as clear as day on the garage door. Being back in the same spot where I'd seen it all happen made me more sure than ever, Ray knew we were going to King's house to burn it down that night, whether or not he was inside.

"Like clockwork," Nissa whispered to me then, and nudged me to look down the street. Jesse walked toward King's house from down the block. "He's come here almost every day since they told us King was dead," she added. We both looked away from him, but it was obvious when Jesse noticed Nissa and I standing out front, he pretended not to see us and kept walking down the street.

I tried my hardest not to watch, wondering if I could tell from a glimpse into his eyes why he'd been so affected by what happened to King. For a moment, I imagined catching up to him and asking point blank, but I remembered Jasmine's sentiment that he should only talk to me when, or if, he wanted to, and I reminded myself that I agreed with her.

"They say the killer always comes back to the scene of the crime," Nissa smirked, pulling me back toward the other end of the block, and ironically, away from the scene of my crime.

When I turned to take one last look at Jesse, he'd disappeared. I panned from left to right as Nissa pulled me around the corner. "Let's go to my house. I have more to tell you!"

"We finally did it," Nissa gleamed, no less than ten seconds after we reached the privacy of her bedroom. "We finally had sex! Valentine's Day sex. I think that might be the best kind."

"You and Ray?" I asked. What a stupid question.

Nissa laughed. "Who else?"

I chuckled along with her, determined not to let it show for a second that the only thing I felt was stunned, not that I had a reason to be. After all, they were dating, and they undoubtedly had chemistry. It was clear to everyone who spotted Nissa grabbing Ray's hand in the hallways, or Ray covering Nissa in his jacket the afternoons he walked her home from school. Plus, it had only been a few months since Nissa and I last sat together at her house talking about Ray, when she was hellbent on seducing him.

She'd finally gotten her wish.

Chin nodding and brows raised appropriately, I watched her gush every detail, careful for my own sake not to actually hear any of it. She lit up with each word, as if she were telling me she found some kind of hidden treasure. But then again, she had, in a way. She officially knew Ray in a way I couldn't say I did, and in the pit of my stomach grew an ache I'd only felt a few times before.

It was envy, and not only for sleeping with Ray, but the sheer delight she felt for doing it. Never in my life had I seen a girl talk about sex the way Michael and the other guys at school would talk about it, with an accomplished prowess like the pride of a hunter catching its prey. I wondered if I would ever think about sex like that, much less even mention it.

My brain worked as hard as it could not to see all the pictures Nissa painted. The modest-but-romantic dinner he made for her at his apartment. The ring he crafted especially for her out of a tiny piece of metal. The way he took every piece of clothing off her body like a sex-starved maniac, and yet made her more comfortable than any guy she'd ever slept with before.

I had to cut her off before the deed itself was described to me in a level of detail that would have made me scream. "Oh damn," I shuddered, glancing up at the clock, "Is it really 4:30? I forgot I promised to pick up some dinner for Sam."

Nissa hopped up and walked me to her front door, throwing her arms around my shoulders before I could leave. "Don't make me hunt you down again, Lukas!" she laughed. As she squeezed me, I caught myself on the verge of crying.

What the hell?

I quickly pulled myself away from her hug and said I'd catch her at school before rushing out of her house as quick as I could to self-assess. I took a deep breath as I walked onto the sidewalk, wondering if the tears pushing their way into my eyes had been triggered by jealousy, guilt, shame, or my own frustrations. Maybe it was all of the above.

Out of nowhere, emerging from the shadows of my soul, another familiar feeling seeped into my veins. I felt physically compelled to see Ray. I asked myself why. What good could possibly come out of that? Did I want some kind of explanation for how he could clearly feel drawn to me and then go all the way with Nissa? Did I want to see if I would be able to tempt him? Was I really that horrible of a person?

Before I knew it, I found myself halfway to Ray's apartment. I stopped dead in my tracks when I realized what I was doing. Nope. No way. It had been over a month and a half since the fire, and King was long dead and buried, but the sight of his red and black body rolling through the emergency lobby at Santana General slid into my every thought eventually. *Ray did that*, I told myself. *Ray killed a man*.

I shook my head, gripping the onyx on my chest, and changed course.

It took Zondra approximately three seconds to notice something was off when I walked into the cafe. She finished pouring a cup of coffee for the customer at the counter and then motioned for me to go sit at the bar before her. "What is it, Lukas?" she asked, and like the perfect antidote, the tranquil sound of her voice melted the ice that had stiffened in my chest.

"I'm sad," I told her. I probably sounded like a six-year-old, and I was surprised at my own simplicity in that moment. But it was the most honest thing I could tell her about what I felt.

She nodded sympathetically, putting a teabag into the mug in front of me and pouring water. For a moment, I waited for her to speak. Then I realized she was waiting for me to continue.

"I feel so stupid, and confused, and completely unsure about what I want. Except I do know I can't wait to get out of this town. But now I can't." Suddenly my mouth working faster than my brain. I didn't even think about everything I was saying. I was just content that with every word, I somehow became more sure I wasn't about to burst into a puddle of tears. So I kept talking.

"I'm screwed. I never accepted the scholarship I got before the holidays, but on top of that, I sold my soul, Zondra. I told my mom I'd stay in Santana because I wanted Sam to stay with us, and that was the only way she could. I don't know what I was thinking. But now there's no way I can leave after graduation."

I paused again, sipping from my mug and hoping Zondra would chime in. But although her brows had risen when she heard the promise I'd made to my mom, she only nodded again, and I realized my turn wasn't over.

To my surprise, my mouth didn't hesitate to keep going. "And, okay. I know I'm extremely stupid for this, because Ray is bad news and we were never an item in any way, but Nissa just got done telling me about how they boned for Valentine's Day, and I thoroughly want to rip all my hair out." At that, Zondra looked like she might finally say something, but she didn't. She nodded again.

I was all out, though. I'd word-vomited everything I needed to expel from my body. "Please say literally anything," I told her, and she laughed.

"I wish I could fix all this for you, dear, and I can't," she admitted. "But I will say you're not screwed, and you're not stupid, Lukas." As usual, her words poured into my soul like warm honey. "I promise you'll end up where you're meant to end up. And the people who are meant to be there will be there. And every single thing that's meant to happen in your life will happen when it's meant to." Then she looked me square in the eye and added one more thing: "And everything that's happened was already decided before it came to fruition, Lukas."

I caught her stare as she spoke. In the caramel glimmer of her eyes, there was a sense of assurance I believed, and I also felt my soul believing that maybe Zondra Devereaux knew everything. Not just about King, but about the future. "You're giving me major psychic vibes," I uttered, still trying to figure out if it could be possible for an ordinary human to have the omniscient powers I suspected stood before me.

Zondra let out a chuckle at my suggestion. "It doesn't take a psychic to have complete and total faith in you, my dear." Then she pensively grabbed the coffee pot. "But it's interesting that you believe it does," she added, leaving me with one more wink before she went off to the tables, refilling mugs and taking pastry orders.

I sat there, warming up under the blanket of encouragement Zondra had thrown over me once again, finishing my tea and replaying her wise promises like a song.

In the days following her calm assurance, it seemed Zondra was right, indeed. Knowing Ray had sex with Nissa slowly transformed inside my head from soul-stinging to emboldening, like a burning cut on my soul becoming a thick, numb scar. It solidified my decision to keep a safe distance from Ray. He was clearly moving on from whatever weird thing existed between us in the fall. I figured I should do the same.

It turned out shifting all my attention to school and the café seemed to ease my anxiety about what happened to King, too. One by one, my mind packed away every memory related to him, from the day he revealed himself as a monster to the day he became my victim, and put it somewhere out of sight. With each new day, I was a little more confident than the day before that life would somehow return to feeling normal.

Sure enough, my scholarship offer from the fall was long gone because I'd never responded. My first instinct was to panic at the lost opportunity, but Zondra and Laura told me not to worry.

"Are you sure you even want to go to college?" Zondra asked me one afternoon. "Right after high school, I mean. I know adults aren't supposed to say this, but you have the rest of your life to go to college." I was struck by her suggestion. I'd never even considered skipping college after high school because my mom made it seem like the next obvious step ever since I was young. She and my dad both skipped college, and I was expected not to make the same mistake.

But what if it wouldn't be a mistake for me?

I was already set to stay in Santana, and there was a small community college half an hour away. When the scholarship fell through, I just assumed that was the next logical option for what would follow graduation. Sam said she could even go with me. Just because she'd be a mom by the fall didn't mean she wanted to give up her chance at an education. We looked at the Fall 2000 schedule in a binder from our guidance counselor and brainstormed the ways we could both go to college, work, and make time for the baby, whose grand appearance seemed alarmingly closer every day.

In fact, we'd only come up with a perfect plan the very night before Sam lost her shit. The sound of her whimpers crept into my room and woke me up just as the Saturday morning sun began casting its early tree shadows onto my curtains.

At first I thought the bawling was my mom's, but I realized it was Sam whimpering in the bathroom when I slipped out of bed and moved closer to the hallway. I quietly tapped on the door, but she didn't say anything. Instead, her cries seemed to harden, realizing she'd failed at keeping quiet. "I'm coming in," I whispered, and turned the knob.

As the door opened, I peeked from the side of my eyes, unsure of what I'd find inside. But it was just Sam, laying in the bathtub, fully clothed, in the dark. I flicked on the lights to see there wasn't even water in the tub. She was just crouched inside as if she were taking shelter.

I knelt down next to her. "What's going on?" I asked. "My mom's going to think you're losing your mind."

"She's not here," Sam cried. "I already checked. She must be at work. I'm sorry I woke you up. I just…" She broke down into tears again, and I hushed her, reaching to unravel a wad of toilet paper for her. "I just had a dream… or a nightmare? I don't know." She took in a deep breath, sniffling herself straight to tell me the details. "My mom and dad came to get me."

"From here?" I said. I wasn't sure it was best to draw this story out, but I couldn't think of anything else to ask.

Sam nodded. "They said it was time to go home," she smiled and wiped her eyes. Her face had been so tear-soaked that when she pushed her hair back, it stayed. "And we went home, to my house. And everything was the way it was two months ago." Her eyes studied the faucet in front of her as she went on. "And all I could think was, *I can't believe I thought they were dead.*" After one more sigh, she looked up, expecting me to say something.

But what's the right thing to tell someone grieving for their parents? I couldn't think of anything especially profound. As much as it annoyed me when Zondra kept quiet so I might keep talking at the café, I found myself doing the same for Sam, and sure enough, she wasn't finished. "I don't know how I'm going to do this," she admitted. "A part of me keeps waiting for my mom and dad to come back and save me. They were supposed to help me. They were supposed to be here."

I nodded. "But I'm still here." It was all I could think to say, finally sure it was time to offer something. "And I'm not going anywhere, remember?"

Instead of the nod of agreement I expected, though, she

only cut me off by asking, "But is that the right thing to do?"

"What do you mean?"

"Staying here. You. Not leaving Santana. Is that right?"

I reverted to speechless. There was no way to sound sure it was the right decision, because I wasn't sure. "All I know is, I'll be happy to be here for you and this kid," I answered. That much was true. If I were to be confined to Santana, then at least it would be for the best reason there was. "You saved my life last year, and if staying here after graduation means I get to be what you need, then so be it," I assured her. Another truth. "I know I'll end up where I'm meant to end up. And so will you."

At that, Sam sprung out of the bathtub and her arms enveloped my shoulders.

I gripped her back, and silently hoped someday I might believe that last part to really be true, too.

For most of the next week, I worked on a mental list of all the reasons staying in Santana was the right thing to do. The main perk, I decided, was that in addition to being there for Sam, I could skip the whole dorm experience at some big university. I never liked the idea of it, anyway.

I put in my application for the community college, and finally stole the course catalogue from the counselor's office so I could obsess on demand, circling the freshman classes that seemed the least daunting. If I was going to be in school all over again, I figured I might as well make it as easy on myself as possible. I must have changed my course selections a hundred times over by that Thursday afternoon, when I pulled the catalogue out of my locker to find a note tumbling out after it and onto the floor. Someone must have slipped it in through the tiny slit on the door.

I bent down and picked it up, unfolding the edges to find a handwriting I hadn't seen in ages.

Swings. Saturday. Noon, it read.

I arrived at the elementary school a few minutes early,

but Jesse was already there, swinging alone in the playground out back. He faced the other way, but I knew it was him. In fact, just the first glance of him gliding up and down on that same swing set we used to love triggered a flood of memories, mostly from the earliest days I knew Jesse. When he and Jasmine moved to Santana and joined our class in the middle of first grade, I became friends with him before anyone else did. All he wanted to do was swing, and I welcomed the excuse to ditch sports with Michael and the other boys.

"Can you believe it's been more than ten years since we first came to swing here?" I asked Jesse, and he turned to me quickly. It was obvious I'd scared him, but he didn't quit swinging. He just nodded his head to the side, and I took a seat on the swing next to him. I pumped myself as high as him, and realized I hadn't been accustomed to the motion for a while. It felt funny. "I forgot how much I like swinging," I added.

Jesse put his feet down at that, his brakes bringing him to an instant stop. I did the same, suddenly confused and unsure whether or not this was a friendly meeting. "Did you do it?" he asked quickly.

I looked at him with no words to speak. My mind was suddenly jumpstarted and the first thing I could find was, "Did I do what?"

"Set the fire," he said. This was a conversation for which he'd come prepared, something I obviously couldn't say for myself.

"No," I answered adamantly, which was the truth. Ray set the fire. Sure, I was there, and I was the reason we ended up at King's house in the first place, but after all the thinking and re-thinking I'd done about that night, the only saving grace to my sanity was that I knew I hadn't set that fire.

Jesse examined me for the next few moments, and then began to swing again. "I believe you," he said. "But I think you know who did it." He looked at me for my response, and I slowly began to push myself back and forth on my

166

own swing, keeping my mouth shut to see what else he'd decided already. "I heard you're friends with Ray Melendez, and you know what everyone says about him…"

"Jesse, why am I here?" I stopped him. I jumped off my swing, landing on my feet in the gravel before me. "Did you ask me to come here so you could drop all these conspiracy theories?"

He followed my lead and jumped off his swing, too. He brought his hands to his hips and observed me some more. He was still as vigilant as ever. In almost every memory I had from our childhood, his watchfulness outweighed his participation, and not much had seemed to change. "I feel like we're not very different, you and me," he said, keeping his stare locked on my eyes.

I looked back at him and found a sense of familiarity in the curiosity that still seemed to live there. It was the same curiosity that watched me cleaning my scraped abdomen on my thirteenth birthday, right before he snuck up on me with his kiss. "Because we're both homos?" I joked.

He didn't so much as chuckle. "Because we both know King deserved what he got. It's the reason you came to my house after Jasmine stood up at the assembly. He did something to you, too, didn't he?" Suddenly the arrogance he'd worn only moments earlier seemed to shed; he looked almost desperate for me to confirm something.

A strange stir twisted inside me. It was true. I wasn't the only one. But for some reason or another, I couldn't think of the right way to tell Jesse. Would it mean I'd have to tell him every detail of it? More than I'd told Michael and Ray? Should I? Would it make me feel better to lay out every second of that sickening visit to King's dining room, and compare each puzzle piece with Jesse to not be alone in the whole thing anymore? No words were going to come, so I nodded.

He sighed, as if letting out a breath he'd been holding for days. "Tutoring?" he asked, and must have seen in my instant reaction that we'd been lured in by the same bait.

167

"Did he ask you to come over because you were failing?" He was two for two. I nodded again. "And once you were there, he…"

"Yes," I answered quickly. I felt I knew enough. I didn't want to know the details of Jesse's encounter – what was different, or what was the same.

He stared past me. "I knew it," he muttered. "I fucking knew it."

"So how do I know you didn't set the fire?" I asked Jesse. "I'd be curious to know your alibi for New Year's Eve."

"You and everyone else. But I don't need an alibi for New Year's Eve because I'm not a suspect," he corrected. "Do you have one?"

"My aunt and uncle died that night. I was at the hospital," I countered. Predictably, that was enough to pause his questioning. When he apologized and asked how Sam was doing, I told him she was fine and that I'd be staying in Santana to help her get on her feet once she had the baby. "And what about you?" I asked, curious if at least one of us would be escaping Santana.

"I'd rather die than stay here. No offense," he laughed. "I'm leaving as soon as I can after graduation. I'm getting me a one-way ticket to San Francisco. They say that's like… a capitol for gays, you know."

I told him I'd heard as much, and nodded along with his plans, listening to his meticulously ambitious timeline. As soon as he arrived in San Francisco, he would find a place to live. Nothing fancy, just somewhere big enough to sleep and paint. Next, he would find a good-enough job, which would supplement his savings to pay bills. And then he'd begin creating art with the supplies he'd been stealing from school over the past year and planned to take with him, eventually garnering enough money from selling his work that he'd live off his passion for art alone.

I wondered how someone could be so confident in their leap from the nest, comparing Jesse's vision to my lack of one. I had no idea where I'd go if I were to leave Santana, much less what I'd do once I got there. "Wow," I said once he finished laying out his next year, "You really have it all figured out, don't you?"

"I have to," he answered. "If I don't think of what comes next, I go nuts. I hate this place. I can't be anyone here. Haven't you noticed that you barely noticed me over the past five years?" His eyes peered at me curiously.

I cocked my head to the side, but quickly realized he was right. It was true that Jesse was all but nonexistent ever since Michael and I banished him from our lives, and I acknowledged as much, asking how he managed to fly under everyone's radar for so long. I was genuinely impressed that I'd never so much as heard a rumor about Jesse, up until everyone suspected he killed King, anyway. "Everyone hated me when the truth came out last year. I couldn't avoid it. It's pretty amazing that never happened to you."

"It's not that amazing. It's because I wasn't best friends with Michael Medina," Jesse scoffed. "The higher you go, the further you fall." He saw my brows scrunch down and he could tell I didn't know what he meant. "You were best friends with one of the most popular guys in school, and then you told him you were this thing that you're just not allowed to be here. And then, look what happened. You came back to school this year and everything was different, Lukas. You weren't sitting with the football players at lunch anymore. They were knocking it right out of your hands."

"And how satisfying was that for you?" I looked at Jesse and wondered if his recollection was accompanied by pride, or pity, or what. "I'm sure it felt good to see me get pushed into the mud after what I did to you when you kissed me way back when. I wouldn't blame you if it made you happy."

"No," he retorted instantly. "It didn't make me happy. I felt bad for you. And oddly thankful that I never ended up on the pedestal you did."

I looked beyond the playground, at a patch of trees whose thin branches were moving with the breeze. I thought back to what my life looked like only ten months earlier, before I'd gotten the nerve to be honest with Michael and my narrow house of cards came toppling down. Other than hiding that secret, I lived a privileged life as Michael's sidekick. I was defended whenever anyone dared to question anything about me, and I was invited to everything in Santana by default, and I was able to block out anything I didn't want to see or remember, including Jesse's very existence.

"Was I your first kiss?" Jesse asked me, looking over with his head tilted in curiosity. "You were mine."

I nodded. "Yeah. Other than Bethany in first grade, but I wouldn't really count that one."

"Well, I'm glad if my first kiss was traumatizing, so was yours," he chuckled. "Is that wrong for me to say? I guess I'm sadistic."

In my head, the kiss replayed three times over, followed by what happened next. I could still feel the force of my hands pushing his body onto the ground. He was so small and skinny then, and it would have taken much less force than I wielded. But I was so damn scared. "I'm really sorry about that," I cringed. "If I could make it up to you, I would."

"Then kiss me now," he answered nonchalantly, and then he laughed at my response. I was speechless and clearly frazzled. "Don't worry, Lukas. I have a boyfriend. Which I will tell you nothing about, by the way. But if you kiss me now and don't push me down afterwards, I'll consider it a do-over."

I wasn't sure what gripped me more: the idea of replacing that awful memory, or knowing there was a guy who was just like me, but had the gall and ability to say he had a boyfriend, whether he'd tell me about it or not. I looked around, double-checking there were no humans to be found, and stood up, pulling Jesse out of his swing. Even though I didn't have feelings for him and I knew he didn't have feelings for me, my stomach fluttered as I drew him in and kissed him on the lips.

It was longer than a quick peck, but still short. Nothing like the felt-out and warm kiss I shared with Ray. When it was over, we both looked at each other with the same surprise as that winter day five years earlier, but this time, it wasn't fear that followed. Instead, we both laughed at how weird, yet familiar, it felt.

Then, before we both went home and resumed our weekends, he said: "Hey, tell him I said thanks." And before I could even ask who *he* was or what I was thanking him for, I knew. Jesse had put it together somehow. *He* was Ray, fire-starter and creep-killer.

"I don't know who you're talking about," I answered. "But I just might do that."

When I came home from the elementary school, it was to an empty house. I thought I'd take Sam to lunch at the diner, but as I looked around the quiet guest room, I remembered she was shopping in Albuquerque with her grandma. It was hard to believe that after so long, Sam's grandma was finally leaving town. Sam was situated with my mom and me, and my aunt and uncle's house had been sold. A part of me was sad Sam made the decision for her grandma to sell their home, but I also understood why she wouldn't be able to go back. Instead, she insisted her grandma take half the money, and the other half was placed into an account for when the baby came, along with the life insurance money she's received.

Ever the nice surprise, the fridge was fully stocked. I made a sandwich and set it next to a handful of chips on a plate to take it to my room.

It was on the floor the second after I opened my door, though. Ray was there, calm and cool, sitting on my bed in his standard black coat. I grabbed my chest, instinctively clutching the onyx. "What the hell are you doing here? How long have you been in my room?" My blood was charging through my veins as I knelt down to scoop the food back onto my plate. I looked up at Ray but he only shrugged, crouching down next to me and picking up the last few chips. He then took the plate and set it on my dresser, letting out a sigh like he needed to talk. "What's going on with you? Did you kill someone else?" I joked, startling even myself. I had no idea where the question came from, or any sense of humor about what happened to King.

To my surprise, he thought it was funny. "No," he chuckled. "Just the one."

We hadn't been alone together since the day I saw him after leaving Sam at the hospital. There was so much I wanted to know about what was going through his mind. I'd been curious since we found out King was dead. But before I could ask him anything else, he told me, "I saw you today, at the elementary school. With that guy."

I felt my eyes squint in confusion. I'd looked around more than a couple times to make sure we were alone. "And?" I said.

"And I saw you kiss him," he added.

I shrugged. Part of me wanted to scream that he'd already slept with Nissa and had less of a reason to care who I kissed now than ever, but I wasn't sure I could have that conversation. Something told me that conversation might undo all the progress I'd made in scrubbing Ray out of my head. The new world I'd begun to build for myself was starting to crack in my chest with every piercing flicker of his eyes.

On the other hand, his presence alone began to send anxiety through my arms and legs, and I knew the discussion was inevitable. "Why are you here?" I asked him defensively. "I know it's not because you saw me kissing someone else. Aren't you and Nissa sleeping together? Haven't you kind of moved on?"

His brows raised. Clearly, he was surprised I knew.

"Yeah, she told me all about it." I felt like an accusatory attorney in some TV show, but I couldn't manage to calm my tone once everything started rolling out. "It really doesn't make any sense to me. You almost kissed me right here in my room, not that long ago. Don't you remember that? And when I kissed you on Christmas, you kissed me back. And you kissed me on New Year's Eve."

"I remember all that. So what?" he asked, perplexed I was questioning his memory.

"So what are you doing kissing Nissa, then kissing me, then sleeping with Nissa, then coming over to my house because you saw me kissing some guy? Are you so desperate to pretend you're not gay like me?"

"I'm not gay like you," he snapped. "Did the thought ever cross your mind that I like you both?"

I was stunned. Mostly because, no, it had absolutely never occurred to me that he actually liked both of us, and even now, I couldn't absorb the idea. "That doesn't make any sense," I said, my brain feeling around for the memory of last prom. It felt so wrong when Lorena Alcantar kissed me that I ran out of the gym. That was the moment I broke, and I was so overwhelmingly sure I was gay that I finally told Michael, because I knew there was never going to be a way around it. "Something's wrong with you."

"What?" He looked at me, even more dumbfounded than before. "I thought if anyone would get this, it would be you."

"Why would I get it? I'm gay! I don't get how you could be attracted to girls if you like me. It's one or the other. You have to choose one."

"Why?" he asked, as if it were the most rational question in the world. "Plenty of people in this town probably think it doesn't make any sense that you like me. Well, not me, because nobody knows about that. But that you're... you know."

"GAY!" I yelled. "I'm gay, gay, gay, gay, gay. I know this about myself. You, though? You just seem confused or something."

"I'm sure enough I like Nissa that I had sex with her. And then I had sex with her again, and again, because I liked it so much," he retorted.

I winced. "Please spare me the details."

"And I'm sure enough I like you that I kissed you back on Christmas, and I kissed you again on New Year's Eve," he continued. "And I'm sure enough I like you, I set a guy's house on fire because of what he did to you." He stepped closer. "And I'm sure enough I like you, I wanted to jump that kid on his way home after seeing you together."

There wasn't a single word I could think of saying in that moment. He probably could have stopped at his comment about the fire and I would have been speechless. "What is it that you want, Ray? You're dating Nissa. You're not dating me. We are not a thing."

"But what if we were?" His eyebrows raised inquisitively. He'd clearly given some thought to this.

"Impossible!" I answered. "We graduate in less than three months. And then I'm assuming you're going to the city with Nissa, and I'm staying in Santana. There's no point."

"But what if I don't go to the city?" Ray stunned me again. I didn't know what to say in response, because I'd barely begun to consider what my life would be like in Santana after high school, much less if Ray were to stay. "Can you really say if we both stay in Santana, we can't work something out?"

He peered at me almost pleadingly, but I couldn't think of anything other than how his gray eyes reminded me of cement. A pool of it. And I'd somehow stepped into this heavy quicksand yet again. There were a million reasons we shouldn't have even been conversing, much less planning any kind of future that involved one another. It didn't matter, though. The fire, Nissa, Zondra. Everything real seemed to evaporate when I was caught up in that damn rocky stare.

Before I could even let myself explore the possibilities with him, we both heard the front door open. "Lukas!" my mom's voice yelled from the living room. "Come help me get this wood down for the stove."

"Coming!" I yelled back, looking at Ray as he zipped his coat. He whispered for me to think about it, and before he opened my window to crawl out and leave, he kissed me. He might as well have thrown a lightning bolt at me. It electrified each and every part of my body, and if the world I'd begun to build without him began to crack the moment I found him waiting in my room, it all crumbled to ruins when his warm lips returned to my mouth after so long.

I stood stunned in the middle of my room until my mom yelled for help again, as Ray hopped onto to the melting snow and jogged out of sight.

The next day, Michael sat at the bar in the café as I closed up, which was a welcome distraction from the memory of Ray's kiss I'd been looping in my mind non-stop.

As it turned out, the same day I talked to Jesse at the playground, Michael talked to Jasmine. Ever twinning, Jesse and Jasmine had slipped notes into our lockers on the same day. Ever twinning, Michael and I refrained from telling each other about the notes in our lockers until after he saw Jasmine and I saw Jesse.

After his Saturday afternoon spent walking around the track behind our school with Jasmine, Michael felt a weight he didn't even know was there lifted from his shoulders. When we were young, Michael shared a certain chemistry with Jasmine that he never quite matched in the years since. Back then, we were oblivious to what that even meant, but now, it seemed so clear. When everything went down between Jesse and me on my thirteenth birthday, the last thing I ever considered was the spark between Michael and Jasmine becoming smothered.

I asked Michael what his note said, and he told me it was the same as mine, succinct with a time and place to meet. When he showed up, she told him she was "checking lists" before graduation, and she had never stopped feeling like there was a bone for her to pick with him. He made her hate him that day in 1995. He chose me over her, as far as she was concerned. Now, she said, it made sense and she figured he did the noble thing, because I was his best friend. But at the time, it broke her heart. Unbeknownst to him, she was thirteen and in love for the first time, or so she thought.

"It made me sad when she said that," Michael lamented, picking at the pastry I'd set in front of him as I wiped down the milk steamers. "I told her I was sorry, and then we hung out all afternoon. I didn't make a single move. We just talked and talked. Between making up with you and making up with her, I feel like I'm becoming all sensitive and shit this year."

I laughed at his self-analysis. "You've always been surprisingly sensitive," I told him. "What you're becoming is mature."

He nodded and asked me about my afternoon with Jesse. I didn't feel like telling him about the kiss because I knew he wouldn't get it. "He knows I had something to do with you-know-what. I played stupid, but somehow he knows."

"No shit?" Michael looked up from the plate with concern. "You worried?"

I shook my head. "He's happy about it. Besides, he's so focused on getting out of Santana in a couple months, I don't think he cares. I'm jealous of him, to be honest. He knows where he's going and what he's doing. I'm not even leaving and I don't know what I want to do after high school."

Michael shrugged. "Why think about it? That's forever away. And you should be glad you're staying here. I've gotten a grand total of zero scholarships, so I'll be here, too."

Zondra came out of the back room, her inventory clipboard in hand. "There's still time to hear back on scholarships, Michael. And there's still time for Lukas to change his mind. A lot can happen in two months."

"Wow," Michael said, more bewildered than anything, "How'd you even hear us back there?"

"For one thing, you're loud," smiled Zondra. "And

that's just the way your ears work after kids. You'll see one day."

"Hopefully *one day* is really, really, far away," Michael scoffed, and grabbed his backpack. In typical Michael fashion, he'd come to the café half-knowing he wouldn't complete his weekend homework, and sure enough, he'd accomplished none of it.

When he left, Zondra took his place at the bar, and for a moment, I thought about asking what else she heard with her supersonic ears, but figured I was better off not knowing. "Speaking of all my kids, you know you're one of my favorites, right?" she winked. I thought back to the film reels she and Laura had been watching the day I came over after fighting with my mom. There were four more of *her kids* right there, and based on the recollections I'd heard over the table the times I'd joined Zondra and Laura for dinner, I knew there were plenty of young people they'd both taken under their wings throughout the years. It was kind of their thing. If I really was one of her favorites, I knew it meant I was special.

"You mean I'm not your number one, all-time, top favorite ever?" I teased.

She shook her head. "There is no number one. But you'd be a contender." She leaned over the bar to take the coffee pot and a mug, pouring herself a cup of decaf as I continued cleaning. "You can meet your competition next week, if you want."

I looked up. "My competition?"

"Two of my other favorites are coming to visit." She blew the steam off her coffee with a smile. "I'm really excited about it, if I'm being honest. I never thought either of them would come to Santana, but they're in the middle of traveling the country, and they're stopping here to see Laura and me." As she sprinkled some sugar into her mug, she peered into it as if a memory were reflecting back at her, and asked if I'd come to dinner the next weekend.

Of course, I accepted, eager to meet anyone who could

give me a glimpse into the Zondra and Laura of the past. I asked who these people were, and she just said, "The sweetest men I've ever known. Their names are Jim and Lady."

It happened that the day Jim and Lady arrived in Santana, March had finally begun fulfilling its promise to evaporate what was left of winter. The sun had become so reliable that Zondra confidently predicted a warm enough evening for us to dine outside. When I asked how I could help prepare for the guests of honor to arrive, she told me I'd be a lifesaver if I could clean up the backyard. She even offered to pay me by the hour, but I turned it down. Zondra was so excited for these guys to show up, I was happy to help however I could.

I began whacking, weeding, watering, and wiping around noon. By three, the yard was immaculate. Zondra came outside to bring me a glass of lemonade, and gleamed when she saw the space resurrected from its wintery hibernation. She told me to go inside and change into the extra pair of clothes I'd brought with me. Then she said I could watch TV while she and Laura worked on dinner in the kitchen. "They should be here soon," she smiled anxiously, glancing at her watch for the umpteenth time. It was adorable to see her so excited. It was the first time I'd seen her look forward to anything, and I felt honored that she wanted me there.

It was about an hour later that a knock on the front door interrupted my thoughtless TV gaze. Zondra hurried into the living room, Laura following behind with an eager grin.

When the door opened, there stood the first pair of grown gay men I'd ever seen outside of a television set, the golden afternoon sun lighting them up like saints. "Holy shit, am I glad to see you!" the taller one gleamed, his beam as big as Zondra's, and pulled her in for a hug. The other man stood behind him, spotting Laura over Zondra's shoulder and pushing his way in to envelope her in his arms. They all held onto each other for a few seconds before switching partners, and then I became the center of everyone's attention.

Zondra came over and put her hands on my shoulders, proudly introducing me to Jim and Lady as if our meeting had been long overdue.

"We've heard so much about you," the shorter one said, extending his hand, "My name's Lady." I reached out and shook it, admiring the circular frames of his glasses and the perfectly-trimmed mustache adorning his lips.

Jim grabbed my hand next. His handshake was firmer than Lady's, and his eyes were the same forest green as his sweater. "It's nice to put a name to the face," he added earnestly.

As much as I would have liked to tell them the same, I didn't feel like I could. Whether they were just being polite or Zondra really had told them all about me, she'd only described them to me a couple of times. I knew she met them about twenty years earlier, when they were my age, and I knew they worked at a bookstore Zondra used to own in the city, which was now theirs. That was about it.

Zondra led us to the backyard, and Laura insisted Jim and Lady have a seat at the table we'd set up on the grass, pulling out a chair for me as well. As they brought out the dishes of food they'd prepared, both Zondra and Laura asked the men about different people and places from their past lives.

Apparently, a lot had changed in their city over the past decade or so, and there was a lot they made sure to quickly explain to me so I'd feel a part of the conversation, but I paid less attention to the verbal details of their discussion, and more to their hardy laughs and happy relief in seeing each other again.

The string of lights streamed above us illuminated our dinner more and more as the sun dissolved into the hills, and it wasn't until after we all finished eating that anyone realized I'd barely spoken two words. "Zondra tells us you're a senior in high school, Lukas," Lady said to me across the table. "Any idea what you'll do next? I was dying to get out of my small town the minute that cap and gown came off."

Everybody laughed and nodded, as if they'd all experienced the same desire to leave their younger lives behind at my age. "Actually," I answered, "I'm staying here after high school." I looked at Zondra and she took a sip of wine to stop herself from voicing her opinion on the matter. Laura looked at me a little more approvingly, but had too honest a face to hide that she agreed with Zondra. "They don't think I should," I smiled, acknowledging what the women didn't think they should say, "But my cousin's about to have a baby, and her parents recently passed away. She was there for me when I came out last year, so staying here and helping her seems like the right thing to do."

They both nodded more politely than honestly, and Jim commented it was admirable for me to make such a selfless decision at my age.

For a moment, it seemed Lady agreed with Jim's acceptance of my answer, but as if he couldn't help himself, he asked, "Is that what you want? I mean, if this wasn't happening with your cousin, is that a decision you would have made?"

"No," I shrugged matter-of-factly. "All I ever wanted was to leave. But it's just not an option now."

Once again, Jim, my only advocate at the table, nodded in agreement. "I could see why you'd want to stay. Family's important."

Lady shifted in his seat, taking a drink from his wine glass. It was clear he was contemplating between agreeing with his partner and saying what he really thought. I looked at him expectantly, and he took it as a sign to speak his mind. "Look, I don't know you the way you know you, obviously, but Zondra's told us a lot about what a hard worker you are, and how smart you are, and what a great person you are, Lukas." He looked at Zondra and she smiled back at him, as if she'd planned for this speech to come out all along. "I just hope you decide to do what's best for you," he added. "And if you decide not to stay here, you always have a place in Levenston, Pennsylvania. Any friend of Zondra and Laura's is a friend of ours."

Jim cupped Lady's hand in solidarity with his offer, and they both smiled at me as Laura reached over the table to refill their glasses. Clearly, this little detour in their reunion had been somewhat planned in advance, and although I wanted to roll my eyes at myself for not seeing it coming, I caught Zondra's eye just long enough to tell her without words that I appreciated the gesture. "Thanks. That's really nice of you," I said to Lady. "If I could, I would. Zondra tells me you run the bookstore she used to own."

"Yes we do," he grinned. "That means you'd have a job, too."

Suddenly, an elaborate escape plan like the one Jesse had created for himself didn't seem so overwhelmingly impossible after all. I pictured myself working at a bookstore in the middle of a big city, aisles of every kind of person imaginable surrounding me, and the muffled sound of traffic outside consistent underneath the smell of fresh coffee and novels.

It seemed too good to be true. "I'll keep that in mind," I said jokingly, half thankful at the offer and half gutted by it, as the possibilities for what my life could be began to seep into my mind. I knew I needed to go before the idea of what I was turning down drowned me alive right there at the table. "Gosh, it must be getting late." The sun had already been gone for a while, and I figured it was an appropriate time to let the old friends continue catching up without having to keep me afloat in the conversation.

Jim and Lady stood up from their seats and came around the table to hug me and reiterate how nice it was for us all to finally meet, and Laura kissed my cheek, making her routine request for me to call when I got home. Zondra told me she'd walk me out, and followed me through the kitchen to the front door before wrapping her arms around me,

...anking me again for my help throughout the day. "I think Jim and Lady really liked you," she added. "I hope you consider what they said."

"Was that for real?" I asked. "Or were they just being nice?"

"Oh, believe me. That was for real," she smiled, before repeating Laura's instruction for me to let them know I made it home. She watched me walk back to my mom's car and only closed the door behind her once I started the engine.

As I drove back to my own side of Santana, I watched the familiar places I'd known all my life pass by, quiet and lifeless in the night, and illuminated by the orange streetlamps. The stores, the houses – everything was pretty much the same as when I was a kid, and I wondered if it would all look the same in ten years, or twenty. And I wondered if anything in all of Santana would ever make me feel half the excitement I felt at the glimpse of what my life might look like in the city.

ELEVEN

When the time finally came and we were blessed by the arrival of spring break, the sky began to darken. The news had warned for days that a big storm was brewing, and sure enough, as we all bustled out of the school, it started to roll in. "Are you sure you want to have this party?" I asked Michael. Although he wouldn't turn eighteen until the first of April, he made the last minute decision to throw himself an early birthday party. His dad had gone to Montana for a funeral and wouldn't be back for a few days.

Michael scoffed at my question. "Are you kidding? It's my last birthday in high school, and coincidentally, my dad's Uncle Salvador finally dies, after 99 years of being an asshole to everyone. It's a sign. We're having the party."

A second later, we turned around when we heard Sam's approving sigh from behind. "Thank god," she huffed. "I need to do something fun."

"Are you sure a party's where you should be right now?" I asked, nodding to her belly. She was only two months away from her due date, and over the past few weeks it had finally begun to seem real when I heard someone call her pregnant.

She rolled her eyes. "I'm pregnant Lukas, I'm not in a

_..na. And besides, I bet Michael doesn't mind if someone's there to take care of whichever one of you idiots drinks too much."

Michael laughed. "Yeah, she's definitely invited."

Thunder rolled, and the new leaves beginning to grow on barren tree branches rattled in the wind. We walked to the grocery store, and as Michael threw bags of chips and boxes of pop into our cart, I looked up at the ceiling. I could hear the wind picking up outside. Clouds continued to cover everything in their shadows as we walked the few blocks to Michael's house, and we only beat the first sprinkling of rain by a minute.

Part of me was surprised Michael invited Nissa since he hated Ray, but I assumed it was because Nissa meant more people might come, and Ray meant more alcohol might come. Sure enough, Nissa gushed about all the people she invited as she pulled out streamers from her bag for decoration, and Ray set down a paper sack, hard liquor bottles clanking together inside.

Jasmine and Jesse showed up next, shaking the rain off their jackets as they stepped in. "I thought you were throwing some big rager," Jasmine teased Michael.

"Hey, people are totally coming," he flirted back. "It's just a little rain."

I wasn't sure he'd have the party he expected, though. Before it was even six, the sky was so dark it looked like night outside, and the rain was coming down so hard Michael turned up the stereo to drown out the tapping. He came into the kitchen as I looked around the drawers for a bottle opener for the beer. "It's on the fridge," he reminded me.

I turned to the refrigerator and plucked the bottle opener off the side when an envelope caught my eye. Above the blue magnet pinning it to the front of the fridge, the tiny illustrated profile of a bobcat hissed. I knew that logo from all the research on colleges I'd done the year before. It was from Montana State University. I pulled the envelope out from under the magnet. It was opened. "What's this?" I asked.

Michael looked over from the cupboard as he pulled out an armful of shot glasses. "Oh, I meant to tell you about that." By the time he finished, I'd already picked out the letter from inside. He'd been offered a complete football scholarship. I felt my jaw drop and I looked back up to him. "I can't believe it either," he said. "I just accepted it last night."

I imagined it wasn't the way he wanted me to find out he was leaving Santana after high school, but it was too late. Now I knew. A voice inside my head reminded me to snap out of my shock and react. "Holy shit," I smiled. "This is so cool."

He seemed relieved to hear it. "Really?"

No, not really, I thought, but I knew it wasn't fair to say that, so I nodded. I knew as well as he did that the chances of this offer coming his way were slim, based on his grades throughout school. I imagined Santana without him and the last thing I'd call it was cool, but it was bordering on a miracle.

Suddenly, Xavier burst through the door, cutting our conversation short and announcing his presence with his signature racket. He pulled back his hood, holding two giant bottles of tequila. "Holy fuck! It's crazy as shit out there!" As he closed the front door and threw his soaked jacket onto the kitchen counter, I looked over at Sam and we both pretended to gag. "Damn dude," he added, throwing his arm around Michael's shoulder and looking around. "Where is everyone?"

I stuck Michael's letter back onto the refrigerator as Nissa came into the kitchen, Ray following behind. I thought of the day they both stood up to Xavier for me outside the school after winter break, and wondered if this situation was about to get ugly. "Oh, it's you," she smirked.

Everyone was silent, a bunch of tense stares shooting in every direction. I surprised even myself by breaking the

...ence, asking who wanted a shot, and taking one of the bottles Ray had set down earlier to hold up. Michael called the others into the kitchen, and I carefully poured a shot of cheap tequila for everyone but Sam, while Nissa sliced a lime. Jesse handed them out, and we all raised them up as Michael gave his own toast. "Here's to spring break, turning eighteen, having a party in the middle of a storm, and getting fucked up! Except for you." He pointed at Sam. "You don't want your baby to come out with three arms."

Sam flipped him off, and we all laughed before throwing back the tequila.

After I swallowed, I took a deep breath. The heat traveling down into my chest felt better than ever. I was ready to excuse myself from the world for a night, and it appeared there was more than enough alcohol for everyone to lose as much touch with reality as they wanted. "I know we're not starting this party with *one shot*," Xavier instigated, quickly darting his glance at each of us, as if to preemptively call anyone a chicken shit who wasn't about to take another shot.

Everybody shrugged, and a minute later, another hot gulp hit my stomach. The second one went down even easier than the first, and I wondered if I was already starting to feel it soaking into my veins. The wind and rain outside barely seemed noticeable anymore, even though neither had stopped, and Michael's Montell Jordan CD that should have run its course weeks ago suddenly sounded better than ever. I didn't even notice my head start to nod along with it, until Sam nudged me on the arm and asked if I was about to get it on tonight, which cracked us both up.

"Another one!" Xavier roared, "Let's do this!"

I shook my head. "Not me."

"Me neither," Jesse winced, looking at the tequila bottle with disgust.

"Fags," Xavier scoffed, and like a reflex, Michael punched him in the arm.

"What'd I tell you about that shit? Watch your fucking

mouth, dude."

Everyone looked at them, waiting for another move. Were they about to throw down? It almost seemed like Michael was about to kick Xavier's homophobic ass out of the party.

To everyone's surprise, Xavier only glared at Michael like he might hit him back for a moment before he switched lanes completely. He peered at me and apologized begrudgingly. I felt a familiar warmth cover my face and my mind flashed back to the first day of school, when Xavier threw that note at my head, Michael sitting next to him, watching me with empty eyes and condoning the whole thing. Talk about tables turning. Now, Michael looked at me waiting for some kind of approval. I knew if I wanted him to, he'd throw Xavier out right there and then, especially because Jasmine was about to slap the shit out of Xavier herself.

"It's cool," I nodded, and Jesse agreed. "You guys should definitely take another shot."

"Make them doubles," Michael said, still looking at me to make sure I was good. And in the same unspoken language, I let him know I was fine. In fact, I was better than ever. The same pride ran through me as the day Michael defended me to his dad when I slept over in January.

As everyone else continued drinking in the kitchen, I walked over to the couch in the living room with Sam and Jesse. They both looked up to see who was coming before continuing their conversation. "Seriously, why is Michael even friends with Xavier?" Sam said quietly. "He's human garbage. I really don't get it."

"Good question," I shrugged. I knew they first became friends because they were on the football team together, but beyond their being teammates, I couldn't imagine what Michael got out of his friendship with Xavier, other than the blind loyalty of a goon.

Jesse seemed unbothered. "I think Xavier just has a lot to learn."

I I both looked at him like he'd just defended ᴜahmer, but he remained unfazed. "Imagine if I judged you by what you did to me, Lukas. Or if you judged Michael by the way he acted at the beginning of the year," he explained. "The only difference between you and Michael and Xavier is that you and Michael know better."

Sam scoffed. "I don't think Xavier will ever know better."

It wasn't long before the fire at King's house came up in the kitchen. We went back in to see what all the commotion was about.

"It's just that I've always wondered why you stood up and said what you did," Nissa said to Jasmine. I could tell from the slight droop in her eyes she had passed tipsy and was drunk.

Jasmine looked back at her with her own buzz, which presented itself in a bit of a squint. I wondered how many more shots they'd all taken in the past half hour. "I said that because we all know he was a creep. Don't we all know that?" She looked around the kitchen to let everyone know it was an open question, but then pointed at Nissa. "Girl, did you not know Mr. King was a creep? I mean I know you're new this year, but did you not know that? I thought everyone knew." She shrugged.

Ray stood behind Nissa, and I could tell he purposefully looked anywhere but toward me. I made sure to look anywhere except his way, too.

Across the kitchen, Michael stared at both of us, his own intoxication barely visible. He'd always been good at handling alcohol. I could tell he wanted to jump in and change the conversation, as the only other person to know King's inadvertent killers were standing on both sides of Nissa as she continued to speculate.

"It's just so totally wild, you know. So many people hated that guy, it really could have been anyone who set that fire. I want to find out who did it!"

"How about another shot?" Michael interjected. I looked at him like he was crazy. I knew he could probably handle another three, and I had no doubt Xavier and Ray would be fine, but Jasmine and Nissa seemed like the last people who should consider another one. "You're taking one," Michael said, pointing to me, "Your break's over." Then he pulled Jesse over to the table. "You, too."

As we all clinked our small glasses together in the middle of the kitchen, Sam sipped on a water bottle and shook her head in the corner, half entertained and half preparing for the inevitable caretaking she'd soon be doing.

And it was soon. It couldn't have been more than three minutes later that Nissa was throwing up in the bathroom. Sam sat on the bathtub next to her, holding a cup of water in one hand, and Nissa's hair behind her in the other. "Just leave her in here with me," Sam laughed. She didn't seem mad at all, which was more than Nissa could say. She cursed herself for being a lightweight as I softly closed the door, trying to escape before she hurled another tequila blob into the toilet.

"Is she okay?" Jesse asked. He, Xavier, and Ray sat as spaced apart as possible in the living room. Xavier turned on some sports game.

"She'll be fine." I looked around the corner and into the kitchen. Nobody was there. "Where's Michael?"

"Getting lucky!" Xavier woofed.

Jesse rolled his eyes. "He and Jasmine went to his room."

It was barely eight o'clock. Some party.

I went into the kitchen to pour a drink, and as I was dumping gin over ice, I looked over to see Ray had followed me. He crossed behind me and looked out the window, and after I screwed the lid back onto the gin bottle, I stood beside him. Lightning still whitened Michael's backyard every few minutes, and the rain hadn't stopped beating on the house.

Ray poured a drink of his own before we went back into

the living room, and for the next two hours, I sipped on my gin and zoned out toward the game on TV.

I must have dozed off. The next thing I knew, I was opening my eyes to the dark. "What the hell?" Ray's voice said. The wild taps on the window quickly announced another wave of rain had picked up outside. The electricity must have gone out. I stood up. Luckily, I knew Michael's house like the back of my hand.

By the time I opened the junk drawer in the kitchen and pulled out a flashlight, Michael had appeared next to me. "Enjoying yourself, Romeo?" I asked.

"Very funny," he said, snatching the flashlight from my hands. He handed me a lighter from the drawer and took down a box of candles from the cupboard over his refrigerator before disappearing back to his room.

"Rude." I opened the box of candles and took one out. I held the lighter up to the wick, and as it flicked out a little flame, Ray's face illuminated next to mine. I jumped back, a vision of New Year's Eve flashing before me: the light of a flame illuminating him just like that night. "Jesus Christ."

I'd scared him too. We both laughed.

I gave him the first lit candle and told him to go check on Nissa and Sam. I lit another one and went back into the living room. I held the candle near Xavier's face. He was sleeping. Then I checked Jesse's. He was asleep, too. I set the candle down on the coffee table in the middle of the living room, and listened to the thunder roll above the rain. When Ray came back, he told me Sam and Nissa had both passed out on the bed in Michael's guest room.

"As long as we're the only one's up…" he said, and picked up a whiskey bottle Xavier had set down on the coffee table earlier. He uncapped it and took a drink right out of the top, handing it to me afterward.

Normally, I hated whiskey. The smell alone made me queasy. But whether it was leftover tipsiness from earlier, or an intoxication from the moment alone with Ray, I took the bottle from him and threw back a few gulps, surprising us both. "You want to see something cool?" I asked him.

We snuck out the side door to Michael's backyard, and ran over to his dad's camper in the rain. The heavy door swung open on my second pull. I knew it wouldn't be locked. I stepped up into the small sitting area behind the driver's seat, Ray following behind. He reached into his pocket to take out a candle he swiped in the kitchen, handing it to me as I flicked on the lighter. As I set the candle down on the small table, Ray and I sat around it, facing each other. I looked at the glow on his face and although New Year's Eve came back to me again, for some reason, the panic didn't.

Instead, I remembered the peak of how I felt that night, in the drunken moment he looked at me before putting his mouth on mine next to his burning graffiti. He was looking at me the same way. For a moment, the only real difference between New Year's Eve and now was that now, instead of vodka, it was whiskey I could smell on my own breath, and would probably taste on Ray's if we kissed again. The heavy swallow I downed before coming outside was starting to warm me up.

"You know, it's been almost three months since that fire and I still think I'm in denial that it ever happened," I told him, looking past him to change the subject of us before it even came up. "It's like… it's such a bad memory, I can't even think about it."

"It doesn't bother me," he shrugged matter-of-factly. He looked into my eyes without a flinch or a second thought.

"How?" I asked. "You… *we* killed someone. We ended someone's life."

"So what? Do you know how many people die everyday who don't deserve to? I'm not sad about some asshole who got what he had coming." Ray reached across the table, taking hold of my arms. "You know what? I'd do it again."

I recoiled. It wasn't what he said that sent chills down

my spine, but that I could tell he meant it. He really would burn King alive all over if he had the chance. Clearly, he hadn't spent close to the amount of time making himself sick over the whole thing as I had. "I wish I could be as heartless as you," I said.

"Heartless? Am I heartless?" His head tipped to the side, and he peered at me through an analytical squint. "Or do I just think you're more important than you do?" He noticed my stare had fallen from his eyes onto his lips. He peered at me even harder. "What? You want to kiss me?" he laughed.

I looked back up into his eyes, and I knew if I wanted to, I could get on top of him right then and there. But I knew better. Even though I had just as many sexual desires pent up in me as any other eighteen-year-old guy, ever since the day I went to King's house, my body wouldn't let any of them come to fruition, even in my head. Of course there were carnal thoughts in my brain when I looked at Ray, the icy slate of his eyes contrasting with his tan skin more than ever in the candlelight, and his unrelenting gaze forever unclothing my soul.

"Is that all you want from me?" I asked instead of leaping forward.

"Couldn't I ask you the same thing?" he countered.

It had never dawned on me that in every situation we'd ever fallen into, I was just as guilty of lust as he ever was. A part of it was that I was too afraid to ask anything about his life or the way he felt, but I knew there was also a selfishness in there, that had captivated me since the night he nudged me awake at the movie theater. Ray had been my favorite distraction over the past year. "I think I'm kind of afraid to know who you are," I said.

The sea of rumors that followed his name all over Santana were overwhelming, and they always made him out to be dangerous. When I first met him, I imagined how many of the stories about where Ray came from were made up. Ever since the fire, I wondered how many were true.

"Why's that? You think I'm some crazy thug like half

this town does?"

I shrugged. "Are you?"

"No," Ray said. "That fire was the worst thing I've ever done. I'm not sorry about it, but it was the worst." Then, on his fingers, he began to count every rumor in town that wasn't true. "I never left anyone paralyzed. I haven't ever blinded anyone in a fight. I didn't kill my family, or anyone else. What am I missing?"

"The scar on your back?" I inquired. I remembered the evening I saw him playing basketball during dusk, and I saw the thick cut, running from his neck all the way down to his shorts. It seemed long-healed, but it was dark and bold. I watched as he turned to look at the rain hitting the window next to us, before looking back at me. "I think I'm afraid to let you know who I am."

I thought back to his irritation at seeing Jesse kiss me at the playground. When he told me about it afterward at my house, I felt annoyed more than anything because he came off as a hypocrite. Now, sitting across from his coy glare, I wondered if he really felt the same way I did every time I saw him hold Nissa's hand. Not only jealous, but curious about why I wasn't good enough, and positive I needed to keep my guard up for when he'd be done with me.

"You want to know something about me?" I asked him. He nodded his head curiously. "Ever since the day King…" I hesitated. There was never going to be a right way to describe what happened that day. "Ever since that day at King's house, I can't…" I faltered again. Whether it was because of the whiskey, or because it just didn't make any sense, I couldn't find the right words to finish the sentence. But somehow, I didn't need to. I looked over at Ray and he studied me knowingly. "I mean, I can, at first. And it's not that I don't want to, you know. I just, can't."

He seemed to understand my frustration and to sympathize with me more than anything else. "You want to, but you can't," he paraphrased under his breath, thinking over what I'd just said, and keeping his stare locked on my

193

eyes. "But if you could, what would you do?" he teased, leaning in again. "If you could do whatever you wanted with me right now, what would it be?"

To my surprise, I felt a familiar swelling in my jeans as he grazed the top of my hand with his finger, and suddenly the cold camper seemed to be warming up. At first, I was speechless. Maybe things were about to change, I thought. As his eyes invited me to answer his question, I let the first thing that came into my imagination escape from my mouth. "I'd smell the liquor on your lips and then I'd lick it off," I told him, "I'd kiss you." By the time I said it, I was a rock. Ray took a deep breath, and from his sigh alone, I could tell he was hard under the table, too.

"And what would you want me to do to you?" he asked.

"Kiss my neck," I answered without hesitation. It was all flickering through my brain like the tiny flame dancing on the candle between us.

He rubbed his leg against mine and pushed himself up, moving over to a long cushioned seat in the shadows on the opposite side of the camper. "So come here." He leaned back onto a pillow, and smiled as I stood up from the table, moving closer until I stood before him.

Within a second of my body falling onto the couch next to him, his lips and tongue began moving all over my neck, and his heat spread all over me as we twisted and moved onto each other like snakes. When he brought his mouth to mine, the carnal urge to take him in burst through me. I grabbed his jacket to pull him closer as his hands slid under the back of my shirt, and he squeezed me. His muscles tightening around me took the breath out of my lungs, and the air I breathed back in was intoxicating. I pulled his jacket off and threw it behind me, and then laid back as his lips began moving from my mouth to my chin to my chest to my stomach.

When I felt his fingers popping the button to my jeans, my heart started to thud. I closed my eyes, trying to convince myself it was excitement. But as he slid his fingertips toward the elastic band of my underwear, I jumped up. "Stop!"

He flinched back, looking up at me to see what was wrong. Suddenly, there was nothing about it that seemed fun. With every gulp of air I took in, the reality of Nissa sleeping across the backyard, and the sensory memory of King pulling down my pants swirled together and filled me up with a dark and suffocating feeling, like tar into my lungs. "Are you okay?" he panted, as caught up in the moment as he was confused.

"What do you think?" I asked defensively. As much as it didn't seem like it, I wasn't mad at him, but the fear of my own body had shaken me.

He could see it wasn't personal. "My bad," he offered. "You just got done telling me you couldn't do that, and I…"

"It's fine." I cut his apology short. "I wanted to. I mean, I *want* to. I just don't know when I'll be able to do that. Or if." I buttoned my pants and pushed myself into a sitting position in front of him, holding my legs to my chest with my arms. "Besides, Nissa's..." I nodded toward the house.

He agreed. "I know." Thunder boomed outside and lightning illuminated everything for a moment. I re-opened the curtains to see if the lights had come back on in the house. Still dark. Ray picked up his jacket from the floor and slipped back into it, keeping his eyes on me and contemplating what to say next. "The scar on my back's from my mom." He seemed uneasy, but confident at the same time. "She was crazy sometimes. Not always, but when it was bad, it was really bad."

I watched his every small move and absorbed every careful word he spoke, as he began telling me about the turbulent years of his childhood.

His dad was killed by a local gang just after Ray was born, leaving his mom to raise him and his older brother alone in his hot Arizona border town. She was mentally ill, although never diagnosed, because doctors are for rich people, he said. She would seem all right for weeks at a time, but when

Ray and his brother would least expect it, something inside her tripped a wire, sending her into sporadic rages, unleashing a firestorm of verbal and physical violence on anyone unfortunate enough to be around when it happened.

The night she drug a broken vase down his back, his life had only been saved by his brother coming home from work at the right time, and pulling Ray free from his mom's grip. He remembered the warm soak of his shirt more than the pain running down his back, as his brother hurried him out of the house.

"He took me to see our neighbor," he recalled, staring out the window as he spoke. "She was this nice white lady who worked at a clinic down the road. She stitched me up. I think she felt sorry for us."

When his brother was old enough to start working, he moved out and took Ray with him. They lived in an old trailer on a bad block, and sometimes, they didn't eat a full meal for days at a time, but Ray was happier than he'd ever been. He went to sleep at night knowing he might hear gunshots at any given moment, but at least the nightmare was finally outside of his home instead of in.

He dropped out of high school to work at a mechanic shop and help his brother pay the bills. His brother told him not to, but Ray insisted on working. He liked the feeling of making money, and he knew that life didn't reward education where he came from the way it rewarded kids on TV. Working made more sense. So, for a couple years, he worked, and his brother worked, and his mom stopped guilting him over leaving, and his life seemed to become normal.

"So how'd you end up in Santana then? Is your brother still in Arizona?" I asked. The escape from his mom's house almost seemed like the end of the story, but something was obviously missing.

"My brother's dead. Gang shit." He shifted in his seat, and I could tell from experience that he was trying to find the right way to phrase the rest. "They didn't just shoot him

196

once, either. The gangs in Arizona are crazy. They waited for him outside a grocery store one day, and when he came out, a group of them jumped out of a car and shot him about ten times each." He let out a deep breath and looked over at me.

I was too stunned to say anything, even some kind of consolation.

"I knew I had to leave town," Ray shrugged. "My brother was involved with shady people and I wasn't sure whether someone was coming for me next. So I packed up, drove all night, and ended up in this nice little town in the middle of nowhere." He gestured out the window.

He brought enough money to move into his apartment, and only a week after arriving, he started work at Santana Motor & Mechanic. "People are afraid because they don't know me," he concluded. His gaze moved over to the candle, and he watched the glow as he went on. "I don't give a shit, though. No one needs to know me. And I like that people leave me alone."

"You and Nissa are so different," I said, strangely perhaps, but it was the first thing that came to mind.

He seemed to understand. "I know. But I like her because she's fun. She doesn't give a shit about anything. She likes to have a good time. And that smile…"

As little sense as it made, I nodded in agreement. The reasons he'd listed were all legitimate. "Same," I concurred.

He let out a small laugh and held my stare for a moment. "And you…" he pondered. "I like that you scare me a little bit. You do give a shit about everything, even though you pretend not to. And from the first time I saw you, when you were sleeping in your seat at the movie theater, I just..." he thought on it for a second. "I just liked you."

A warm mix of flattery, pride, and longing seemed to pump into my chest, and for a moment, I thought about kissing him. The urge came to me like an instinct. But outside the camper window, we noticed all the lights in the house flicker back on.

We hurried across the yard and quietly came back into the house, pushing our muddy shoes off and heading our separate ways. He went to sleep on a cot set up in the guest room next to the bed, and I went into the living room.

But I stopped dead in my tracks as soon as I came in. The couch where Xavier slept earlier was empty, and so was the chair where Jesse had curled up. They were both on the floor now, Xavier's arm wrapped around Jesse's body, holding him close to his chest. I was so floored, I took a step back, and thanks to someone's shoe, I fell onto my ass.

Jesse woke up first, propping himself up and looking back at me. I could see the panic in his eyes immediately. Clearly, I hadn't been meant to see the two of them on the ground together. He jumped up onto his feet, quickly trying to explain what I saw. "We… this isn't what it looks like."

Xavier's eyes opened next and he sat up, still drunk, looking up at Jesse and then at me. He slowly pieced together that I'd seen the aftermath of whatever had occurred between Jesse and him, and pushed himself onto his feet as I stood up, still trying to piece it all together myself. He came face-to-face with me, and I was pretty sure he didn't know what he felt anymore than I knew. He seemed angry, as if I had done something wrong. But he also looked scared, like he'd been caught doing something wrong.

"If you tell anyone, I'll kill you," he threatened, careful to keep his voice low. His brows came down over the tops of his eyes.

I turned away from the boozy stench of his breath. "If I tell anyone what?" I asked, still genuinely confused. But when I looked at Jesse in the next moment, and then back at Xavier, the whole situation began to come into focus. "Are you two…?" Suddenly, Jesse's vague bragging at the playground made sense. He had a boyfriend, he'd said, but he wouldn't tell me a thing about it. And he wouldn't tell anyone where he was on New Year's Eve. I peered at

Xavier, and I could feel my jaw becoming heavy at my own astonishment. "No fucking way."

"I'm serious, Bradley," Xavier grunted, coming even closer than before. "I will fucking kill you."

It was true that he could kill me if he wanted to, or if he had the nerve, but I was just drunk enough that the fear he might make good on his threat was overthrown by the sheer satisfaction building up in my lungs. "Oh, this is hilarious," I laughed. "You are such a fucking joke, Xavier." I pushed him aside, which I knew would normally trigger an immediate punch to my face. Not now, though. "And for the record, I don't think you're in a place to make any demands with me." I looked over at Jesse, unsure whether I admired or pitied him. "How long has this been a thing?"

Xavier started to say it was none of my fucking business, but Jesse interrupted him. "A couple years, on and off," he said defensively. "Please, Lukas. You can't tell anyone about this."

"So you're telling me, the entire time this shit sack was throwing notes at me and pushing my lunch on the ground... the whole time he was calling me a fag, he's been..." I still couldn't believe the words as they came out of my mouth. I turned back toward the kitchen to find my red plastic cup. I poured some more gin into it, and when I threw the drink back, Jesse and Xavier both watched anxiously. "Why shouldn't I go to Michael's room right now and tell him you're a fag just like me?" I asked Xavier.

"Because you know that's wrong," Jesse said, stepping between us. "And I don't want anyone to know, either."

"Fine. But Xavier? Of all people?" Disgust boiled up in my throat. "Jesse, you should really have some self respect." I poured another splash of gin into my cup before heading back into the living room.

I turned off the light and went straight for the couch Xavier vacated. He knew better than to stop me, and rested his body back down on the floor. Jesse curled up in the recliner. Within minutes, I could hear the breaths coming

199

out of them become deeper. They'd both fallen asleep.

The boxy green numbers on the VCR clock seemed to glow brighter than ever, each minute blinking into the next. The rain had settled some and became a quiet static behind the snores in the living room. 1:00 came and went, and then 2:00. I got up to pee twice, my buzz beginning to wear off, and my body becoming more and more awake for some reason. When 3:00 rolled around, I was still staring blankly at the VCR.

It must have been sometime between three and four when I fell asleep, because the next thing I knew, I was sitting in my room somehow. The world outside my window was dark, and the only light in sight was a quiet flame across the room. I sat up in bed and peered at the tiny glow, trying to figure out where it came from. My feet touched the ground and slowly took me closer, until I made out the faint outline of Nissa's face, gazing coldly at me. "What are you doing here?" I heard my voice ask her.

She didn't answer me with anything but a disappointed scoff, shaking her head and walking the flame over to my bedroom door. She held the light up and I could faintly see some words spray painted onto it. Before I could decipher what anything said, she set the paint ablaze. Even though panic spilled into my blood, my body was frozen still. No scream could make its way out. The flame crawled up my door and began swaying onto my ceiling, but my legs still wouldn't move.

I looked around to find Nissa was gone as the fire began to make me sweat, and finally, the adrenaline speeding through me put my feet into motion. I ran over to my window and opened it, preparing to crawl out and run away from my house, but as I pushed up the glass and looked out, suddenly, there was nothing before me but night sky, and the thunderous gush of El Maldito below, roaring over a voice yelling up at me. As if my bedroom were perched up at the top of the waterfall, I looked down and saw Ray waving his arms, telling me to jump. My mind quickly began calculating the chances of surviving the fall, but was interrupted by a crash behind me. My closet door was cracking open like glass. When I turned back to the window, Ray was running out of the water beneath me to save himself. I yelled his name, but he didn't look back.

"We need to get the hell out of here!" I heard from behind me. By then, my room was completely engulfed in flames, and somehow Jesse appeared next to me, and pointed up. Above, the ceiling had vanished. Michael knelt on a single moonlit cloud, throwing down a thin chain, shouting for me to take hold of it. I felt around my chest to realize it was my necklace he'd thrown down. It didn't seem possible, because it was long enough to drop all the way from Michael to me, but I knew it was my necklace. I could even see the black onyx stone dangling in the center. I yelled that there was no way I could climb up my necklace, and looked around for Jesse to confirm I wasn't losing my mind, but instead, Sam was now standing next to me, urging me not to worry and just climb.

I grabbed hold of the skinny chain and miraculously, pulled myself up. In the first moment I was stable, I repositioned myself to look back down. Sam was gone. But when Michael pulled me up, he pointed out that she was safe, and indeed, she had somehow ascended onto another cloud, waving at me with Zondra standing beside her. I waved back and noticed Zondra was tapping her chest. I felt beneath my neck. The chain was there again.

"Are you ready?" Michael said with a nudge to my arm. I looked at him, still so spun around in my mind, I couldn't gather enough words to ask what he meant. I opened my mouth to try, but instead of allowing my response, he yanked the collar of my shirt and we both dropped off the cloud and tumbled toward the earth.

My heart was pounding when I sat up and looked around to find myself on Michael's couch. Jesse was still curled up on his chair, and Xavier was still snoring on the ground. Sweat soaked the back of my shirt. 5:50 AM, the VCR clock read. I pulled as much air as I could into my lungs and stared outside. The rain had stopped, and although the darkness was beginning to light up into morning, it was still a dim and cool blue. I stood and walked over to the window, and no more than thirty seconds later, Sam tiptoed into the living room, as if she'd been waiting to hear the first semblance of life inside the house. "Oh good, it's you," she said. "Can we go home?" She reached behind her and wearily rubbed her lower back. "I swear that bed was not made for human beings. And did you know Nissa snores?"

I laughed to myself, and we quietly found our jackets and slipped into our shoes before sneaking out into the fresh coolness of the morning.

TWELVE

Spring break ended as quickly as it had begun, just like everything else during senior year. On my last evening of freedom before the final few weeks of high school, I worked with Zondra at the café, enjoying that after the big storm, spring had officially finished making its way into the trees, their leaves fully formed and fragrant. We kept the windows cracked all evening to let in the cool green breeze, and Zondra put a new record on in the back. Slow, cozy jazz was over, she said. It was time to kick some spring into our step.

Michael's party had left me with everything to think about, and working at the café almost every day since was more therapeutic than a waste of my break as far as I was concerned. I was thankful Zondra had given me so many hours, even though she barely needed the help. By then, I figured she knew, either consciously or subconsciously, that I felt better when I worked. My time, we'd learned, was better left occupied.

"Have you thought any more about Jim and Lady's offer?" she asked me, as the last few customers shuffled out the front door.

"There's not much to think about," I told her, not

looking up from the counter as I wiped up some splattered mocha. "Sam's having that baby no matter what, and I already promised I'd stay to help."

Zondra reached across the bar and took hold of my hand, stopping me mid-wipe. "Lukas, if you go, Sam can have your job." She gazed at me with concern, as if to tell me I was making the wrong decision. "Laura and I love Sam. She's a great girl. We'd be happy to help her with the baby, you know."

"It's not even about the money or babysitting," I explained, admiring how long it had taken Zondra to follow up after the dinner party at her house. Everyday since, I'd half-expected her to start this conversation, and I'd already planned every defense I'd need when she would try to convince me to move to Levenston after high school. "It's about being there for her as her life changes, the way she was there for me. I owe her that."

"But this situation is completely different, don't you think? When you told Michael you were gay and everyone seemed to turn against you, you had nobody but Sam. She'll have a support system, whether you're here or not." Zondra kept her inquisitive eyes locked on me, but she could tell my perspective was unchanged. She went to her purse and picked it up. "What if we consult these?" she added, pulling out her deck of tarot cards.

The sight of the cards took me back to the last time I'd seen them, when they warned Ray would lead me toward some kind of disaster, and then he did. I shook my head. "No way," I answered.

"Were they wrong?" Her head cocked to the side, answering her own question with a raised brow. Although we never discussed New Year's Eve, I knew she knew. "What's the harm in a sign? You know what they say: *Que será, será*. Whatever will be, will be." She fanned the cards in front of her, inviting me to pull one out.

Maybe she was right, I thought. In the end, I did believe whether I'd known it was going to happen or not, Ray was always going to set the fire at King's house that night. I was meant not to stay away from him on New Year's Eve. King was meant to die that night. All the cards had done was provide some kind of heads up, not that it did me much good. I reached out and picked out a random card, handing it to her face down.

She flipped it over on the tabletop, and as soon as the card was visible, she looked up to calm me down. "Don't panic, Lukas."

"What do you mean *don't panic*? It's a Death card!" I looked down at the illustration. Its meaning seemed pretty self-evident. On the back of a white horse rode Death itself, cloaked in black and carrying a sickle.

"It's not necessarily what you think, dear," she smiled, leaning in and folding her hands in front of her. "It doesn't actually signify the death of a person, so much as the death of normalcy. I think a big change may be coming."

"I could have told you that," I said dismissively. "I'm graduating from high school, and Sam's having a baby. Not to mention, Michael's leaving town after graduation. And Nissa." Suddenly, Ray's face appeared in my head. What if he and I were the big change? "Believe me — that card doesn't mean I'm going anywhere after graduation."

Zondra nodded along with every word I said. "All right," she agreed.

But her smile persisted from the moment she'd flipped over the card to her sly goodbye, as she slipped out of the café and went home for the night.

The next day, the hot topic in the halls of Santana High was the countdown to the end. There were only six weeks left until summer. Some kids were checked out as if graduation were overdue, and some were already reminiscing about high school as if it had come and gone. I was moving from class to class more quietly curious about the end than anything else. Zondra's latest card reading had proven to be the perfect cherry to top my mangled mental mess sundae. It was all I could think about the night before, and throughout most of the day.

"*A big change is coming.*" Zondra's voice echoed through my mind as I walked home after school, and once again, I had to stop myself from adding to the list of possibilities her Death card could have represented. The scariest of which, I'd decided, besides someone actually dying, would be for Ray and I to finally get caught for the fire at King's house.

There was no smoking gun, as Ray put it, but I was raised Catholic. I couldn't help but anticipate the truth coming out sooner or later. It always did in the end, my mom taught me, as far back as I could remember. I pictured us both in handcuffs, he the murderer and me the accessory.

Just in time to thwart my twisted daydream, Michael appeared next to me, catching up from behind. "Do you have work today?"

"No," I answered. "Why? No plans with Jasmine?" As soon as I said it, I heard the bitchiness tucked under my words, and it took me by surprise just as much as him. Michael's birthday had come and gone over spring break without him having any time to hang out, because he spent so much time with Jasmine. I didn't think it bothered me, but suddenly, I wasn't sure.

"Are you mad or something?" He looked confused, too. I shook my head. "I'm just tired."

As we walked the rest of the way to my house, Michael wished he hadn't wasted so much time ignoring Jasmine after what happened all those years ago between Jesse and me. He wondered aloud what could have been between the two of them, adding that he felt more and more sad over the past few weeks, knowing they'd soon go their separate ways, so shortly after reconnecting.

Once again, I could feel the irritation building in the pit of my stomach as we stepped onto my front porch and threw our bags down, sitting in the sun instead of going inside. What about the fact that he was leaving Santana so shortly after making up with me? Maybe it didn't seem like such a big deal to him, but ever since he told me he was accepting his scholarship and heading to Montana after high school, I'd been feeling more and more down about it, for the same reasons he'd just mentioned. My best friend finally knew who I was, and he was finally okay with it, and now he was leaving. It mattered to me but I wasn't sure it was the same for him.

"Well, I think Ray's staying in Santana next year," I said, looking at the far-off hills. "At least I won't be completely alone here with Sam and the baby once you leave." The truth was, I didn't know whether Ray had decided to stay in Santana, but I knew it would satisfy my sudden urge to irritate Michael.

He scoffed. "Okay, seriously. What's your deal?" He had turned to face me, but I kept staring at the hills, which only irritated him more. "What's your plan, Luke? Start hanging with Ray because I'm going to college? That turned out great for you last time, man. You sound like an idiot."

I could tell he expected a fiery response from me. But I was a different kind of mad than that. The kind of mad starting to crawl through me felt more calculating and sly. I looked at him for a second before rolling my eyes back to the distance.

"Why can't you be excited for me?" he asked. "I'm getting out of here and maybe I'll have some sort of chance to be something. Are you jealous of that? Because you could get out, too." He examined my face for some kind of sign I'd give in and react, but I didn't feel compelled to give him the satisfaction. "You know, Jasmine was supposed to go to California with Jesse after high school. But when Jesse found out she accepted her scholarship for soccer, he was happy for her, even though it changed their plans. Because he's excited about what he's doing, he can be happy for her. Why can't you be like Jesse? Just because you're too much of a chicken shit to leave this town, don't blame it on me."

That was it. He found the button he'd been looking for. "Are you fucking kidding me?" I snapped. "You know why

207

I'm staying here? Because you made my life such a living hell when I came out, Sam had to hold me together. I owe her because of what you did. I'm not staying here for me."

Michael got up and threw his backpack over his shoulder. "Keep telling yourself that," he said, before he walked back to the sidewalk and disappeared into the afternoon. As I watched him go, I replayed the words I'd just thrown out. I could hear the uncertainty in my own voice.

The next evening, I sat across from Jesse after finishing my shift at the café. He was there to get some homework done, but when he ordered from me, he asked why I was in a bad mood. I said I'd tell him about it later. He listened to me mull over everything Michael told me, from saying I should be happy for him – like Jesse was for Jasmine, to accusing me of staying in Santana because I was really afraid to leave.

"First of all, the world would be a much better place if everyone were a little more like me," Jesse smiled, sipping his latte. He'd recently bleached his hair, and I couldn't stop looking up at it every few minutes. *The look of the new millennium*, he called it. I called it *the look of an Art Kid with too much access to Clorox*. "I'm joking," he added. "But did you ever think maybe he knows you well enough to be right, even if he sounded like an asshole when he told you?"

"Of course I considered that," I told him. That was the reason I was in such a bad mood. My commitment to stay in Santana had already become an uneasy itch I couldn't seem to sooth; when Michael pulled the covers off the real reason I was probably doing it, I felt weak. And there were few things I always hated more than feeling weak.

"Oh, believe me," Jesse nodded. "I get it. When Jasmine told me she was taking the scholarship, I was actually terrified at the thought of going to California alone." He peered out the window. "I still wish Xavier would come. I have this dream of us getting out of here, and starting a

208

whole new life where we can both be ourselves." He sighed and pulled his attention back inside the café. "I guess half the dream coming true is better than nothing."

I tried to imagine Xavier ever living out of the closet, but I couldn't picture it. In fact, if I hadn't seen him enveloping Jesse in his arms at Michael's party with my own two eyes, I wouldn't believe he wasn't straight. "Can I ask you something?" I said quietly to Jesse, and when he nodded, I leaned in. "How the hell did that even happen? No offense, but you might be the oddest couple I've ever seen."

"You're not wrong about that," Jesse laughed, and asked if I remembered Xavier working at Brando's, a seasonal ice cream stand over on Zondra's side of town, two summers earlier. I shrugged. Even before Xavier became my personal bully at school, I stayed away from him as often as possible. "Anyway," Jesse explained, "We both worked there the summer after sophomore year."

As his story unfolded, he looked up at the ceiling, allowing himself to admire each scene he painted for me. After three weeks of working the same shift, they finally had their first conversation one June night, while they closed up the stand by themselves, and it didn't take long for Jesse to sympathize with Xavier's tumultuous homelife. He didn't say specifically what that meant, just that it all made Xavier seem like a real person.

By the end of that month, Xavier started asking Jesse if he wanted to go hang out at the lake by the hills, to smoke pot he stole from his brother. By July, he'd built up the courage to kiss Xavier at the lake. By the time school began to near, they were hooking up on the dark shore almost every other day.

But as the summer break of 1998 came to a final stop, so did their fling. Xavier pulled away first, and Jesse knew it was because there was no rational way for the system they'd created to continue into the school year. Jesse had already figured out he was gay, but Xavier looked at their whole summer as some kind of situational pastime, instead of the defining relationship it was for them both. He told Jesse it would be best for them to pretend nothing ever happened, and said they should go back to school and rejoin the cliques they already fit into before that summer. To his surprise, Jesse agreed. He didn't want anyone to know about it any more than Xavier did. Ever the introvert, the last thing he ever desired to be was the subject of Santana's gossip mill.

"Well, going your separate ways obviously didn't work out," I teased. It wasn't lost on me that Jesse's experience with Xavier mirrored mine with Ray in many ways. The secrecy, the shame, and most of all, the clear addiction.

Jesse smiled. "I'll have you know it lasted for one whole semester." He looked back to the ceiling, picking the right place to pick up their history. During the winter break of our junior year, their families both went to church for the same Christmas mass, and happened to sit near each other. They made enough small talk to somehow stumble upon a plan to meet up. Sure enough, it was only the next day Xavier parked his truck in some cluster of snowy trees near the lake, and Jesse leapt out of the passenger seat and onto Xavier's body. Their mouths anxiously reacquainted after what felt like years.

I'd begun fanning myself with the menu from the table. "Jesus Christ," I said. "You should write a book."

Jesse playfully rolled his eyes. "That's pretty much the story," he replied, explaining that over the year and four months since their Christmas tryst in the woods, he and Xavier decided to see each other, in secret, until high school was over. Then they agreed to go their separate ways and never see each other again. It seemed they needed to give themselves a deadline and a punishment in order for them to let it go on, which made me sad for Jesse. Maybe even for Xavier.

"I just can't believe I never saw it," I sighed, trying to find any memory in my brain of Jesse and Xavier so much as looking each other's way before Michael's party.

"I'm sure we miss a million stories a day," Jesse

shrugged. "We all have our own shit going on."

It was hard to fathom so much time passed without anyone uncovering their secret. The weird attraction between Ray and me couldn't even be kept a secret from Zondra or Michael, and it had barely existed for half a year. "Does it ever bother you that no one knows? Not even Jasmine?"

"No." He'd spoken quickly, without giving it a second thought. "We're not a firework show," he said carefully, attempting a perfect metaphor of his relationship with Xavier. He thought on it for a few seconds more before adding, "We're a lake. That lake, where we found our spot no one ever sees, that's us. And we are just for us. And I feel like that's good enough for me. I like that a part of him is for my eyes only. Maybe it's sick, but that's the way I feel." His eyes scanned the air as if he were still approving his own explanation, and then he smiled. It was approved.

If I'd unloaded half the questions I had about my future when I sat down with Jesse, I'd picked up just as many after hearing his story. Surprisingly, it had become easy for me to see what Jesse got out of the time and feelings and patience he had invested in Xavier. I wasn't sure I could say the same about Ray. And yet, I still knew the way I felt about Ray was the same, like it could never go anywhere, and yet none of it seemed like a mistake or a waste of time.

By the end of April, Sam not only caught up on everything she missed after her parents' accident, but somehow, for the first time ever, she had pushed herself to earn better grades than me. "Maybe you should be doing the tutoring," I told her over the kitchen table one quiet evening. English was the only grade she needed to raise in order to end the year with straight A's, and after reading the essay she'd written about expecting a baby without the support of her parents, I was sure the perfect GPA wasn't out of her reach.

When we finished going through it, I gave her the

handwritten essay, all the changes we'd just discussed highlighted and scribbled onto the pages. She quickly scanned it over with satisfaction before going to her room to give it one more in-depth review. As she walked out of the kitchen, Richie came in.

"Is she an early bird like your mom?" he asked. Over the past few months, Richie's friendly grin had become somewhat endearing to me. He was always a neutral party when my mom was in a bad mood, and genuinely seemed to be happy for Sam and me as we anxiously prepared for graduation. He even offered to bring his computer over to our house so we could use it once college started, instead of relying on the two computers at library.

"She's just finishing up homework," I said, gathering my books into my backpack.

Richie pulled out a seat at the kitchen table, though, and sat across from me. "Hey, can I ask you something?" Suddenly, his easygoing smile seemed to be replaced by curiosity. I nodded, zipping up my bookbag, and he lowered his voice. "It's actually about the night your aunt and uncle passed."

My stomach sunk. It had been so long since anyone in my house discussed New Year's that it caught me off guard. "Sure," I said cautiously.

"I was thinking about that night earlier. I think about it a lot," he explained, peering into me. I knew this was going somewhere I didn't want it to. "I remembered something."

In my head, I was frantically running from drawer to drawer, trying to find every memory I had of that night. Even though some of it was tattooed onto the back of my eyes, there was plenty all the vodka I drank that night had distorted or erased. "What's that?" I asked.

"When we were all in the waiting room at the hospital, you made a phone call." He shifted in his seat, leaning in and keeping his eyes glued onto mine. I tried my hardest not to blink at his recollection, even though the memory of my call with Ray was replaying in my head, and my mind was already spinning and spinning, trying to draft the perfect explanation as quickly as I could. "Who'd you call?" he said.

"Zondra," I answered. It came to me so quickly, I'd even surprised myself. "I can't explain why but for some reason, I just felt like I needed to talk to her right away. My mom was so sad. I just… that was who I called."

He nodded sympathetically. For a moment, I was sure I'd extinguished his burning question. Richie wasn't a rookie, though. He was already three steps ahead of me. "It's just that I checked the phone number. And it wasn't Zondra's house, Lukas."

My guts twisted like gears and the air seemed to be vacuumed out of my chest, but I tried my hardest to keep solid. "Yeah, I called the wrong number. I guess I was just so shaken up." It was the best I could come up with.

"You accidentally called the apartment where Ray Melendez lives?" Richie said, more astounded than accusatory.

"What are you trying to say?" I snapped back. As lightly as I treaded, it dawned on me that I might have already stepped on a landmine.

Richie shrugged. "I'm just saying I find it interesting. Thanks for letting me know." With that, he pushed himself up from the table and told me to have myself a good night, waltzing back into the living room to watch TV. I watched him until he turned the corner and then let out all the air I hadn't even realized I was holding in my chest. My heart was racing, and in my mind, there was nothing but a tabletop baring one single item: Zondra's Death card.

I grabbed my bag and went into my room, closing the door quietly behind me and dropping myself onto my bed. The ceiling seemed to be lower. The walls seemed to be closer together. I closed my eyes to summon Dr. Carver's voice, and I let my lungs open and close until I could feel my chest relax. Eventually, the room opened up again.

For the first time, I thought about telling Sam everything. I trusted her, and I knew she'd do anything she could to help, but I couldn't drag her into this mess. There wasn't room for anything else on her plate.

Next, I thought about sneaking over to Zondra's house and coming clean. The thought of her reaction stopped me, though. There was still hope in my soul that what she thought she knew about that night wasn't as bad as the real truth. I didn't want her to think less of me.

I opened the window and pulled in some fresh air. The night was quiet and calm, and the smell of spring was a welcome visitor to my bedroom. But suddenly, the night I opened my window to find Ray's Christmas card flashed through my head. I winced. After Michael's party, I'd done my best to stay away from him again, his hand linked with Nissa's almost every time I noticed him at school, and whatever existed between us once again sealed into a bag toward the back of my mental closet. No matter what, though, there was no escaping that what happened on New Year's Eve was coming back from the dead, and he needed to know our futures were on the line.

Over the next week, I watched Nissa and Ray like a vulture, waiting for an opportunity to catch him without her so I could warn him Richie might be onto us. It seemed the closer graduation inched, the tighter their grip onto each other became. I started to lose count of how long it had been since I saw them apart. Since Nissa's parents seemed to be forever out of town, she'd even begun staying at his apartment.

The right afternoon finally came along when Nissa would be busy at a prom-planning meeting after school. I knew Ray's schedule at the mechanic well enough to know he wouldn't be working. After school that day, I snuck over. When he answered the door to find me standing in front of him, his lips perched into a satisfied grin. "It's not what you think," I said, pushing my way past him. "My mom's boyfriend is onto me about New Year's. I think we're in big trouble."

He pulled out a chair for me at his kitchen table. We sat and I watched him spin his wheels, deciding whether or not to feel concerned. "I'm not worried," he concluded. He could see quickly that I was baffled at his nonchalance. "If there was any evidence against us, we'd be busted by now," he added. "Think about it, Luke. There's no fingerprints anywhere. The footprints were too jacked up for them to even get a shoe size. We're obviously not confessing. And no one knows why you or I would even be there."

"I see you've thought about every little thing," I told him. "But Richie knows I called you at the hospital that night. He checked the hospital phone records. He's not an idiot. He solves crimes for a living." I started looking around Ray's apartment, replaying every image from that night leading up to the fire, and then I peered into Ray's eyes, his drunken rage at what King had done to me still lingering quietly somewhere.

He shrugged. "If it comes down to it, what do you have to worry about? You didn't set that fire, I did. And if you want, you can blame it all on me. Say I scared you into keeping quiet about it."

I felt my brows scrunching over my eyes. "You'd do that for me?"

"It's the truth, isn't it?"

As rare as it was for me, speechlessness held my mouth hostage for a minute. I couldn't believe what he was saying, and for some reason, his offer wasn't as comforting as I would have predicted it to be. I shook my head and he asked what the matter was. "I still don't want that to happen," I said. "I don't want you to…"

"You don't want me to go to jail?" He cracked a smile, scooting his chair around the table and next to me. "Why's that?"

I shot up from my seat. "Anyway, has there been any news on Nissa's plans after graduation?"

He knew very well I'd been avoiding Nissa, punishing myself by withholding her friendship. There was no part of me that felt worthy of it. "She got into some school in Las Vegas and her dad got her an internship with a lawyer. She decided that's what she wants to be." I imagined a future Nissa, absolutely dominating a courtroom and looking like a supermodel doing it. She had never mentioned wanting to become an attorney, but it seemed like such an obvious job choice for her. I watched Ray look out the window. I could tell he wasn't happy about it. "I told her I'm not going," he said.

My jaw dropped. "You did? Why?"

"Why do you think?" he asked without a second thought, and looked at me with a peer indicating I should know the answer was me. When he could tell their whole situation was still lost on me, he explained they were going to enjoy being together for the rest of the school year, but she accepted he wasn't going with her when it was over. It seemed crazy to me, but then again, their whole relationship seemed crazy to me from the moment Nissa recruited me to help her get a date with him. "After she's gone, I guess we'll see what happens here," he added with a mischievous wink.

I hated my body for reacting to it.

Everything he'd just said seemed to unseal that mental bag where I'd been storing the idea of him and me. I looked at his gray eyes and the light stubble above his lip and his perfect teeth under it, and all the feelings I'd locked up again unleashed themselves and swirled in the pit of my stomach. I knew I had to leave before the incident that had taken place in the camper at Michael's house repeated itself. Having fulfilled my goal of warning him about Richie, I got up and told him I'd see him at school before walking home.

Unsurprisingly, Richie's interest had seemed to snowball since he asked me about the phone call I made on New Year's Eve, and it was only a few nights later there was a knock on my bedroom door. He asked if he could talk to me for a minute. If it were up to me, I would have told him

I'd really rather not, but I figured that wasn't the wisest move, and I also knew it was imperative to know where his curiosity had taken him next. I put down the book I was reading as he sat on the corner of my bed. At least the door was closed and he'd waited until my mom was in bed again, I thought. Though if he were really smart, he wouldn't have hidden his questioning from her; she was one person who could probably put the whole night together, her nosiness and ability to read my lies sharper than anyone else's.

"I hate to bring up New Year's again. I know it was a really hard night for everyone in this family," Richie started. "Hell, it was a hard night for me. Your Uncle Carlos and I have known each other for a long time."

While I appreciated the soft introduction, I just looked at him, waiting for his question.

"I can't believe I've never asked, but where were you before your friend found you and brought you to the hospital?"

Luckily, I'd been waiting for him to ask for an alibi ever since he made it clear he was still hunting for the truth about New Year's Eve. I knew I couldn't say I was at home, and I knew I couldn't say I was with Sam, and I knew I couldn't say I was with Michael. So I said the most logical answer. "I was with Zondra and Laura," I lied. As prepared as I was to answer Richie's question, my heart still began to beat a level quicker, knowing the chances of keeping everything from Zondra were officially zero. When I saw her next, I'd have to explain everything and hope to God she'd be willing to lie for me.

Richie kept his stare hooked on me for another moment. He was looking for the slightest crack I might give, but I could feel a strong mask of confidence covering me. "All right," he nodded, and continued to look me over for just another moment before adding, "So if I were to call Zondra right now and ask her, she'd tell me you were there before the hospital?"

If there was an emergency case of calm, I'd have cracked

the glass to access it right then and there. The question of where I was before the hospital I'd anticipated, but I thought I'd have time to talk to Zondra before he could get to her. There was no other choice but to double down on my answer, though, so I kept my mask on and shrugged. "Sure."

Without saying another word, he got up and opened my bedroom door, and before I knew it, I was following him to the kitchen, my chest thudding faster and faster as I realized he was really about to call Zondra. He reached into his pocket and pulled out her phone number. I had to stop my jaw from falling open. Somehow, he knew what my answer would be. Richie picked up the cordless and punched in the phone number, asking me one more time if she was going to back me up. I couldn't think of any other answer but to nod again.

I heard the ringing tone in the silence of the kitchen, and prayed that if there was any kind of God out there, no one would answer. But a few seconds after the ringing had begun, I heard a muffled voice speaking into Richie's ear. "Hello, Ms. Devereaux?" he asked into the receiver.

"Yes, this is she." Zondra's voice seemed so close and so far away at the same time. I wished she could see me because I knew if she could, she'd somehow know to cover for me. But this was genius on Richie's part. She had no idea what was happening.

"This is Richie Velasco. I hope I'm not disturbing you." He looked at the clock. It was 9:30. I knew Zondra never went to bed before eleven, and I wouldn't have been surprised if he somehow knew that, too, the way things were going.

"Not at all," Zondra's voice said. "What can I do for you? Is everything all right?"

"Yes, yes. I was just hoping I could ask you a question, if it wouldn't be any trouble. It's about New Year's Eve."

"New Year's Eve? Well, I'll try to help, but that was nearly five months ago. What's the question?"

Richie looked at me one more time, his final, silent offer to end the whole thing if I were to tell him where I really was on New Year's Eve. Something told me not to budge, though, and I returned his look expectantly, nudging him to ask Zondra the question. "I was hoping you could tell me what you did that night," Richie said.

Zondra paused for a moment. "Let's see. New Year's Eve." My heart was beating in my ears and every nerve in my body exploded as I anticipated her answer. "Well, I worked at the café that day," she began. "Lukas was there, too. In fact, he helped me close..." She paused again, recollecting the evening.

I remembered her telling me to go home, shooing me out the door with her recommendation that I tell Ray it was over between us forever. I remembered talking to myself in the mirror. I remembered walking to Ray's. Drinking with him. Going to King's. The fire.

"And after he helped me close," Zondra continued, "I asked if he'd like to come over to the house and celebrate with us at midnight. He went home to change and then when he came over, oh I'd say around nine o'clock, Lukas and Laura and I played some games for a while. But Lukas didn't feel well, and he went home around eleven. So at midnight, Laura and I watched the ball drop on channel 7 before we went to bed. That's all I really remember."

Richie gazed at me, his astonishment weakly hidden in comparison to mine. As shocked as I was at what Zondra said, I forced a look of annoyance at Richie as he thanked her for taking his call, and told her to have a good night. Every ounce of me felt like a flower blooming, just as awakened by the surprise of her answer as I was proud, and grateful beyond words.

When he hung up the phone, Richie continued to look me over, still floored that the conclusion he'd begun to build in his head about what might have happened that night was just flicked over like a house of cards. "I don't know what to say, Lukas. I'm sorry for doing that."

I rolled my eyes. "Where did you think I was?" I said, as strange as it was, asking him to admit he had discovered the truth.

"I don't know." He shook his head and stared at the floor for a moment before saying he was going to bed. When he was gone from the kitchen, I caught my breath just like I had the week before, relieved to have cleared what I hoped was the final hurdle I'd need to about that night.

I returned to my bedroom and stared at the ceiling in bed, mystified and saved yet again by Zondra Devereaux.

When I walked into the café for my shift the next morning, Zondra looked up from the pastry display she was organizing. "Good morning," she smiled with as much serenity as ever.

"Hi," I yawned. I'd been up all night, wondering how on earth she knew what to tell Richie when he called. I joined her behind the counter and as I tied my apron around the back of my waist, I wasted no time trying to get to the bottom of it. "How'd you know?"

She smiled, still using a pair of tongs to turn the pastries in their case until the presentation was up to her standards. "I just did. How is irrelevant."

I sighed. Somehow, I knew this would be her answer, and ironically, even though I'd spent the whole night trying to figure it out, I knew she was right. It didn't matter how she knew, it just mattered that she did, and that she came through when I needed her. For a moment, I considered asking what else she knew, but it was obvious her answer would have been the same. It was irrelevant. "Well, thanks," I told her.

Zondra looked around the café, at all the tables full of chatty customers. When she was sure no one was about to come up to the counter, she said quietly, "I told you before, Lukas, I'm on your side. I don't need to know every detail about whatever's happened to know that I trust you. You're a good person. I know this to be true, and it's enough for me." She put her hand on my shoulder for a moment, looking into my confused, thankful stare to make sure I understood. Once she was sure I did, she told me there was a pile of dishes with my name on it.

"Believe it or not, there's only one week left before the last day of school," Mrs. Jimenez told our English class the next week, in the final few minutes of fifth period. She came around to the front of her desk and patted the top of the hourglass she kept on its surface. "As you may remember, I promised at the beginning of the semester there won't be a final test for this class." She smirked as everyone in the room seemed to lean in. It sounded like she was about to take back her vow. "Don't worry. There really is no test!" she laughed.

Instead of a test, she explained, our final assignment would be to make something for a class time capsule. The idea was that all these things – letters, songs, videos, whatever – would be put into a box, which would be kept at the school until our ten-year reunion in 2010. "I suggest you think about what questions you have for your future self," Mrs. Jimenez grinned, and then gave us the rest of the period to work with each other and brainstorm.

Nissa pushed her desk next to mine. "Who in their right mind would come back here in ten years?" she joked, before remembering my plan to stay. "Not that it's a bad place. And it will totally be amazing to see everyone by then."

"It's fine," I chuckled. "I would hope that 2010 Lukas is out of here, too. That seems like a million years away."

She nodded. "Anyway, we can use my dad's camcorder to make tapes if you want. You should come over this evening and we can get it done! I have more prom planning to do after school, but I should be home by five. Ray can help us. This is actually going to be so fun!"

Before I could get a word in, she began to tell me about her Las Vegas college plans and how excited she was to move out there, get a fake ID, and live her best life over the summer. She didn't even mention Ray for a while, and I figured she had come to accept she'd be living her best life without him. But once she brought him up, it was clear she assumed he would be there. "I didn't know Ray was going with you," I told her, and she laughed.

"He says he's not, but why wouldn't he?" She explained that her parents had already signed an apartment lease for a year, and it would almost be too easy for him to come stay with her. He didn't want to go to college, but that was fine, she said, because he could easily find a job with his experience. They could both do their thing and they wouldn't have to break up after graduation.

I nodded along, never having felt more guilty, or thankful for the dismissal bell.

Sure enough, when I showed up to Nissa's house that evening, Ray answered the door to let me in. In typical Nissa fashion, she'd decorated an entire side of the living room for us to use as a set. Paper graduation caps and diplomas were taped up, and she'd cut out big letters to spell out "Class of 2000" across the wall. It was only then that everything about graduation seemed real. It had been this invisible finish line for so long, seemingly so far in the distance, it had come to feel like I'd never be on the other side. But just like Mrs. Jimenez's hourglass at the end of English everyday, the last little bit of sand was starting to wither away to nothing. It was really about to happen.

"This is kind of amazing," I told her, running my fingers over the cutouts.

"Thanks! Ray helped me with the letters!" she said.

Ray came to the wall and looked his work over. "That's why they're so ugly," he chuckled.

She playfully pushed his arm before picking up her dad's video camera from the coffee table. "Okay. I've thought about what I'm going to say. I'm ready. How about you, Luke?"

I hadn't given the project a second thought since we

222

walked out of English earlier that afternoon. There was nothing I felt particularly inclined to say to my future self, other than he'd better have escaped Santana, and I'd never forgive him if he came back to see this stupid video in ten years. "You go first," I told her, shrugging on the couch as she put the camcorder into Ray's hands, quickly pointing at the buttons he'd need to press to record and stop the tape. He aimed the lens toward Nissa as she stepped back, adjusting her skirt and flipping her hair. When she felt camera-ready, she asked if he was recording, and he gave her a little nod to start.

It was as if someone had plugged her into an electrical outlet, the way a giant smile suddenly lit up her whole face. "Hi everybody!" she beamed. "Nissa Delfino here. Santana High School, Class of 2000! Go Falcons!"

Ray watched her from inside the viewfinder. I could see him smiling behind the camera.

"I know I haven't spent as much time at Santana as most of you, but my senior year here was so much fun. I'll never forget it. I made so many amazing friends! I really hope that right now, we're all crowded around the gym watching this at the reunion, and it's 2010, and cars can fly, or something cool like that. Anyway…"

Before she could finish her message, there was a ring in the kitchen. "Dammit!" she yelled, and Ray put the camera down. She raised her finger as she picked up the cordless, and rolled her eyes almost immediately after answering. "What? You're kidding me." She grunted in frustration and put her hand over the receiver, mouthing to us that she'd be right back before she vanished into the kitchen. Somebody was apparently hysterical on the other line.

Ray set the camera down on the coffee table, and then collapsed onto the giant chair next to it. "Still have your panties in a bunch about your mom's boyfriend?" he said jokingly, quiet so Nissa wouldn't hear from the kitchen.

"No. You were right," I told him, as much as it pained me. "There's no proof we were ever at King's house that night. Richie's last trick was basically asking where I was when the fire happened, and thankfully, Zondra covered for my ass."

"See?" he grinned, sneaking his hand onto my knee and squeezing it playfully.

I jumped and looked toward the kitchen, paranoid at how close Nissa was, even though we could still hear her trying to calm down whomever had called. "What's wrong with you?" I asked. "You have a girlfriend and we are literally in her house."

He pulled back his hand unapologetically, his mischievous grin lingering on his lips until Nissa popped back into the room. "The school is flooding!" she exclaimed. Ray and I both instinctively stood up as she went on, rushing to grab her jacket. "A pipe just broke and the whole gym is a mess! All the decorations we've been working on for prom are ruined!"

Ray and I followed Nissa out the front door, and we all ran back to the school. By the time we reached the parking lot, everything the prom committee had prepared was being drug out the gym doors. Cardboard palm trees had been melted from ornate to soggy, and the giant paper mural a bunch of art kids huddled to complete over the past few weeks was totaled. If Nissa's head could fume from how pissed she was at the whole scene, I was sure it would.

We all went into the gym and helped everyone who'd quickly shown up, pulling the rest of the prom supplies out of the school. It was clear Nissa was no longer in the mood to film our project. She was beginning to list all the people on the prom-planning committee she needed to call and assign tasks to salvage what was possible, and reconstruct the rest over the next week. "We'll do the project tomorrow, okay?" she told me, excusing me for the evening before grabbing Ray's hand so he could walk her back home.

I smiled as I made my way to my house. I wasn't sure when Nissa had become the executive producer of prom, but of course she did, and I wondered how she did it. Just calculating all the time I'd seen her working on everything stressed me out.

More than anything, though, I admired her for it. My heart swelled with pride that our last big hurrah would be a Nissa Delfino original. She was a natural leader, and her personality was still so monumental to me, even after the months and months since she first appeared in my math class. I hoped that in ten years, the future Lukas would be half as confident.

I stopped Nissa in the hall the next morning to let her know I'd write a letter for the capsule, since I had to work at the café after school. She seemed to be so stressed with prom that she was short. "Whatever," she shrugged, and told me she needed to get back to planning.

Later in the afternoon, I asked if there was anything I could do over the next week to help, but surprisingly, she said everything was taken care of. Once again, she cut our conversation short, leaving me at my locker as she clicked away in her heels.

The next week seemed to flash by in the snap of a finger. I worked as many hours as Zondra would let me at the café, and Sam kept me up late studying for finals almost every night. I was so tired by the night our last final was over, I spent most of it in my room listening to the radio and staring at the ceiling.

Everything seemed to be passing by faster and faster, which seemed ironic, because at the end of this whole rush would be an anticlimactic summer. Nissa, Michael, and Jesse had all indicated they were getting out of town right after graduation. Sam would have a baby and would be home all summer. I would still work at the café with Zondra. As excited as I felt to be close to the finish line with school, it also felt like that was the only good change on its way.

When there was a soft knock at my door, I could feel my every muscle tense up by instinct. I knew Sam was in bed, and I was worried Richie was coming back for more investigating. To my surprise, though, it was my mom. "Can I come in?" she asked quietly.

"Sure." I sat up as she pushed the door closed behind her and pulled out the chair from my desk, sitting beside my bed the way I'd seen her prepare to talk to her patients at the hospital. "You're freaking me out," I told her. She never came to my room to talk, and I assumed something was wrong.

But she smiled, calming my nerves by telling me everything was fine. "There are just some things I want to say to you," she said.

I reached over to my radio and turned it off. The deafening silence made me even more nervous, but it felt like the best way to let her know I was ready to hear whatever she needed to say.

She seemed to appreciate the gesture, and took a deep breath. Then she looked me square in the eyes, and told me if I wanted to leave town after graduation, I could.

"In fact," she said, "I think you *should*." I must have been as floored as she had been when I told her I would stay in Santana a few months earlier. All I wanted to do was ask where her sudden change of heart had come from, but I was dumbstruck. I couldn't move. "Sam and the baby can stay with me and Richie," she added. "Between what we make, and the money she gets from her trust, we'll be okay."

I nodded along, but I couldn't help remaining silent, dazed as if she might take it all back after a second thought. But she didn't. She kept talking. "I'm really happy with Richie. He's a good man, and he makes me think about things," she explained. "Like you."

She looked over at my wall, admiring the collage of magazine cutouts I'd haphazardly constructed over the past year. "I think you should find what makes you happy. And I don't think you're going to find that here."

I knew I needed to say something when nothing followed, but I was so taken aback, no words came to me other than, "But I promised…"

She didn't even let me finish that thought. "I should have never let you do that. You're too young to be promising your life to anybody," she admitted. "Don't get me wrong, Luke. I'm so happy I married your dad and stayed in Santana my whole life. That was my dream. I always wanted that for myself. But it's not what you've ever wanted, as far back as I can remember. And this town is never going to make you happy." She shrugged at the plain truth. "I'm not saying you have to go anywhere," she clarified. "But I want you to know that you can. And if you do, it's okay."

Out of nowhere, I felt tears leaking into my eyes and my mom became a blur as quickly as she reached out and pulled me into a hug on the edge of my bed. I wasn't sure what had done it, the granting of my oldest wish, or the validation of feeling seen, but every part of me was overwhelmed with love for her in that moment, even though it wasn't lost on me that she still didn't understand everything about me.

Tolerance is the first step toward acceptance, I heard Zondra's voice echo between my ears. That's what she always said about my mom when I'd complain that she'd done the bare minimum by not throwing me out when she learned I was gay. *One day your mom will surprise you*, Zondra promised. I always thought it was lip service, like an obligatory statement to pacify my teenage angst toward my mom. I never thought it would really happen. But there it was.

Surprisingly, though, when I moved past the cloud of shock from her offer, I discovered a cliff of doubt. It would be easier to stay, I realized. Michael had been right. I had grown more comfortable than I cared to admit with the idea of staying. I'd all but extinguished my fiery desire to get out. My mom could see I needed some time alone, and told me I didn't need to decide then and there.

"I'll talk to Sam about it tomorrow," I agreed, as my mom nodded and left me in my room to think. I turned the radio back on and let my head fall back down to my pillow, the air somehow feeling lighter, and the summer looking more like a giant question mark than I'd imagined.

THIRTEEN

"It's the last day of school!" Sam yelled into my room first thing the next morning, waddling back out before I could even see straight.

I rubbed my eyes and looked at my alarm clock, grunting at that last five minutes I had left, and pushed myself up out of bed. My mom and Richie had already gone to work, but luckily for me, had left some coffee in the pot. As I poured myself a mug, Sam twirled into the kitchen, pregnant belly and all, and told me she'd been up since five. "Probably because you go to bed at seven these days," I moaned, sitting across from her as she grabbed a banana from the fruit bowl and began to peel it.

I remembered my conversation with my mom, but I couldn't even bring it up to Sam before she started to gush about how excited she was for the summer, and that she couldn't wait to see me attempt holding an infant. I smiled along, and decided it wasn't the right time to ask if I could erase that picture she'd just painted.

By our last day as Santana students, our tests had come and gone, our lockers had been cleaned out, and all that remained was a visit to each class one last time to sign yearbooks before prom that night. Unlike most schools, Santana's prom marked the end of our school year. Every senior class complained it was stupid to hold off on prom until the night before graduation, but I figured it was more genius than anything. If there was one way to keep a bunch of seniors out of trouble on prom night, it was to make sure they had a reason to get up the next day.

Of course, that didn't stop anyone from making after-prom plans to get completely fucked up. Even though Michael and I had only talked a few short times since pissing each other off, I knew he was calling a truce by asking if he should still come over to get ready before the dance. "I guess," I smirked, and as only Michael could, he grinned at what I really meant: I wasn't mad anymore. He told me he'd be at my house by six.

As he sauntered away, taking Jasmine's hand and walking her down the hall, my mind flashed the memory of the year before. For as different as everything was back then, it started out exactly the same. Michael had come to my locker to ask what time he should come over, and it was six last year, too. We got all dressed up, and as the sun set, we let my mom take a bunch of photos as we waited for our dates to pick us up. I'd thought more than a few times of how happy everything must have looked to everyone but me that day. Nobody knew about the cloud of anxiety that followed my every move, all the way until that moment I told Michael the truth behind the school.

This year, Michael knew. Everyone knew. And even though there would always be idiots, I survived, and I'd continue to survive.

Unlike the last year, I felt a real sense of confidence in my own strength, instead of the defiant defensiveness I had mistaken for strength nine months earlier, when I had to face Michael after our summer apart. Now, as if the final pieces of a puzzle I didn't know I was constructing had fallen into place, a wholeness I never knew poured through my veins as the bell rang, and I walked out of Santana High as a student for the very last time.

Outside, I saw Nissa waiting for Ray by the flagpole. "Hey!" I shouted with a wave, but when she turned to find it came from me, she immediately looked away. Something was still up with her. I'd tried asking about it earlier, but she told me she didn't have time to talk. I figured it must have been one of two things: either the prom was really stressing her out, or she was upset her parents canceled their trip to Santana for graduation. She acted like she was happy about it all week, letting everyone know she was officially hosting an after-prom rager, but I knew it had to make her feel like shit. The icy attitude that came over her during the past week stung, but I tried to understand.

"What are the chances you don't have a date tonight?" Jesse's voice abruptly asked behind me. I turned around, an eyebrow raised.

"Why? You asking me out?"

"You wish," he laughed. "We actually need more help than we thought. Apparently, a whole person has to be designated as the punch monitor."

We walked through the parking lot as I told him I was sorry to decline, but I was taking Sam to the dance, since she was my most appropriate date. "Santana's only out homo and his pregnant cousin, what more iconic couple can you imagine walking into a prom? Besides two homos, maybe. But that would be impossible," I said.

Jesse nodded. For the past two years, every time a school dance came around, he dreamt of Xavier taking him. In a perfect world, they'd be able to go together, but we didn't live anywhere near a perfect world.

"Is Xavier taking a girl to the dance?" I asked.

"Stephanie Alfaro and I'm not bitter at all," Jesse joked. "But on the bright side, he's all mine after prom. Booked a hotel room and everything. Eat your heart out, Stephanie."

If there was one mature thing about Michael since we

were kids, it was that he was early for everything. At half past five, he knocked on my front door and I came out of my room to find my mom hugging him, showering him with her usual compliments and asking all the standard questions, from "How excited are you for graduation tomorrow?" to "Is your dad just devastated that you're leaving town for college?"

Michael appeased my mom by giving her all the obligatory answers before joining Sam and me in her room. She had already wiggled her way into her custom prom dress, joking she owed her life to Sally at the antique store for her tailoring skills, and I'd put on the same suit I wore to prom the year before, and to my aunt and uncle's funeral in January. It felt new, and just like the other two times I'd worn it, I couldn't master the tie. "I see you still don't know how to tie that," Michael joked, pointing at me. "I'll fix it in a minute."

He went into my room to change into his suit, and I sat on Sam's bed, admiring her every swipe as she brushed on her makeup. I thought again about bringing up the conversation my mom had with me the night before, but she seemed so excited about everything that I couldn't do it. When Michael was all suited up, he came into the room and fixed my tie, as Sam put the final touches on her hair. Then we let my mom take about a thousand pictures out front, before Jesse and Jasmine showed up and she took about a thousand more.

When we walked into the gym, it was instantly clear that Nissa had worked every last bit of her magic. The Hawaiian theme was honored at every corner, from the resurrected palm trees, to the giant island mural, to some Elvis movie projected onto a huge screen above us all.

Michael and Jasmine branched off toward all the dancing couples, and Jesse reported to the committee to see where he was needed. "What are you in the mood for?" I asked Sam. She tilted her head toward the left, and I looked over to see the food table. I cracked up and told her it was the best idea she had in years. We piled as many snacks onto our plates as we could, and moved to the bleachers.

"He's coming soon," Sam said, biting into a little sandwich square and rubbing her belly at the same time. "If he comes tomorrow, I'm going to be so pissed."

"Do you feel okay?" I asked.

"Just hungry and tired," she answered. I felt bad. She had been looking forward to prom and graduation for so long, but now that it was finally upon us, it was clear she was pushing herself to be present for it all.

"I won't be mad if we can't stay the whole time," I told her, trying my best to come off more supportive than pushy. "Just let me know."

She nodded and continued eating her food. In the end, she was happy to be there, even if we watched more than participated. I scanned the gym for Ray, and eventually saw him dancing with Nissa toward the front. She looked as gorgeous as ever, and the sight of him in a suit was a welcome surprise I never knew I'd like so much. They swayed back and forth, and although I knew he didn't see me, when Nissa caught me looking their way, she pulled him in and planted a kiss on his lips before looking back at me.

Suddenly, my stomach dropped. I wasn't sure how, but she knew about Ray and me. It was crystal clear. I thought back to the past week and re-watched every slight and quick glare. It wasn't prom that was making her act like that. She knew about us.

My suit became hot and I fidgeted. Sam asked if I was okay, and I told her I was, even though I was dying to talk to Ray more than ever before to ask what he knew. I pulled in air and slowly pushed it out, telling myself that if she knew, it was out of my control now. I could hear Dr. Carver telling me if there was a plan I could make, to make it.

I cooled myself down, concluding that I would come clean before graduation. I would beg her to forgive me, hoping she'd believe how tortured I was for what kept happening, and that I never meant to hurt her.

Every time she faced me, her stare was like a knife in my stomach, so I tried to look somewhere else, hoping for any distraction.

Dancing not too far away from Nissa and Ray were Xavier and his date. I cringed, remembering how I felt when I was in that position last year. I hated every minute of it so much that I couldn't help but pity Xavier, at least a little bit. And I felt even worse for Jesse, who was trying, and failing, not to watch Stephanie take up a space meant for him.

I shook my head for us all, wondering if things like this happened in big cities, and if things would be this way here forever. If we could all be who we were and do what we wanted, the world might be way less of a mess.

"Okay," Sam said, interrupting my gaze. "Here's what I want." She set her plate down next to her and stood, pulling me up with her. "I want to go get our awkward prom picture in front of that ugly mural, and then I want to go home. But I want you to stay here. I can call your mom to come get me."

I tried to convince her I wanted to go home, too, but she knew better. She cupped my mouth and told me not to argue with the pregnant girl. Under her hand I smiled, and then led her to the makeshift photo set. We took the most standard, hilarious prom picture imaginable, before she asked Mrs. Morales if she could call my mom from the office. I told her I'd check on her later, and before she left, she commanded me to have enough fun for both of us.

Once Sam was gone, though, I wasn't sure why I'd chosen to stay. Michael was busy slow dancing right into Jasmine's smile, and it was clear Nissa wanted me dead, for as much as she mysteriously clung onto her other deceiver. I walked over to the punchbowl and stood next to Jesse. He asked where Sam had gone, and when I told him she went home for the night, he looked pensive for a moment. Then he asked the kid he was working with if he would watch the punch for a few minutes.

"Follow me," he said, and I walked behind him toward the bleachers, still wondering what he was thinking when he turned his hair into that awful yellow. Instead of going up the bleachers, though, he led us behind them. I looked around. It was dark, the only light coming in through the small slits between the seats.

"What are we doing here?" I asked warily.

"Don't make this weird, Bradley," he laughed back, pulling me in to slow dance with him. We stepped back and forth, one of my hands linked with his, and the other around his back. As strange and surreal as it felt to be dancing with a guy, and so close to everyone else at school, something about every move we made felt oddly familiar and natural.

Just like the day in the park when we kissed, there was no romantic chemistry between us. I wasn't about to catch feelings for Jesse and he didn't have any kind of spark for me, but what I did feel glowing between us was a mutual sense of respect. It felt right in the way a pair of shoes feels right; they go on two different feet, but they are the same.

We danced through the rest of the song, and I tried my hardest to notice every detail of how it felt to be in his arms, however platonic it was. For a moment, I closed my eyes and let myself imagine it was Ray in front of me, and I wondered if Jesse was imagining I was Xavier. It may have been pathetic, but I knew it was exactly what we both needed, and apparently, so did Jesse.

When the Usher song and our little break from reality were over, he stepped back and smiled. "There. Two guys danced at prom." He winked, giddy at the small taste of rebellion.

"Clever," I told him, and he patted me on the shoulder before we left the underworld of the bleachers and reentered the cardboard oasis that was our gym.

I poured myself a cup of punch. As I drank it, I noticed that once again, Nissa had her eyes locked on me. I wondered if I should talk to her, but before I could make up my mind, Michael walked to where I stood and asked if

235

we could talk. I nodded, looking back one more time as I followed him out of the gym. Nissa's stare was threatening me, but I couldn't tell with what.

Michael led me out the back doors of the gym and we moved to the football field. I gazed up at the moon and remembered the year before, when I chastised that pitiful face after running out to the same spot Michael led me toward now. It was a bit warmer than I recalled it being the last year, but otherwise, it was like stepping into a memory.

I looked around, trying not to let the last year's conversation into my head, but that was exactly what Michael wanted to bring back. As the music thudded in the background, and a cool breeze moved over us, he looked at me and it was like déjà vu. "You don't like girls," he said. "You're not like me." He paused, thinking back. I recognized the wording from the memory I'd played over and over the summer before. They were my coming out words to him. "What I should have said was that you were never like me," he added.

It almost felt like I should say something back, but I could tell he wasn't finished. "What I always liked about you is that you were weird to me since the day I met you," he laughed. "Remember when you couldn't figure out how to pump air into your bike tires for the life of you? Or when Selena died and you cried for a week? Or when you would read books during my football games because you were so bored?"

I thought back and nodded. All those things were true, as much as they didn't seem like compliments.

"If you think about it, we were never the same. That's what made us the coolest best friends. I learned how to be a better person because you made me do things like teach you how to pump air into a tire, and because I saw that you were able to cry about something you care about, and because you did what you wanted, even when it wasn't what everyone else did."

I couldn't think of a more contemplative thing Michael

had ever said. I was as struck as the night before when my mom told me I could leave town, finding myself in the middle of a conversation I never thought I would live to see.

"You're braver than I am," he said then. "I don't even want to go to college. I don't even want to play football anymore. But I do want to get out of Santana so I don't end up like my dad, and I know that going to Montana will make him happy, so I'm doing it. It's the easy thing."

Just when I'd thought he couldn't surprise me anymore, he had. I never imagined Michael giving up on football. It had become such a major part of who he painted himself to be, picturing his life without football was like picturing him without arms. I never would have guessed he had done it for anyone else, let alone that he was going to college for anyone else. But I did know from personal experience that getting out of Santana was the best thing anyone who wanted a better life could do. So as tempted as I was to convince him to stay with me, I couldn't.

"I think you're doing the right thing by going," I said. "And I'm not brave. You were right. I wanted to stay in Santana because the closer graduation came, I was too scared to leave. At least you're going somewhere." He looked as surprised at what I said as I had been at his whole speech, which was fair, because I was never the type of person to enjoy admitting I was wrong about anything. "And if you wanted a do-over for last year, consider it done-over."

He lit up. That was exactly what he wanted.

As I looked at his proud grin, I remembered a fight we had when we were ten years old. I wasn't sure what the fight was even about, but the defining moment of it all was when he angrily stormed out of my room, taking the collection of rocks I had accumulated that summer and leaving my house with it. He felt so guilty, he snuck back over that night, and tapped on my window to give it back before biking home.

"Can we go inside now?" I said, clenching my folded arms. "It's chilly out here." He laughed, and back into the gym we went, the prom scene from Hell finally corrected.

When the dance was over, everyone went to Nissa's house. I was unsure whether or not I should go, and tried to tell Michael I should call it a night since we had to get up early the next morning. But he and Jasmine dragged me with them. The party would be big enough for me to keep a safe distance, I figured, and since she hadn't already confronted me about anything, I leaned into the possibility that I was just being paranoid. We went to Michael's house to pick up the beer he'd convinced his dad to buy for the occasion, and then headed to Nissa's.

The Hawaiian theme seemed to have flowed over into the afterparty. Leftover decorations from prom were scattered on the walls and tables, and by the time we walked in, most of the crowd had been given grass skirts and coconut bras as party favors. "Remind me not to get drunk enough that I end up with either of those on my body," I told Michael, before branching off and finding Nissa's phone in the kitchen. I took it to her dad's den and called my house. Sam was fine, my mom assured me, and told me if I needed a lift to call the police station. Richie was working, and would give me a ride at any time, free of questions about who was drinking. I told her thanks for the offer, but I was probably going to sleep at Michael's, since he lived within walking distance of Nissa's.

I came out of the den and put the phone back in the kitchen, making a drink while I was there. "Has Nissa been acting weird to you?" I heard from beside me. It was Ray. Quickly, I scanned the room to make sure Nissa wasn't around. "Don't worry, she's changing. She won't be out for a few minutes," he said.

"I think she knows about us," I told him, and he recoiled, visibly confused.

"No way." He shook his head. "Not if you didn't tell her."

"I didn't tell her anything." I was still watching around,

ensuring my voice was low enough for no one to hear. "But I just have a feeling she knows."

"Why wouldn't she say anything?" he asked.

I shrugged. I told him I wasn't sure what was going on, but I wanted to stay out of her way, and I should stay away from him, too. I left him in the kitchen and found Jasmine, watching Michael play beer pong with some of the other football guys. She took my red cup and sniffed it. "Tequila? Gross," she cringed, holding up her can of beer. I joked she was a weakling, and we watched Michael toss his ping-pong ball into a cup. Everyone cheered.

Beyond the game, I saw Nissa eye me when she entered the room. As much as I wanted to work up the nerve to go settle whatever was wrong, I didn't have it in me. I threw back my whole drink, hoping for any courage I could get. There had to be a least four shots worth in there. Jasmine looked at me and took my cup away. "Woah," she joked, "Slow down there, cowboy."

I took a deep breath, my veins soaking in the heat I'd just poured down my throat. I knew it wouldn't be long until the weight of my nerves started to relax.

"I'm glad you and Jesse made up," Jasmine said. "Is it crazy that I wish he ended up with you instead of Xavier?" She chuckled when I looked at her, the surprise that she knew about them clearly visible in my eyes. "He hasn't told me, but I'd be stupid not to know after so long. Plus, that night at Michael's house, I heard you find them in the living room. Michael was sleeping, but I was standing at his door. I heard everything."

My jaw was heavy, and I wasn't sure whether it was from shock, or how impressed I was. "Damn," I told her. "You're going to be a good mom one day. Is that weird to say?"

She laughed. "Yes, that's weird!"

I was already beginning to feel lighter. I snatched my cup back from her and went into the kitchen. Lo and behold, I ran into Jesse. "What are you doing here?" I asked, lowering my voice. "I thought you and Xavier were going to a hotel?"

"We have all night for that," Jesse said. "He wanted to come for a while, so we're here."

I looked back into the living room. Xavier was already playing beer pong at the table with Michael. I must have passed him without even realizing it. I second-guessed pouring myself another drink, but as Jesse finished making his, I took the bottle and dumped some more tequila into my cup, ignoring his raised brows.

He shrugged and looked the other way as I mixed in some juice and then cringed at my first taste. It was stronger than the one I'd just finished. The benefits of it were beginning to flow more heavily through me, though, and I knew I could handle it.

Jasmine was happy to see that Jesse was at the party, and we all watched the football guys drink until it got boring enough for us to retreat to the backyard. String lights and tiki torches illuminated the entire area, and there were people playing volleyball in one corner, lounging by a fire pit in another, and drinking at a makeshift bar by the window.

When I finished my second cup of tequila, I knew I couldn't drink any more if I didn't want to end up sicker than I had become on Halloween. Besides, I also knew I didn't need to drink anymore to work up the nerve to talk to Nissa. It had been worked up. I told Jesse and Jasmine I'd be back. As I was walking away, Jesse grabbed my hand. "Are you okay?" he asked, looking me over. "Are you sick?"

I pulled away from him. "I just need to do something."

Jesse yelled that he'd come check on me in a few minutes as I marched away, back into the house, looking from left to right throughout the kitchen. Nissa wasn't there, but the tequila bottle was. I picked it up and drank a few more glugs straight out of it, ignoring my body's warning that I'd already had enough, and then went into the living room. Nissa was there, watching Ray play at the beer pong table. "Hey," I told her, touching her arm. "I need to talk to you."

She looked at me with such a piercing glare, it would

have slit my throat if looks could kill. Ray looked over from his game as she drank the rest of whatever was in her cup, and I could see a faint trace of panic in his eyes as she grabbed my arm and took me to the hallway.

Nissa pushed open her bedroom door and threw out the couple kissing on her bed, slamming it shut behind them. Her arms crossed in front of her, and she continued to stare me down without saying a word, cracking that nerve I thought had solidified in my chest. She could see that I was suddenly feeling less bold, and I knew she had my number. "You said you needed to talk, Lukas. So talk." A devious grin overtook her lips, and I couldn't believe she could ever look so mean.

"Why are you mad at me?" I asked, almost regretting it instantly, as Ray came into the room. It was as if he were right on cue, and like it was his biggest mistake at the same time.

"Oh, I'm glad you're here, babe," Nissa smiled eerily at Ray, telling him to shut the door behind him. He was confused, but he did what she said, and then she turned back to me. She peered at me for another second, before her hand flew across my face.

The smack was so loud, my first thought was that everyone in the house had to have heard it. And for the moment immediately afterward, all three of us froze and everything seemed freakishly silent. My hand covered the cheek she'd just slapped, and it felt hot under my palm. I was in shock as much as I knew I had it coming.

"What the fuck?" Ray asked, and then she slapped him, too.

"You're both trash," she grunted, careful not to yell for the sake of her party. Her breath was heavy, as if all the pent up anger she felt for however long she'd known the truth was pushing its way out through her lungs. "What's wrong with you?" she asked Ray.

Like me, he was holding his face, surprised at the slap Nissa just laid on his cheek. Unlike me, his eyes were filled

241

with rage. I could tell he'd already drunk a lot, because the way he looked wasn't far from his angry gaze when I told him what King did to me on New Year's Eve. Whether he was mad we were caught, or that she hit him, he didn't answer her. He looked at me, and for a second I thought he was going to say something.

But panic was bubbling up in my chest as the shock was dissolving out. "Nissa, I'm so sorry. It was a mistake. I wish it never happened. I hated lying to you. You've been such a good friend to me. I never should have done that to you. It wasn't worth it." I threw out everything I'd thought of saying all night long, if my hunch about her knowing the truth was right, and looked beggingly into her eyes, as she caught her breath from the rush of adrenaline that had just possessed her.

Then, I looked at Ray. His eyes widened at my apology. His silver stare was hurt, and betrayed, as if I'd just invalidated every minute we'd ever spent together, from the theater to the waterfall to the fire to the camper. Suddenly, the guilt erupting over me doubled. He took in a deep breath, like he was about to scream, but then he just left. He ripped open the door and stormed out of the room, catching Nissa and I both by surprise.

She shut the door behind him, then looked at me again. I could see the tears of angry embarrassment beginning to take over her eyes. I opened my mouth to continue my apology, but before I could say another word, she went over to the TV on her dresser and turned it on.

A blue screen illuminated, and when she pressed the play button on the VCR underneath, the picture appearing on-screen was a shot of her living room window. At first, I was confused. But then I heard my voice. "There's no proof we were ever at King's house that night. Richie's last trick was basically asking where I was when the fire happened, and thankfully, Zondra covered for my ass."

A dark cloud of surprise doom punched me in the stomach and knocked the air out of my lungs.

"See?" said Ray's voice.

And then a few seconds later, I came through the speakers again: "What's wrong with you? You have a girlfriend and we are literally in her house."

Nissa stopped the tape, and it was as if she'd just seen it for the first time, an angry squint of disbelief accompanying her words. "You know what I was going to do tonight?" she asked quietly, and it was clear she was still working to suppress the rage shaking in her. "I was going to take the Elvis movie off the screen at prom and put this on."

My jaw dropped. The thought of the whole school watching that tape made me sick. I wanted to ask why she hadn't, but I couldn't even speak, I was so floored.

Maybe Nissa could see it in my eyes, because she answered that question. "And then I saw you, and for some reason, I felt sorry for you, even knowing that you and Ray…" She couldn't finish the sentence. She just took the tape out of the VCR and waved it in front of me. "Maybe I should take this to the cops right now!" she taunted, and I could smell whatever fruity vodka she'd been drinking on her breath. There was no doubt in my mind she was drunk enough to do it.

Every instinct in my body told me to leap forward and snatch the tape from her, but in the pit of my stomach, all the tequila I'd consumed suddenly bubbled up into my throat.

I fell over and threw up onto the carpet. Nissa shrieked, and within a moment, Jesse barged into the room.

"What's going on? Are you okay?" He knelt down next to me and yelled out the door for someone to bring me water. I sat back and tried to catch my breath, focusing with everything in me on calming down before I spiraled into a panic attack. Jasmine ran into the room with a water bottle from the kitchen and put it in my hand. I threw it back and swallowed as much as I could. "Lukas, what's going on?" Jesse repeated. Jasmine stood behind him, and I noticed Nissa was gone.

"Where did she go?"

"Nissa?"

"Yes! Where is she?"

They both shrugged and asked what was the matter. "She has a tape. She's taking the tape to the police!" I panicked. Jesse's eyes widened, and Jasmine closed the door.

"You're not making any sense," Jasmine said.

Jesse somehow understood, though, and sprinted out of the room. I pushed myself up and made my way out of the house after him, Jasmine following behind and telling all the people watching to mind their business. We all ran out onto Nissa's front yard. As we looked down the street and called out her name, there was no answer. She was gone.

She only lived about four blocks away from the police station. "She's probably almost there by now," I said in horror. I could feel my heart thudding underneath my stained shirt.

Jasmine ran inside to get Michael, and Jesse asked what he could do. I just shook my head. There was nothing he could possibly do, I told him, because I was officially fucked. And so was Ray. Everything was officially fucked.

As Michael came running out of the house with Jasmine, I felt my stomach clenching up again under my ribs.

And then, nothing.

FOURTEEN

"It's my honor to welcome you to the graduation for Santana High School's Class of 2000," Mr. Kramer announced into the microphone at the front of the gym. Before him, a sea of maroon caps and gowns cheered, which might as well have set off a pack of firecrackers in my head. I'd only been awake for half an hour. Michael's alarm clock didn't wake me up, and once he shook me out of my dead sleep, I only had enough time to throw up one last hurl in his bathroom, drink the coffee he handed me, and get dressed in my cap and gown.

I cringed at the seemingly everlasting hoots and hollers surrounding me, catching a glimpse of Nissa about ten seats away. I'd been wracking my brain since I woke up, trying my hardest to collect the pieces of what happened the night before and put them together, but I didn't have any luck. The second Nissa's glare caught me, though, I heard the echo of her drunken threat the night before: "*Maybe I should take this to the cops right now!*"

I winced, and I could see her wagging the tape in front of me. Was I really so drunk I couldn't jump and snatch it from her hand? *Oh, that's right*, I thought, *That was when I threw up all over her bedroom floor.* She looked away from me and back toward the front, and I couldn't help but think there was no way she actually delivered the tape to Richie. *Wouldn't I be in jail right now?*

My eyes frantically scanned the bleachers, desperate to locate my mom and Richie. Sure enough, they sat next to Zondra and Laura, and all four waved from their seats when they saw me looking their way. I grinned back. I could tell my mom didn't know a thing. Richie, though, was harder to read. Maybe he had no idea about the tape. Or maybe he was waving to his future stepson, accessory to murder, graciously allowing him to graduate high school before locking him up and throwing away the key. My fingertips grazed my necklace, and I gulped down the nausea boiling up under it.

Then I glanced behind me, to see if Ray was there. He wasn't. An empty seat with his name written on a sticky note was all that filled his spot.

Sam sat a couple seats from his, rubbing her giant belly. She noticed me turn around, and threw both thumbs up, silently mouthing, "You okay?" I nodded.

Not far from Sam, Michael caught me looking around from the corner of his eye. As he examined me from afar, I could see the sheer pity in his eyes for my current state of disaster. I obviously looked as rough as I felt. His brows jumped to make sure I was all right, and I nodded before turning back to Mr. Kramer at the podium.

He optimistically predicted how bright our futures would be. What wonderful things we would achieve. How many lives we would touch. *So many hopes and dreams for a couple hundred kids from Nowhere, USA*, I thought.

And then, like clockwork, I wondered why Ray wasn't there, strumming through my memory of the night before, trying to remember anything about where he'd gone, or if he ever came back to Nissa's house. Nothing. Maybe I could sneak away to look for him later, I thought. I could tell Michael I needed to spend time with my family, and tell my family I needed to see Michael.

246

"And now, our graduates will line up in alphabetical order to receive their hard-earned diplomas!" Mr. Kramer declared, lifting his arm to welcome the line of us assembling next to the stage.

Dr. Carver's voice calmly reminded me to breathe inside my head. "*Feel the air being pulled into your lungs, Lukas. Then slowly push it all out. You are in control.*" I could feel her smile from inside.

My name was called seventh. I stepped onto the stage, took the small leather folder from Mr. Kramer, and posed for the obligatory photo of us shaking hands before I waved at the cheers coming from my mom, Richie, Zondra, and Laura.

When I returned to my chair to watch the rest of my class take their diplomas, Dr. Carver's voice seemed to have been replaced by everyone else's in my head. All at once, Sam asked if I'd ever be happy in Santana, and Ray said he'd kill King all over again if he could, and Nissa growled that I was trash. Richie interrogated me. Zondra warned me.

I could feel my heartbeat revving up, and for some reason, I became thirsty. The room seemed darker. I felt like everyone was watching me. Was it a hundred degrees? Were the walls shifting? I closed my eyes and tried to push out everyone but Dr. Carver.

But what I heard then was a wave of gasps all around me, and I felt Charlie Buck elbow my arm. I turned to him and he pointed up at the stage. "Maybe you should go up there," he said.

When I looked forward, I saw Mr. Kramer and Mr. Garcia supporting Sam by her arms, helping her to a seat. Without giving it a moment's thought, I pushed my way through my classmates and dashed to her side on stage, kneeling to ask if she was okay, just like on New Year's Eve at the hospital. Only now, she wasn't in shock so much as she was entirely pissed off.

"I knew this was going to happen!" she yelled, grabbing me by the collar of my gown. And in the next moment, as she threw her head back and burst into laughter, and the rest of the gym followed suit nervously, I breathed an ironic sigh of relief.

Everything was fine. Nobody was about to die. Sam's water just broke, right there, at her own graduation, in front of all of Santana.

Joe staggered onto the stage behind me. "I'm going to be a dad," he said, clearly in a state of shock. He made his way to Sam's other side, and knelt down to help her up out of the chair. "I'll drive you. I'm ready for this."

I could feel the astonishment showing on my face. I wasn't sure when Sam and Joe had conversed enough to move past the fact that their month-long relationship ended disastrously eight months earlier, much less enough for him to be ready for this to happen, but I was glad to see someone else taking charge, because I was beyond unprepared to help. Even my mom and Richie looked pleasantly surprised, as they stepped on stage to see if everything was all right for themselves.

Once we got to the hospital and Joe learned the labor process would take hours, he felt confident enough he wouldn't miss anything to go home and get his camera. I assured him I would be there in case anything happened, and took a seat next to Sam's bed as he rushed out the door.

That was when Sam asked if I was all right letting Joe sit in the room with her until the baby was born. Originally, the plan was for me to be the one present. I was never thrilled about the idea, but I had hesitantly agreed, even though I maintained that my mom would probably be better company, since she was a nurse.

I told her it was fine by me if Joe wanted to take my place. The demon that took over her body every time the contractions came freaked me out, and as selfish as it may have been, I was relieved to pass off the job.

We watched TV as we waited for Joe to return, and

during a commercial break, I heard her sigh beside me. "Can you believe I'm going to be someone's mom?"

"Stop," I grimaced. "That makes me feel so old." I looked up at her. "Do you think you'll get to come home today?"

"Probably tomorrow," she shrugged, before drifting into another, more serious lane. "Luke, there's something I need to tell you."

I felt my whole hungover body tighten up, unsure of whether I could handle any groundbreaking news. "What's wrong?" I asked.

She laughed. "Nothing's wrong. It's just that Joe and I have been getting along over these past few months. And things are good." She said every word thoughtfully, clearly careful to get it right. "We're not getting back together, but we do want to try raising this kid together. He's going full-time at the grocery store this summer, and I have enough money from my trust that we can get a house and everything."

There it was. The final crack in my imaginary glass cage.

I didn't have to ask Sam if I could leave town, because she was telling me she didn't need me after all, and as much relief as it brought me, it also made me sad. Nobody needed me anymore. My last excuse not to escape Santana had officially disintegrated before my eyes.

That was, if I wasn't in jail by the end of the day. I looked out her hospital room window. Everything seemed surreal. My mind was working to figure out how it could all be possible.

"Are you mad?" she asked.

I shook my head. "Just surprised. But not in a bad way." I leaned forward and hugged her.

"You really should go somewhere, Luke." She squeezed me back before letting me go, as Joe reentered the room. "I'll be fine," she said with confidence. Her eyes peered sternly into mine to let me know she meant what she said. I nodded. Of course she would be fine. "Now, please go enjoy our graduation day for both of us. Joe will call home when this baby comes. There's no use in spending the whole day in the waiting room."

Joe nodded that it was all right for me to go, but I still asked one more time to let them insist. A part of me wanted to stay because I knew Sam had to be scared, but I could also see there was nothing I would do for her that Joe wouldn't. And at the end of the day, it was his kid she was having. He deserved to share that moment with her if it was what they both wanted.

Before I left, I added one more line of advice. "Hey, if you can do this, you can do anything." Then I kissed her on the forehead and went.

I only made it halfway down the hall before I ran into Nissa.

Before I could ask what she was doing at the hospital, she pulled me into a corner. "For the record, I'm still mad at you," she said hurriedly. "Like, really, really mad at you." She looked around to make sure no one was near us, and I leaned in. Her makeup could barely conceal the dark circles under her eyes. She was suffering from the night before just as much as I was. "But I am sorry I gave that tape to Richie. I was so drunk and mad, and I didn't know the whole story..."

My stomach pinched up as if I'd just downed another cup of tequila. I imagined Nissa bursting into the police station, drunkenly handing Richie the VHS after her outburst at Ray and me. I pictured him watching it, and the flood of satisfaction that must have come over him as he realized his hunch about New Year's Eve was right. "Are you sure he's already watched it?" I asked.

She nodded. "He found a VCR and played it right away. And while it was playing, Jesse showed up and tried to stop it all, but it was too late." She was tearing up. "He told Richie what Mr. King did to him and to you, and I am so sorry, Lukas. I had no idea. If I did, I wouldn't have taken that tape to the police. I really wouldn't have."

"It's okay," I told her. It most certainly was not okay, but I couldn't handle a full-fledged Nissa breakdown right before my eyes, and I was still trying to reconstruct the night from my memory and my imagination. I had no idea Jesse ran to the police station after I got sick.

My brain was still spinning when Nissa added that her parents had surprised her by coming into town early that morning, and she was leaving later in the afternoon to spend the summer with them in the city before college. "This isn't how I pictured our goodbye," she said sorrowfully. "You did a really messed up thing, but I get it," she added, taking my hands in with hers. "Ray's like, really hot. And technically, you knew him first." She shrugged and I couldn't help but laugh at her logic. I pulled her in for a hug and thanked her for telling me what happened and forgiving me in a way only she could.

"Whatever you do, I hope you love it, Lukas Bradley." She squeezed me one last time and kissed my cheek before taking another look at me and disappearing, her unzipped gown hanging off her shoulders, flowing behind her like the cape of a queen.

I stood in the dark corner for a moment before peeking through the window into the waiting room. Richie and my mom were there. Something inside me knew that my mom had no idea what happened. For some reason, Richie must not have told her yet. She sat beside him without a care in the world, laughing with Zondra and Laura over paper cups of coffee. As much as I wanted to go into the waiting room and confront Richie to get whatever he had in store for me over with, I quickly moved away from the visiting room door instead, sneaking out the hospital's back exit and into the May sun.

I got off Main Street as soon as I could, walking myself over to the side road that would take me to Ray's apartment. Even unzipped, it wasn't long before my gown was being baked by the sky and I took it off, crumpling it into a ball and carrying it under my arm as I paced all the way there.

My fist banged quickly on the door when I arrived, paranoid to be outside. There was no answer. I banged again, and when no one opened the door, I went to the window and put my hands and face up to the glass.

The apartment was empty.

Not just empty like Ray wasn't home. It was empty like Ray didn't live there. The same surprise cloud of doom that had knocked the air out of me the night before came back and choked me. I returned to the door and twisted the handle. It was unlocked, and as I stepped into the apartment, I looked from right to left. The sheets had come off his bed. The closet door was open and all that remained were a couple hangers. There was an envelope on the counter. I walked over and pulled a folded paper from inside of it. In his quick handwriting, Ray told the landlord to keep his deposit. He was gone.

Slowly, I put the letter down and moved to his mattress, sitting on the corner and looking down at the bed. The memory of our kiss on Christmas Eve sparked through my brain like a lightbulb ready to burn out. It all seemed so close, and like none of it ever happened at the same time. My body was running on empty; even though I wanted to cry, nothing came. Not even a frown.

I wearily stared at the table where Ray's old TV used to sit, trying to remember exactly what I'd said the night before when I begged Nissa to believe everything I'd done with him was a mistake. But in a second, I realized the words were irrelevant now. The sting of betrayal in Ray's eyes after I said them was all I needed to know about why he was gone.

There was nothing in me before I'd come to his apartment, and yet, somehow I felt even more hollow, yet another possibility plucked away. It must have been half an hour I sat there on the corner of his abandoned mattress, soaking in the idea that I'd already said my last words to Ray

Melendez, and they weren't even to him.

The emptiness occupying my body was what took me over to the phone on Ray's kitchen wall after enough time had passed. I was ready to face Richie and find out what he was going to do with the tape. After two rings, my mom answered the phone at my house, asking where I was. "Coming home soon," I told her. "Is Richie there?" A second later, Richie's voice came through. I asked if he could come to Ray's apartment without bringing my mom.

When Richie's truck pulled up outside, I felt as sick as when I'd woken up that morning. I noticed Nissa's tape in his hand as soon as he stepped out, and opened the door to Ray's apartment before he could even knock. "I'm guessing you want to talk about this," he said, holding up the cassette. I looked up at him and realized that the cruel satisfaction I expected was instead a look of concern.

I let him into the apartment and he looked around. It was obvious he knew it had been Ray's apartment, but he was clearly learning Ray was gone in the moment, just like me. Richie pulled out one of the chairs at the table Ray left behind, and I sat down directly across from him. He set the tape on the table in front of us. "What do you want me to know?" he asked.

Fear trickled through me as I realized this was all really happening. Richie knew everything he needed to about New Year's Eve, and I was the only one left to face whatever was on its way because of it. I wasn't in high school anymore. Zondra's cards, once again, had been correct. My life was on the brink of changing forever.

"We did it. We set the fire. You were right." The words came out of me like water. I was so tired, the dam was leaking. "We went there, drunk, and spray painted his house. Then Ray set the paint on fire. But it wasn't all his fault because I was the one who told him…" Suddenly, something in me patched that dam right back up. I looked at Richie, and more than anything, he seemed disturbed. I turned away from him, the embarrassment flustering me like a bag over my head. "Well, I know Jesse told you about Mr. King."

"That's enough," Richie said, taking in a deep breath.

He stood up and walked over to the drawers in Ray's kitchen, opening them one by one to see what was left. Nothing he was looking for, apparently. He went into the bathroom. Nothing in there, either. He sighed before stepping out the front door, and came back in with a big rock from beside the stoop. Then he stood above the table, lifted it up, and smashed the rock down onto the tape. The crash was so loud, I jumped back.

Richie smashed the cassette with the rock again, and again, and again, and then he tossed the rock back outside, returning to the tape only to rip out its plastic guts, wadding them into a filmy ball before throwing the whole thing in the trash can behind him. He panted, gazing down at the black plastic to make sure it was completely and utterly destroyed, before looking up at me.

My eyes had widened as much as my jaw. I looked back at him, his stare hard but assuring. "Isn't destroying evidence kind of against the rules for a cop?" I asked, still shaken. I'd never seen Richie do anything he wouldn't do in front of someone sleeping. He had become the most calm person I knew. His violent execution of that tape was the last thing I would have ever expected.

"Cops break rules all the time." Richie sat back down at the table. "I became a cop because I believe in justice, Luke. Lots of people think that means following the law. But I don't think that's always true." He looked up, and I imagined he'd decided hours earlier what he was going to tell me, but it still came out as smooth and honest as it could. "What that guy did was sick, and we both know he didn't just do it to you and your friend. You did the world a favor. You served justice. Even if you didn't mean to. I don't give a damn if that man is dead, and I'm sure as hell not going to let him affect your life any more than he already has. Does that make sense to you?"

I could feel my brows pushing down on my eyes, still accepting what had just happened right in front of me. It appeared Richie didn't think twice about it, and as much as I tried to look past his relief at what he'd done to see if there was even a speck of hesitance, I couldn't find any. "Sorry, I just don't know what to say," I told him. I felt like I should be profusely thanking him, but I had exceeded the level of shock I could handle, especially on a hangover, and I was motionless.

He looked at me, clearly not oblivious to the way I was feeling, and told me I didn't need to say anything. "We should get you back home. Looks like you could use a shower. No offense." We looked at each other and I couldn't help but laugh. Not even because it was funny. I was just so tired. And he was right. As we stepped out of Ray's apartment, I breathed in the sunlight coming down, another surprising inch closer to freedom.

When Richie and I got home, I called the hospital and checked on Sam. My mom assured me the baby wouldn't be coming anytime soon.

I hung up the phone and breathed out a sigh of relief, knowing it was the perfect time to head to my room and finally take a nap. But as soon as I stared at my bedroom ceiling, my hangover was overpowered by the excitement possessing me. There was no way I'd be able to sleep for a single minute, so I got up, took a shower, and headed back out into the sun.

"We were hoping we'd see you today!" Laura gleamed proudly, greeting me at the front door.

Zondra came up from behind her and pulled me into the house, pushing me into the kitchen for a glass of cold lemonade. "It's too hot out there for you to be walking!" she scolded, and I smiled as she set a cup down in front of me at the dining table. For a moment, we just looked at each other. Somehow, it was once again clear to me there was little to explain to her. "I decided I'm leaving Santana," I told both Zondra and Laura, and each of their faces dropped into a pretend state of shock.

"I can't believe it," Zondra whispered jokingly. "Where will you go?"

Truthfully, I still hadn't thought much about that, since the real possibility of leaving Santana was still so new. As much as the idea of blindly venturing out into the world all by myself didn't feel great, I knew I couldn't go to college with Michael, and I didn't see myself in California living out Jesse's artist fantasy. Nissa had her own things to accomplish in Las Vegas. Ray didn't leave so much as a scribbled goodbye. "Maybe I'll just get on a bus and see where it takes me," I shrugged.

Zondra and Laura looked at each other, and Laura nodded, passing Zondra a square envelope from the counter. She took it and handed it over to me. "We had a feeling you'd say that," she winked.

I tore the top of the envelope and pulled out a card. *Our graduate*, it read in gold print. When I opened the front, two hundred dollars and a folded paper fell onto my lap, revealing Zondra's big, fancy cursive underneath. *Lukas*, it said, *This is your bus money. The future starts now.* I picked up the folded paper and looked at them. "What is this?"

"A bus schedule," Zondra said. "Look at it."

I flattened the schedule in front of me. There was a listing of departures that went from Santana to Albuquerque, to Denver, to St. Louis, and finally, to Levenston. At the top, the date caught me by surprise. "This is the schedule for tomorrow," I said, confused about what it meant. Surely, they didn't expect me to leave town the day after graduation.

"Why wouldn't you leave tomorrow?" Zondra asked, as if I were the irrational one.

I looked back at her, unable to come up with an answer, other than I didn't have a place to stay or anything planned. Laura chimed in. "What if we told you we own a small studio in Levenston, and it's all yours until you can find a place of your own?"

"And that Jim and Lady are waiting anxiously for the bookstore's new coffee guy to arrive?" Zondra added.

I was stunned yet again. Just when I thought there was nothing else I could take in, I absorbed what they were suggesting.

Every part of my brain felt obligated to resist the idea, but my soul couldn't think of a single reason not to leave Santana as soon as I could. That was, after all, what I had promised myself I would do over and over again. High school was finally finished, and every shoe that had dropped over the past day indicated I had every reason and right to be free. "Am I dreaming right now?" I asked them both. "Can I actually leave tomorrow?"

They laughed joyously at my surprise, their last nudge their biggest, and their final gift to me their greatest.

As they enveloped me in their arms for the last time, we all cried a little. For as many young people as I'd come to learn they nurtured over the years, I was sure it was always their latest they felt the most proud of, and devastated to let go. And as for me, I knew there would never be another woman who looked out for me the way only Zondra Devereaux could.

As the sun painted the sky orange over my walk to Michael's house that evening, I wondered how long it would be before I'd see another Santana sunset. The knowledge that I would soon be over a thousand miles away terrified me as much as it gave me a sudden adoration for Santana's physical beauty. I knew it was mostly nerves, but I leaned into it anyway, and breathed in the sweetness that could only be leftover from a hot Santana day.

"You missed the party," Michael told me as I came around his house and walked into his backyard. The only people present were Jasmine and Jesse. They sat around the firepit his dad made when we were kids, and for a moment, it felt like walking into a summer evening in 1994. We spent almost every night that summer laughing around that firepit until our parents made us go home.

"How are you feeling?" Jasmine asked, cozying up with Michael on the grass in front of the flames.

"It's a miracle you made it through graduation without throwing up," Jesse laughed from a lawn chair beside them. "You were a mess last night."

I sat myself down on the ground next to his chair and leaned against it, facing Michael and Jasmine. "I'm fine," I answered. "I'm better than fine, actually." I told them about Nissa forgiving me, Ray's disappearance, Richie's surprise act of mercy, and the sudden offer to leave Santana I'd received from Zondra and Laura. They were all as speechless as me at every turn things had taken. "I know it's crazy, but it's actually happening. I'm leaving tomorrow. It doesn't feel real," I admitted, staring into the firepit.

Jesse would only be in Santana one more week, and Jasmine was leaving in two. Michael, as it turned out, would be the last person in town. He wasn't heading to Montana until the end of June. We all wondered what our lives would be like in one year, or five, or ten, and before long, we were thinking about life a year before, or five, or ten. We laughed at all the fun we had, and we acknowledged how stupid we all were for spending the last five years split in two, each half pretending the other didn't exist.

When the sun disappeared and the sky faded to black, the twins said they needed to go home. Jasmine hugged me goodbye first, joking she hoped I'd find a good friend in the city to take care of me the next time I got my hands on a bottle of tequila.

Jesse swooped in next, and we clung onto each other a bit longer. The same glow from our dance at prom lingered there. In some ways, I would miss him most of all, because there was the most lost time between us. "Good luck," he smiled. "Don't be an idiot."

"You too," I laughed, and then quietly promised I'd find

a way to call him soon. He knew it would be to check up on him after his inevitable goodbye with Xavier. I felt so bad for him, it almost made me happy Ray skipped town without a goodbye between us. If I'd come to learn one thing about whatever existed there, it was that the highs always felt better, and the lows always felt worse.

Once Jasmine and Jesse were gone, Michael put out the fire, and we went inside to his room. The day I spent sleeping in there after staying at the hospital with Sam came back to me. I remembered him defending me to his dad, and the small bucket of relief it provided against the inferno of anxiety I felt over the fire at King's. We both sat on his bed, aware that we were about to say goodbye for the first time in our lives. Even after prom the last year, there was a small part of me that knew we weren't done with each other forever. This felt different, though.

One thing we always had in common was that we hated serious conversations about ourselves, which was why every hurdle we had to jump throughout the past year was so hard for us. I couldn't think of a time we ever hugged, or a time we ever said we loved each other, even though there was an entire unspoken world that was ours, constructed of the love that was indeed there, and held up by the ways we saw our little world the same. Not to mention the years and years of knowing the other was never too far away, save for the last summer.

"Are you happy?" Michael asked.

I looked over at him, thinking about his confession the night before that he didn't want to go to college. "Yeah, I'm happy," I answered. I wanted to follow with some kind of encouragement for him to do whatever would make him happy, but I knew he was going to college to make his dad proud, and that was a rock too heavy to ever get Michael out from under. Since we were kids, I knew pleasing his dad was his greatest goal, even though he'd never admit it. I always hoped he would outgrow that, mostly because I never liked his dad, but it appeared he still had some growing to do there. "You're going to have so much fun at college. Sometimes I wish I was going," I lied. There was actually no part of me that wanted to go back to school after the week of finals I'd just survived.

He knew I was full of shit. "It'll be fine," he said. I wasn't sure whether he was talking to me or himself when he said it, though. It killed me that I had suddenly become so lucky in finding a ticket to my dream future and he was clearly dreading his, and in that moment there was nothing I wanted to do more than tell him to forget college, and to come with me to Levenston.

But in the way I had committed my future to Sam for as long as I could, he had already pledged his to his dad. And unlike Sam, there was no way Michael's dad would ever permit him to stop pushing forward with his commitment.

I also wanted to throw my arms around him the way I had Jesse, and tell him how much he meant to me. I wanted to tell him I'd never forget him, and that I hoped one day we'd live in the same place again, and that we'd be best friends until we were old. But beside the fact that it just wasn't our style, it made me too sad, because it made me realize that we might not be best friends after I got on that bus. For all I knew, I wouldn't see Michael again. He would fall into a whole new life in Montana, and I would build a new one in Pennsylvania. Even if he came back for holidays, I couldn't say whether I would.

"I should get home," I said instead, and stood up to leave. He followed me through his house, and as we passed his dad watching TV in the living room, I told him goodbye only to be met with an obligatory head nod. Good enough for me.

When Michael and I stepped out onto his front porch, the moment of truth was upon us. We looked at each other, both knowing there was everything and nothing more to say, and like an instinct, pulled each other in for a hug. He squeezed me and said he'd always be there if I needed him, and I couldn't say anything in return without crying, so I didn't. I just squeezed him back harder. When we pulled away from each other, I started walking away before we could start another conversation. I was spent in every way, and as I walked back to my house, I wiped the tears off my face, thankful more than anything that I knew someone I would miss as much as Michael Medina.

"It's a boy!" my mom gleamed into the phone when I got home from Michael's house. My instinct was to run back into the night, but it was too late. Sam was exhausted. She'd already gone to sleep for the night.

"So," my mom segued, "Did you see Zondra today?"

"Yeah," I answered, "Actually –"

And just as I was about to explain my abrupt decision to leave Santana, I realized she already knew. And as much as I wanted to ask when and how a conversation about my future had ever occurred between her and Zondra, I realized that like most mysterious things, the details were unimportant.

"Do you think I'm crazy?" I asked her instead.

"No," she answered. "I meant it when I said you should do what feels right. If this feels right, then it is."

A warm and welcome relief rushed over me, and as I laid in bed after hanging up with my mom, I watched the moonlight coming in through my window fade calmly to black.

MAY 20, 2000

I woke up when my bedroom door creaked open. It was still dark outside, but the faint light seeping in from the hallway revealed it was my mom standing at the foot of my bed, and I could tell she'd tried not to wake me up. "Go back to sleep," she said softly, and then crawled onto my covers, laying herself behind me and wrapping her arms around mine. I was so tired, I left my eyes closed, but I still instinctively asked if everything was okay. She hadn't gotten into my bed to hold me since I was a kid and she mourned the loss of my grandma. She hadn't even done this when my dad left us.

"Everything's fine," she whispered. "I'm just sad about my baby leaving today."

"Are you going to work?" I asked, my body already shutting back down. I felt a comfortable heaviness under her arm, and as she answered I wasn't sure I was even awake.

"Yes. I can't be here when you leave. It's too sad for me. I hope that's okay with you," she said. I heard her but I didn't answer. "I'm leaving you some money on the kitchen counter and you have to call me at every stop on the way there, okay?" She knew I'd fallen asleep, but somehow, she knew I heard her, and I'd call. "I love you so, so much," I heard her whisper next.

And the next thing I knew, it was 8:00.

I sat up in my bed and looked around. My mom had gone to work hours earlier, but it seemed like she had been next to me only minutes before. A part of me wanted to cry because I already missed her, which didn't make any sense after the year we'd just gone through, but it didn't matter. The same instant panic of a baby who can't see his mother flooded through me for a second. And then it passed, and I smiled, holding myself and somehow feeling her presence in my chest. It almost felt like a dream, as if I didn't have any right to feel as serene in reality as I did.

I took a shower and packed my bags, calculating how much time I had left every five minutes. When I was done, I looked at the clock. It was nine. Three hours until a bus would take me away from Santana forever.

Richie looked up from the newspaper when I came into the kitchen. "Good morning," he said. "You ready to go change the world?"

"I feel like throwing up, actually."

He laughed, setting down his coffee. "You're just nervous. But you'll be fine. You have a plan, right?"

Yes, I had a plan.

For once in my life, I had an entire, detailed blueprint of every minute for the next month planned out. The first bus to Albuquerque, the next bus to Denver, the next to St. Louis, the last to Levenston – plus all the stays I'd need to budget in between. It would take me over four days to get there, but I'd mentally prepared for that, and thanks to Zondra, I also knew what to do upon arriving. I'd stay at Zondra's studio long enough to find an apartment I could afford, and for work, I'd begin at Jim's bookstore as soon as possible.

I'd saved enough money to make it all work, and I knew

Jim and Lady would be waiting for me on the other side, there to support each move I needed to make. But I was still worried sick about failing. What if one thing went wrong and derailed the whole plan? What if my anxiety snuck up and threw a dark bag over my head? What if this, what if that? The uncertainty of it all made me queasy. But it also thrilled me. It was a rush I'd never felt in my life, because I'd never done anything so big as to leave the only home I'd ever known.

I sat down across from Richie and poured myself a cup of coffee, going over my plan again and again, unable to shake the feeling something was missing. I was three sips in before I realized. "If you're not busy today, could you take me to the bus station?" I asked Richie.

He looked surprised. "You want me to take you?"

"Only if you have time," I said. "I can ask Zondra, but I'm not sure she could handle another goodbye, and Michael's probably already on his summer sleep schedule. Won't be up 'til noon."

Richie told me he'd be happy to take me, and asked if I'd like to go with him to the hospital to visit Sam first. I finished my coffee, picked up the envelope my mom had left for me on the counter, and went to my room, unzipping my bags one last time to try filling whatever empty space was left. I couldn't fit much more than I needed, but I convinced myself it was for the best.

Richie and I walked into Sam's hospital room to find her flipping through TV channels, and Joe standing next to her bed holding their new baby. My eyes widened. For as long as I'd known Sam was going to become a mom, it still felt like a bizarre dream to see it right in front of me. "This is Carlos," Joe said, facing the baby toward Richie and me.

Richie asked how it felt holding his son, and Joe gleamed that it was awesome, his eyes bright and fixed on his boy. I believed him. It was apparent he and Sam were both more excited than anything when they looked at their tiny son, and as selfish as it may have been, it mostly gave me comfort in my decision to leave. It felt right, all of us jumping off the cliffs of our youth and into our own separate rivers of life.

Joe carefully placed Carlos into Sam's arms before slipping out of the room to give us some privacy. "Can I get you anything from the cafeteria?" Richie asked Sam, clearly looking for an excuse to do the same. "How about a Coke?"

"That would be amazing," Sam begged eagerly. "Now that I can have all the caffeine I want, that is *all* I want."

Richie smiled he'd be back in a few minutes and left the room. Sam and I both looked down at the baby's little round face. He slept without a care in the world, oblivious to everything. "Can you imagine just being a day old?" I said to Sam. "Literally a whole new life."

"That'll be you in a few hours, won't it?" she replied, and looked up at me. "Literally a whole new life."

Clearly, she'd heard about my plans. I nodded, and looked back into her eyes. "I guess you're right." We just stared at each other for a minute, and I could only assume that like me, she was trying to process we wouldn't be seeing each other longer than we'd ever gone without seeing each other our whole lives. "Are you sure it's okay that I'm leaving?" I asked.

"I'm as sure as you are," she said knowingly. "This is what you've wanted forever, Lukas. I'm so excited you're getting out of here. I mean, I'm sad Carlos won't get to grow up with you, but luckily, I have plenty of stories to tell him."

We reminisced about the time she threw up on my shoes after we egged Joe's house, and the moment she told her parents she was having the baby. In just ten minutes, we laughed and we cried, and my heart emptied out and filled back up again in knowing I was about to take myself miles and miles away from the best cousin I could have ever asked for, the most consistent friend and solid ally.

"I'm fucking scared," I confessed. "Like, really, really fucking scared."

"Same here!" she joked, lifting up the baby. As always,

she made me laugh in the most serious of moments. "But we've survived scary shit before, and we'll survive scary shit again." I bent down and wrapped Sam and Carlos in my arms as Richie walked back into the room with her promised can of Coke.

He set it down on the table next to her bed, and looked up at the clock. "You want to go to your mom's unit and see her before you leave?" he asked me.

I shook my head. "Nope," I told him, remembering what she said that morning when she crawled onto my bed with me. I knew she needed that to be her goodbye: quiet, calm, and on her own terms. "I guess it's time to get this show on the road."

Sam and I hugged one last time, and as I followed Richie out of her room, she said, "Hey, Lukas." I turned around and she smiled. "If you can do this, you can do anything."

The bus station was surprisingly busy when we arrived. Lots of visitors leaving after graduation, I figured. I felt relieved for getting there early as Richie pulled into a parking spot. "You want any help with your bags?"

"No thanks," I told him, my eyes glued to the station. I peered through the windshield, trying to figure out if I'd realized this was all happening yet. It felt somewhat like a dream. But then again, maybe the foreseeable future was meant to. Everything was about to become unfamiliar, and knowing as much made my head feel a little light. I took a deep breath and thanked Richie for the ride.

He smiled reassuringly. "You'll be great," he said, and as I got out of the truck and pulled my suitcases out, he added, "Do me a favor and call your mom when you get to Denver, okay?"

"Of course," I said. I knew calling my mom would make me feel just as relieved as it would make her feel. And beyond that, as far as I was concerned, Richie had the right to ask any favor in the world after what he'd done for me.

"Just remember to always do what'll let you sleep best at

night. You follow that rule, and you'll be all right." He smiled encouragingly. I thanked him for everything again before shutting the door, and taking a moment to feel the sun radiating down on me before I went inside.

"That'll be $29.46," said the gruff cashier when I bought my ticket. "The bus leaves in twenty minutes, but I'd go pick a seat now if I were you." He slipped me the ticket and handed me the change from the fifty dollar bill I'd given him before calling up the next customer. I took my things to the small lot of buses out back, and looked for the one heading to Albuquerque. It was the second one in. Bus #34.

The driver took my suitcases to load them into the lower storage compartment, nodding that I could keep my backpack. When I stepped into the rows of seats inside, there were plenty of spots to choose from, so I headed to the back, as if the further away I sat from the exit, the less likely I would be to change my mind and dart right off the bus before it pulled out.

I set my bag down beside me and closed my eyes. Everything was going to be okay, I told myself. I had a plan. I took in another deep breath and pushed it out. And that's when I felt my bag being lifted up and tossed onto my lap. I jumped and looked up as Michael dropped himself onto my seat. "Scoot over," he grinned, pushing me toward the window.

I had no words. I just stared at him as if he'd come back from the dead. "What are you… I…?"

"Fuck it," he laughed. "I don't want to go to college. So I'm not. My dad's pissed but he'll get over it."

"You're not serious." My head was slowly shaking back and forth, as I pieced together what he'd just said. I felt like someone just pushed me off a building, and like I'd just won the lottery at the same time.

"Oh, I'm serious." He laughed again. "Did I surprise you? Are you mad?"

"Surprised? Yes! Mad? No fucking way!" I understood

why he asked, but the amount of exuberant joy overtaking my whole being immediately canceled out any desire I ever had to start this new life by myself. "How'd you get here?" I asked.

Michael pointed out the window. Zondra and Laura waved from the parking lot outside, and if the shock running through my veins had allowed me to feel anything else, I would have cried. I waved back at them. *Thank you*, I mouthed. Zondra winked.

I rested my head back in disbelief. "This doesn't make any sense."

"Maybe not," Michael agreed. "But if you're doing what feels right, then so am I. So let's do this."

As I looked into the excited, eager eyes of my best friend, everything suddenly felt colored in. "Is this real life?" I asked.

The bus engine rumbled on.

"This is real life," Michael smiled.

We pulled out of the lot a few minutes later, and waved to Zondra and Laura one last time before they became smaller and smaller out the back window. Finally, they disappeared, along with the rest of town.

And it was only a few moments afterward that I finally read the words I'd been waiting to drive by for so long:

You are now leaving Santana.

ABOUT THE AUTHOR

Kameron Tyler is a family guy, a best friend, a worker bee, a storyteller, a Betty Who stan, and your fellow human.

He believes storytelling will save the world, and he wants you to know that if he can do it, so can you.

If you or someone you know is feeling hopeless or suicidal, contact The Trevor Project's TrevorLifeline 24/7 at 1-866-488-7386. Counseling is also available 24/7 via chat at TheTrevorProject.org/Help, or by texting START to 678-678.